TRACI STEAD

THE SPIRIT SERIES

The
Shepherd *of* Shotton Cross

THE SHEPHERD OF SHOTTON CROSS
The Spirit Series

———

DEDICATION

The United Kingdom's 1842 Mines and Collieries Act banned women and girls from working underground. Boys had to wait until age ten to be sent under. It stated that mines had to be tested for gas and qualified mining inspectors appointed. The act was mostly ignored since many colliery owners were also magistrates who sat on the cases. The act was amended and revised several times, but the results stayed the same.

In 1913, Welsh coalfield production peaked at 57 million tons of coal from 620 mines. But coal mining was extremely dangerous in Wales, and everyone knew it. Explosions, fires, cave-ins, and mechanical injuries were common. In 1937 alone, 175 men and boys were killed, and 25,947 were injured, even though there were no major colliery disasters that year.

The worst mining disaster in British history involved an explosion at the Universal Colliery in 1913. It created 205 widows and 542 fatherless children. The colliery manager was fined £24 for breaches of the Coal Mine Act. That's about £600 in today's currency, or less than $1,000 US.

Not all owners and managers were this negligent or abusive. Some good men and women fought for the rights of the miners. This book is dedicated to those who gave their lives to the cold darkness of the earth so that we might have warmth and light.

" SHOUT IT ALOUD, DO NOT hold back.
  Raise your voice like a trumpet.
Declare to my people their rebellion
and to the descendants of Jacob their sins.
For day after day they seek me out;
they seem eager to know my ways,
as if they were a nation that does what is right
and has not forsaken the commands of its God.
They ask me for just decisions
and seem eager for God to come near them.
'Why have we fasted,' they say,
'and you have not seen it?
Why have we humbled ourselves,
and you have not noticed?'

"Yet on the day of your fasting, you do as you please
and exploit all your workers.
Your fasting ends in quarreling and strife,
and in striking each other with wicked fists.
You cannot fast as you do today
and expect your voice to be heard on high.
Is this the kind of fast I have chosen,
only a day for people to humble themselves?
Is it only for bowing one's head like a reed
and for lying in sackcloth and ashes?
Is that what you call a fast,
a day acceptable to the LORD?

"Is not this the kind of fasting I have chosen:
to loose the chains of injustice
and untie the cords of the yoke,
to set the oppressed free
and break every yoke?

Is it not to share your food with the hungry
and to provide the poor wanderer with shelter—
when you see the naked, to clothe them,
and not to turn away from your own flesh and blood?
Then your light will break forth like the dawn,
and your healing will quickly appear;
then your righteousness will go before you,
and the glory of the LORD will be your rear guard.
Then you will call, and the LORD will answer;
you will cry for help, and he will say: Here am I."

Isaiah 58:1-9

Unjust laws exist; shall we be content to obey them, or shall we endeavor to amend them…?

Henry David Thoreau

CHAPTER 1

Wales: 1925

COLD WIND BIT WILLIAM'S FACE. He tucked his chin deeper into the wool scarf and squinted. Last year's weeds were trampled and fallen, killed by heavy hooves and heavier frosts. The land sloped like sleepy, old men toward Afon Tywi, its waters dark in the coming dusk.

"Did you hear it?" Amaryllis asked, stopping beside her father.

"No. Just wondering where I'd go if I wanted to warm up."

He scanned the hills again.

"I'd go home," she said.

"Ahh, but you aren't a sheep. Sheep don't use logic."

"Well, if I'm being illogical, I guess I'd head for the river."

"You might be right." He pointed toward a tangle of brambles. "There's a drop-off just past those briers. Might be hunched down there out of the wind."

This land was all that William had and all that he wanted. Hunting down stray ewes in late February wasn't his favorite part of shepherding, but you took the bad with the good, Taid Williams had always said. Taid had taught William everything he knew about shepherding while William's own father worked his life away in the mines.

"There's Ian Roi Bugail." Amaryllis pointed toward the hedge line. "Maybe he's seen her." She waved her arm over her head and shouted into the wind. "Ian Roi!"

"He'll not hear you. Run on over and ask what he knows."

Long waves of black hair rolled out behind the girl as she ran across the field. William kept walking toward the river, its own dark waves whipping crests of white foam in the wind. The sun was nearly down now, and the ewe would soon be lost in the darkness.

Desperate bleating drifted from the river. William picked up his pace and headed toward the sound. Just as he supposed, the ewe had climbed down the ridge. The first slivers of spring grass, sheltered against the embankment, had enticed the ewe to venture down the steep hill. Now she was stranded on the ledge, unable to turn without losing her footing.

"Greed got you into this mess. Now what you going to do?"

William sat on the hillside and scooted down to the ledge. The pregnant ewe was bulky and awkward, refusing to be turned up the hill. Man and beast struggled in a war of knowledge and fear.

"Need some help?"

William looked up to see Ian Roi Bugail smiling over the edge of the bank. Amaryllis stood next to him, blowing on her hands.

"She's not wanting to budge," William said.

"That's the thing about sheep. They seem to know exactly what they ought to do, but they try their hardest not to do it." Ian Roi shook his head and chuckled.

"At least she's out of the wind down here."

"Can't leave her there, though. Where's your rod?"

"Back at the barn. Amaryllis and I were out walking when I noticed a hole in the wall. My count found this one absent."

"Sing her on up, then. You know the way."

A shot rang out from the woods. William jolted and fell to the ground.

"Dad?" Amaryllis called down. She leaned over as far as she could.

"You're alright, William. Just Thomas over in the trees. They've had some badgers on his farm."

William stood up and dusted his trousers. "Sorry 'bout that. Can't seem to get over it."

"No worries. Now bring her on up."

William stooped beside the ewe and looked her in the eyes. He started singing, soft and gentle:

"When summer's radiant months are come,
And leaves and flowerets spring,
When mid the trees all white with bloom
The feathered warblers sing."

William stood and turned up the path, dark against the dry brown grasses of winter. The sheep fell in line behind him and followed up the hillside.

"'Twas thus a youth of courtly mien
At springtime in the grove,
Told to the hamlet's blushing queen,
His tale of faithless love."

Amaryllis wrapped her arms around the ewe's neck as it sprinted over the edge of the bank. Ian Roi handed William a long stick.

"This will help you home. See you later, friend."

"Thanks." William took the long beech rod. "I'll come by tomorrow and return it."

"No need. I have more at home." Ian Roi walked into the darkening meadow. "Better get her back before she goes to wandering again."

William prodded the sheep and headed home.

"Were you afraid in the war?" Amaryllis asked, walking beside her father.

"Yes."

"What if there's another? Will you go back?"

Amaryllis took her father's hand. He put it in his pocket with his own.

"Many years ago there was a Welsh shepherd lad who went to London to seek his fortune. One night he was walking along London Bridge when a Welshman stopped him.

"'Where'd you get that hazel staff?' the man asked.

"'Back home in Wales. It grows on the hillside where I keep the sheep.'

"'Lead me there and I'll show you wonders beyond your imagining,' the man urged the boy.

"They hurried back to Wales, and on the hillside where the hazel trees grew, the man led the shepherd boy to a secret entrance below ground. They crept inside, and in that dim cave the boy saw a prince and all his mighty warriors.

"The prince awoke and called out, 'Does Wales need us? Has the day come?'

"'Not yet,' the man answered, and the prince went back to sleep."

Amaryllis rested her head on her father's arm. "So you would go back to war."

"There'll not be another war; the Great War has

ended all wars. But, yes, if I was needed, I would go."

"But you're afraid. Why would you go?"

"For the same reason the knights can sleep in the hills. I'm a Welsh warrior—awake and ready to serve."

"Would Ian Roi go with you again?"

"I'm sure he would, but we would both miss the sheep. We prefer the sound of sheep over the sound of shot."

William stopped and pulled his daughter close. They watched the last light fade away over the hillside. Woodsmoke from the stone cottage along the lane scented the evening air. An owl hooted from the tree line.

"Why did God make Wales so beautiful and the life of a shepherd so short?" William said, then sighed.

"Wales is beautiful … but you're old." Amaryllis laughed and took off running for home.

William followed behind, guiding the sheep.

———

"Where've you been? The littles are in bed already."

"Sorry, Eileen." William kissed her cheek. "There was a hole in the wall and one of the ewes made a break for it, she did." He sat on a kitchen chair and pulled off his heavy boots. "Amaryllis and I found her over by Afon Tywi."

"Ian Roi helped us get her out," Amaryllis added.

"Was she safe, then?" Eileen stood with her hands on her thin hips. The fire that had flashed in her eyes was only glowing embers now. Eileen loved William, but his sheep were only business to her. They paid the bills—nearly. A missing ewe would mean missing shoes or clothes for her children.

"Yes, she's safe back with the rest of them. I'll fix the wall tomorrow."

"I won't be able to help. I'm going to town tomorrow. I cleaned twenty fish this afternoon and they'll bring close to a pound, I bet. Amaryllis, you head up to bed now."

Amaryllis kissed her mother and headed for the stairs.

"See you in the morning," Eileen said.

*He has shown you, O mortal, what is good. And what does
the LORD require of you? To act justly and to love mercy
and to walk humbly with your God.*

Micah 6:8

CHAPTER 2

Judah—near the Dead Sea:
circa 760 BC

"JUST SEEMS THEY COULD FIND somewhere
else to go." Kediah stood on the ladder halfway
up the tree. "We're being overrun with their like."

Amos looked across the orchard. Small tents dotted the outer region of trees. Two women stirred pots
while children poked the fires with sticks. He glanced
back up the ladder.

"There aren't that many," Amos said. "We were
foreigners once as well." He gave the ladder a shake.
"How's it looking?"

"They're big." Kediah wrapped his hands around a
fig and then held his hand up for Amos to approve.
"The king will be pleased."

"The king doesn't eat sycamore figs. Likely they'll be
served in the lower kitchens, but he will appreciate the
payment." Amos smiled. "Come on down. We'll start
the cuttings tomorrow."

The sinking sun glinted off Kediah's white smock

as he jumped off the ladder halfway down. He liked reminding his master how much younger he was, spry and limber as a house cat.

Amos laughed and patted him on the shoulder. "Since you didn't have three days' travel, go on and plate up my dinner," Amos said. "I'll be there in a moment."

Kediah's shoulders slumped. It wasn't the compliment he had hoped for.

Amos ignored the young man and walked toward the tents. He had been to the orchard in spring to make sure the fertilizers had been applied. There were no tents then. He clasped his hands behind his back and walked like a lion gauging its surroundings, nonchalant but ever watchful.

Five tents were circled around the fires. Ten to fifteen people per tent, Amos reckoned. Seventy-five wanderers could be a problem, but they obviously weren't all men. He waved to one of the children as he neared. A woman looked up and shoved the youngster behind her skirts.

"Shalom." Amos smiled and extended his hand to an elderly man who came forward. "I'm Amos, dresser of figs and herder of sheep."

"Shalom." The man smiled and clasped Amos's forearm. "I am Elelbet. I also have been a herder of sheep. Now I am a wandering old man."

"Why do you wander?" Amos gestured toward a fallen log and the two men sat together.

"The only reason any man would leave his home: war has driven us from our fields and pastures." He sighed and rested his elbows on his knees. Talking seemed an effort. "We have been driven from the land by both North and South."

"You're from Gilead." Amos knew the accent from

some of his business deals.

The old man nodded.

A boy approached with two bowls of thin broth. He handed one to Elelbet and then held the other to Amos. The men took the bowls and nodded dismissal to the child. They slurped the soup and chewed on their thoughts.

Elelbet broke the silence. "Gilead is a land of plenty, pastures for sheep and cattle, but not for Israelites." He glanced at Amos. "We are still Israelites … brothers."

"You're welcome to stay." Amos patted the man's thigh. "How many men do you have?" The lion was still on the prowl.

"Only twelve. The women have worked as hard as any men." The old man sighed. "We won't be trouble. Most of them are children. The Ammonites made sure there were no fathers or mothers left."

Amos looked around the small compound. Women and children watched through lowered eyes. There was movement at the door of one of the tents.

"How long have you been here?" Amos asked.

"The Ammonites burned our village in the spring. Ripped my granddaughter open. It would have been her fourth child." Silent tears slid down Elelbet's face. "I was in the hills with the first of the lambing. The children found me. There was nowhere to go but across the Jordan. We found a haven in your orchard in late spring as the sycamores bloomed."

"And the twelve men? What have they been doing?" Amos looked at Elelbet but also noticed the tent flap pulled farther aside.

"Hunting in the hills, fishing in the river, running from our brothers." The man pursed his lips in a half smile. "No one sits to talk or share a bowl of soup."

"You're safe here." Amos stood and offered his hand to Elelbet. "My men will begin cutting the figs tomorrow. Tell your *twelve men* in the tent not to bother my people, and you won't be bothered either."

Elelbet nodded his head. Amos turned back to the trees.

———

"You aren't hungry?" Kediah stood near the table while Amos picked at his dinner.

Amos blinked up at his servant. "I had some broth earlier." Amos took a deep breath as Kediah furrowed his brow. "The Gileadites in the tents." He scooped some bits of meat onto his bread. "There's an old man and a lot of women and children. There are young men too. He says twelve. Have you seen them?"

Kediah nodded. "They came soon after you left in the spring. I thought they would leave when I gave them no lodging."

"Why did you not offer them hospitality? It's the Lord's way." Amos eyed his servant.

"How could I know if it was safe to let them in? What if they took my master's things and harmed me?" Kediah raised his shoulders, helpless.

"I doubt they could do much to harm you. A flock of women and a herd of children is what it looked like. I told them they could stay. You're to leave them alone. You hear me?"

Kediah shifted his weight from left to right and nodded to his master. Amos was a careful man but sometimes too friendly. Kediah didn't trust as easily as his master.

"It's been a long day, and my bones aren't as fresh

as yours." Amos smiled at the young man. "I'll go to bed and we can start early tomorrow." He stood and stretched before walking toward the bedroom.

"Sleep well, Master Amos." Kediah began clearing the table with his wife. "I'll wake the men early."

———•———

The morning air was pleasant streaming through the open window. Amos loved coming to the sycamore orchard during harvest. His soul breathed deeply in the mountain air of Tekoa, but it was the warm air of the river valley that helped him exhale. He sat up in bed and looked through the window. The sun was just peeking through the trunks of the trees.

"You're up." Kediah knocked gently on the half-open door and came in. "The men are finishing breakfast now. I think it will be a profitable harvest, Master. Will you stay through the whole season?"

"Of course. I shouldn't be needed in Tekoa before rutting season. Elroi will come in a few weeks to report on the flock." Amos stood and scratched his belly. "What's for breakfast?"

"Leah has made all of your favorites. She thinks you appreciate her cooking more than I do." Kediah looked at the ceiling.

"And do I? The way to a woman's heart is through her ears, Kediah." Amos began dressing. "Do you tell her how marvelous her melons are?" He grinned and watched the young man.

"Come when you're ready." Kediah was bright red. "I'll help the men with the ladders."

———•———

Amos slurped a cup of water from the bucket and surveyed his plantation. Men hung from tree branches and ladder rungs. They grasped each fig tightly and gouged the side before moving on. Wasps and bees flew around their heads in the warm autumn sun.

Children stood along the tree line, watching the process. When they saw Amos looking at them, they hid behind the trees. He wiped his mouth with his sleeve and put the cup back in the bucket.

"Some trees need to be replaced soon, my lord." Kediah appeared at Amos's side. "I hear there are new ones coming from Egypt by ship."

"And how do you hear these things?" Amos's eyes narrowed.

"I've been watching my master." The young man grinned. "He's a wise businessman."

"And what have you learned?"

"That I can't look after trees alone; I must listen to those who pass through. The Moabites have been buying trees from Gaza. They traveled through all winter getting ready for the spring planting."

Amos nodded and crossed his arms. "And how many of these Moabites crossed my land?"

"Maybe ten or twelve groups." Kediah shrugged. "I didn't count."

"Seventeen. Leah counted." Amos's eyes danced. "She was rather put out with you having her cook for so many. Said she thought she worked harder than you, but you kept all the money."

"We didn't use any of your food, Master Amos. Honest." Kediah flushed red and then turned ghostly white.

"It's alright." Amos laughed and put his hand on the young man's arm. "But I think you better get a new dress for Leah when the next caravan goes through."

"Yes, sir." His color returned. "But the trees. The winter was hard on the section near the foothill." He pointed toward the tents of the Gileadites. "They used a lot of the old wood for fires."

Amos took a deep breath and nodded. He exhaled and turned back to the men as he said, "I'll see what I can do. Perhaps a trip to Ashdod this winter. I won't have time to go all the way to Gaza. Ashdod is safer anyway."

Charity begins at home, and justice begins next door.
Charles Dickens

CHAPTER 3

MARCH WAS COMING IN LIKE a lamb. Yesterday's biting wind was today's nibbling breeze.
The sun was warm on Eileen's bare head as she carried
the heavy basket of fish toward town. The rolling hills
would soon be emeralds inset with the white pearls of
lambs. She found beauty in the ordered countryside,
but the shepherd's life was a hard one and times were
harder now that wool prices were down.

"Anyone to home?" Eileen knocked on the first
wooden door in town. "Fresh trout!"

She could hear children playing around the back of
the house. The door cracked open and a pale woman
looked out.

"Good morning, Doris. I've got some fresh fish, I
have. You're my first stop. Pick of the bunch." Eileen
smiled and lifted the basket higher.

"I buy over at the company store," Doris said.

"I can beat their prices. What do you pay over there?"

"It's not that." Doris tilted her head. "They might
hear I bought from you, and Charlie'd get in trouble."

"They can't tell you where to buy your fish." Eileen
snorted and furrowed her eyebrows.

"Just the same, I don't want any. Thanks."

The door shut, and Doris appeared at the front window. Eileen waved a small salute of understanding and moved onto the next house. The story was the same. The company store had noticed Eileen's fish business last fall and decided to shut her down.

By the time she made it to the schoolhouse, her basket was only three fish lighter. She crossed the street to the company store. She pushed the door open and walked in.

Bob stood guard behind the counter. He raised his eyebrows at Eileen's basket, then went back to writing on his tickets. Eileen walked around the store a minute to prepare for the fight, then approached the counter.

"What do you think you're doing telling people not to buy my fish? It's still a free country from what I know, or did my husband take three bullets for nothing?" She plopped the basket on the stand and glared at the middle-aged man behind the counter.

"Now, Mrs. Williams, what do you mean? No one's stopping you from selling fish." Bob put his pencil behind his ear and stared at Eileen. "In fact I might be interested in buying some, I might. Let me have a look."

He uncovered the heavy basket and poked through the fillets.

"Already cleaned and cut," Eileen said. "Too early for the sea trout, but these brown trout will be tasty on your table." She knew how to talk up her sales.

"Not my table," Bob said. "I'll take them for the store. Ten shillings for the lot."

Eileen's eyes popped wide open. "What? They're worth twice that and you know it. You'll not have any of my fish at that price." She covered the basket and grabbed the handle.

"Your loss, not mine."

Eileen huffed and stormed out of the store. The children were outside for morning recess across the street. Eileen walked to the play yard and waved at them. Allen was involved in a ball game and Iris was skipping rope. She turned back up the street and headed home.

Three blocks from the edge of town, Eileen turned east toward the river. The little whitewashed house facing the street looked dingy and sad. The thatch roof sagged. Eileen took a deep breath, exhaled, then trotted up to the door.

"Constance, it's me," she called. She opened the door and walked in. "Constance?"

"Back here I am."

Eileen headed toward the back of the house where the dark kitchen was hidden. "Can I interest you in some fish?"

Constance stood over a pot of boiling water with a large wooden stick, pushing shirts in the soapy water. She wiped her arm across her forehead, and strands of light-brown hair stuck to her skin. She smiled at Eileen and said, "The children would love it, but you know I can't pay you."

"I'd rather give it to you for free than sell it for nothing." She set the fish on the counter. "Should I put it in the icebox?"

"Thanks. I'll stew it when I get done with the laundry. Enoch Evans pays me to do up his laundry since his wife died."

"That's good, for you and for him. How's Enoch doing these days?"

Constance blew hair out of her eyes and kept agitating the shirts. Eileen opened the icebox door and moved things aside for the fish. She shut the door and crossed the floor to the stove.

"He's getting along. The children are having a hard go of it. He says they aren't doing well at school. Alice told me they get in trouble a lot."

"Alice ought to know how it feels. She's old enough to remember." Eileen took the paddle from Constance. "Sit down a minute. I can handle this."

Constance smiled and handed the washing stick over. She sat at the table and sighed. "It's hard on the children, that it is. Alice remembers her dad. The boys know his pictures. That's all Morgan has of course." She smoothed her hair back and pulled her sweater tight around her bony shoulders. "Enoch's children will remember their mother for a long time. They're angry." She strummed her fingers on the table. "Cup of tea?"

"No thanks. I can't stay long. I just wanted to check on you and give you the fish. William will need me home soon." She sighed, thinking about the unprofitable morning. "He's mending a wall now. One of the ewes escaped last night."

The women stayed silent a few minutes, lost in their own problems.

"These are done," Eileen said. "I'll be off now."

"Thanks for helping." Constance rose. "I'll take that."

———◆———

"Look who came for dinner," William said as he and Allen burst through the door.

A blast of cold air banged the door against the wall. William shut it while Allen stood grinning ear to ear. Iris ran over to stroke the tiny lamb wrapped against her brother's chest.

"It's the first of the season," Allen said. "His mother

had triplets. Can you believe it?" He put his cheek against the lamb's black head. "She won't take this one. Dad says I can bottle-feed it and it can sleep behind the stove."

"Already?" Eileen sighed in exasperation. "Do we have to start nursing babies in the house the first day of March?"

"How would it survive if we left it outside, Mum?" Allen asked. "It's too cold in the barn this early." He looked up at his mother.

She couldn't think of an answer, so she said, "It's your responsibility, then. You'll run home on lunch hour and feed it, not playing with your butties and expecting me to be nurse in the day."

Allen grinned up at her, but Eileen knew it was useless and went on, "And you'll clean up its messes, you will."

"Yes, Mum. I'll take good care of it. You'll never even know it's here."

"Get out the nursery box," Eileen said, then turned. "Amaryllis, you know where the warming rags are. Dinner will be ready soon."

Eileen twisted her lips and stared at William. She turned on her heel and walked back to the cookstove. William came behind her and circled her waist with his arms.

"You're a good woman, Eileen."

"And you're a cold man, William Williams." She slapped at his hands. "Go wash up for dinner."

He kissed her ear and laughed. "Triplets on March the first—Saint David's Day. It's going to be a good year, yes it is."

"Thank you for Wales, for Dewi our patron saint, and for the birth of the three little lambs," William prayed. "Your abundance is our blessing. Amen."

"Amen," they all agreed.

"Fish and turnips." William dished out a heaping spoonful and passed it to Amaryllis. "Did you sell all your trout today?"

Eileen shook her head but said nothing. She handed a slice of bread to Iris.

"Mum came by the school today," Iris said. "I saw her when I was skipping rope." She looked at her dad. "She looked angry."

William raised his eyebrows and looked at Eileen.

"Eat your dinner, Iris," Eileen said. "And pass the turnips, Allen. I wasn't angry. I was … I was indignant." She nodded her head and took a bite of brown bread.

"What happened?" William asked.

"The company store told the miners that they have to buy their food there. They evidently didn't like my competition last year. Bob offered to buy my basket for half what it was worth. I told him not on his life and left." Her eyes flashed.

"No one would buy from you?" William licked a piece of fish from his lip.

"A few did, but the rest were tucking their tails and shutting their doors. I tried talking to Bob at the store, but he's toeing the same line."

"So we'll be eating all that fish for a while." William smiled.

"No, I took it over to Constance. Figured I'd rather help her than help old Granville Jones. She needs my fish more than he does."

"Granville's just trying to make a living like the rest of us. But this is our year. We'll be fine without the fish money."

The lamb bleated behind the stove.

Love and compassion are necessities, not luxuries. Without
them humanity cannot survive.

Tenzin Gyatso, the 14th Dalai Lama

CHAPTER 4

THE FIRST OF THE FIGS were ready for picking.
The autumn nights were getting cooler, but the
days were still summerlike.

Amos sorted through the basket of fruit. "A good
crop to pay King Uzziah's tax," he said.

Kediah's teeth flashed white in his tanned face. He
had struggled all winter to fertilize the aged trees.
Their broad bases and clumps of roots were difficult
to work around. Now the effort had paid off with a
compliment from his lord.

"The wagons are ready to carry them to Jerusalem,
Master."

Amos nodded and looked at the donkeys standing
with their loaded carts. The perfume of ripe fig was
rich in the air. Amos handed the last basket of fruit to
Kediah for loading. "You earned your wages this year,
Kediah. May the Lord bless you."

"Thank you, sir."

Amos held his hand up to shade his eyes. A man was
coming down the hillside along the western path.

"Elroi!" Amos called and waved his arms.

Kediah turned to look.

"Elroi is here," Amos went on. "You can handle this without me." He patted Kediah's back and started down the road.

———

"How many are still in the upper fields?" Amos asked Elroi.

"It's been a warm autumn. Most of the shepherds are still grazing their flocks there." Elroi licked his fingers and looked at Leah standing by the table. "This is a tasty dinner. The bread I brought from Tekoa is stale."

"I'm glad you enjoy it." Leah smiled and bowed her head, eyes on the floor.

"Leah has been feeding Moabites all winter, I've discovered." Amos winked at Elroi. "She'll cause another war when men hear how well she cooks."

A giggle escaped the young woman. She turned back to the kitchen.

"Moabites, huh?" Elroi asked. "Is that who's camped at the edge of your land?"

Amos shook his head and tore his bread in half. "Gileadites. Been camped there all summer from what I can gather."

"Pushed out?" Elroi asked, watching Amos.

Amos sopped up gravy with the bread and nodded. "There's an elderly man, several women and children, and perhaps twelve men. The men didn't show themselves. I'm not sure how much I can trust them."

"You know there's trouble in Gilead. Has been for years. Why would they lie to you?"

"Winter will be here in a few months." Amos shrugged. "They'll need some food. Might get desperate."

"How many of your men headed to Jerusalem just now?"

Amos stroked his beard and looked at the old shepherd. A slow smile spread across his face. "What are you suggesting?"

"You're short workers." Elroi raised his eyebrows.

"How can I trust them? I don't even know them."

"They're your brothers, are they not? And have they caused trouble this summer?" He turned his head to the kitchen. "Leah, have the Gileadites been a nuisance this summer?"

Leah popped her head through the door. "Excuse me?"

"The Gileadites." Elroi looked at her. "The ones at the edge of the orchard. Have they caused trouble for you and Kediah?"

"Not at all." Leah brushed a stray hair from her forehead. "Sometimes I hear the children playing in the stream, but noise isn't a bother."

"Did you lock up everything at night?" Amos asked, eyeing the young woman.

"Should I have?" Her face turned red. "They seemed harmless. Nothing went missing, except for the time a group of Moabites came through. Kediah couldn't find his shovel the next day, but I think that was before the Gileadites showed up."

"Thank you, Leah." Amos waved dismissal, then looked the shepherd in the eye. "So you think I should hire these men for the harvest."

"It's your fig harvest ... your money. But they are foreigners and brothers alike."

"And it's the right thing to do," Amos said, then sighed softly.

Elroi clasped Amos's hand on the table and gave it a

squeeze. "Helping others less fortunate than yourself is never the wrong thing to do."

———————

"How are you, Elelbet?" Amos sat down beside the old man. "Are you warm enough at night?"

The old man sat in a fading sunny spot near the fire. He nodded his head. "The children curl up to me and I sleep like a hen on a nest. We're all warm." He rubbed his hands together. "I see your harvest is going well."

"Yes. The king will be pleased. And now is my turn to be pleased. The second cutting begins tomorrow. Can you spare some men to help?"

Elelbet's face remained unchanged, but a glimmer of hope brightened his eyes. "My men are shepherds, not fig-dressers. They don't know how to cut the figs."

"It isn't difficult. They'll learn in no time." Amos glanced around the small compound of tents and campfires. "Are they here?"

"They'll be back soon. They found day work in a neighbor's field."

"Then they do know more than shepherding. Quick learners too, I bet. All shepherds are." Amos stood and held out his hand. "Send them over tomorrow."

"How many?" Elelbet asked as he shook Amos's hand.

"Six?"

"Thank you. They'll be there." The old man smiled and pulled his cloak tighter.

"Better gather your chicks, Elelbet. Once the sun is down, it'll be cold." Amos laughed. "Tomorrow." He turned and walked home.

———————

"Sir?" A knock sounded on the door. "Sir, are you awake?"

Amos stretched under the covers. He took a deep breath and opened his eyes. "Morning already?"

"Yes, my lord." Kediah walked in the room. "There are men at the barn gate. They say you told them to come work the figs."

"Ahh … yes. Gileadites?"

Kediah nodded.

"Mm-hm. I thought we could use some help, what with the men on their way to Jerusalem." Amos sat up in bed.

Kediah shuffled his feet.

"Is there a problem?" Amos asked.

"No. … Yes." Kediah twisted his hands.

"What's the matter, Kediah?" Amos threw the covers back and put his feet over the edge of the bed.

"Do we need them? We didn't hire extra hands last year."

"You're such a good farmer, the crop is bigger than last year."

"Thanks, sir, but I don't think it's that plentiful. Their wages will cost the extra profit." Kediah took a step forward and opened his hands. "You won't make any more money."

"You're worried about the money." Amos started dressing. "That's a good businessman."

"Yes, the money." Kediah exhaled.

"Well, I don't think it will cost me more than the extra I'm making." Amos sat on the edge of the bed to put on his shoes. "And since I fared well enough on last year's income, I think it will be alright. Put the men to work, Kediah." Amos looked up at his servant.

"But—"

"The Lord provides so that we can provide."

"Yes, Master Amos." Kediah bowed and left the room. His sandals slapped down the hall and out of the house.

———

Amos watched the men climbing in the trees. Their legs dangled from branches as they swiftly cut each fig with their curved, metal tools. The early-morning sun glinted off the dewy grass and tiny spiderwebs.

"I'll be heading back today," Elroi said.

Amos turned and saw his old friend holding a hot cup of broth. "So soon?"

"The sheep will be coming off the mountains by the time I get back. They'll need some direction." Elroi grinned. He had been guiding shepherds through the passes and meadows for as long as there were sheep. "The Gileadites working out?" He lifted his cup toward the orchard.

"They're good workers." Amos turned halfway to look again at his trees. "I can't imagine what they've been through."

"War is a pestilence, an evil from beyond." Elroi blew across the cup of steaming broth before taking a sip. "It was right for you to take them. They were sheep without a shepherd."

"I just hope I'm not the one who gets fleeced."

———

Men's voices echoed off the house wall. Leah kept the table filled with meat, bread, and vegetables. The men filled their plates and then found a seat. They sat on benches and a few chairs outside the main entrance.

Amos and Kediah were stationed at the end of the

house, ready to pay the men. They had managed to score the figs in record time and the next harvest should begin in less than a fortnight. The regular hired hands joked together, eating and laughing. The Gileadites sat together in a group, dry leaves crackling into dust.

"You take care of this," Amos said as he handed the ledger to Kediah and walked over to the men. "How's your meal, Jacob?" he asked the oldest of them.

"Fine, sir." Jacob stood and wiped his mouth with his sleeve.

"Your brothers are very quiet. Is there a problem?" Amos looked Jacob in the eye.

"No, sir." He had no expression.

"Sit." Amos motioned to the chair where Jacob had been seated. Amos pulled a chair up next to him. "Tell me your plans. What will you do now?"

"We'll look for more work. Some of us are thinking we'll go to Jerusalem for the winter. Maybe we can find work there. The women and children and Elelbet will stay here of course." Jacob bit his lower lip. "It doesn't feel right to leave them, not after what happened. I worry if they'll be safe."

"They should be safe enough. Kediah and Leah are here year-round. A few of the men will stay and help as well. There might be some piecemeal work for whoever stays behind." Amos stroked his beard. "What about the children? Any strong enough to pull a plough? Maybe they could help turn the fields for some meals."

The air changed immediately. Jacob sat stiff and his brothers' eyes slanted.

"You'll not take our children," Jacob said. "They're all we have left. Ploughs would only make it worse."

"What do you mean?" Amos furrowed his brow.

"The Syrians came down from Damascus. They lined up the captives and took every third one for their play. They lay the men in the fields and ploughed over them, metal teeth biting their flesh and piercing their lungs. They died in a field of blood." Jacob spoke plainly, emotion dried up in the scabs and scars of time. "We eat what the Lord provides and not what our plough can turn. It's too ..." His voice trailed off. No description could satisfy.

"Of course." Amos touched Jacob on the arm. "I won't ask again. My men will be back from Jerusalem soon. They'll pick the second harvest and then head to Tekoa." He looked at all the men. "What's left of the third harvest is to be shared with you. You can work beside Kediah and keep what you need." He nodded to each of them. "The third harvest is never great, but it will help you through."

Jacob nodded in return. "Thank you, Master Amos. You're very kind."

"You can gather your pay when you finish eating." Amos stood. "I'll have Leah pack a bag of sweets for the children."

Labor to keep alive in your breast that little spark
of celestial fire called conscience.

George Washington

CHAPTER 5

"TURN YOUR PAPERS IN NOW. Up to the front, there you go."

The students passed their tests to the front of the row and then started gathering their things. School was more than reading and writing. There were games of Oranges and Lemons to play, and the girl who caught the right boy might get to hold his hand through an entire round.

The morning fog had burned off and left the schoolyard in sparkling diamond droplets. The crowd of students broke off into groups as they left the schoolhouse. Oranges and Lemons was always played near the patch of flowers that the teachers tended without success.

"Oranges and lemons, say the bells of Saint Clement's." The grade-nine students sang. "You owe me five farthings, say the bells of Saint Martin's."

Amaryllis followed the line of students passing under the arch of Thomas's and Owen's arms. They always wanted to be first so they could rock everyone they caught.

"Here comes a candle to light you to bed, and here

comes a chopper to chop off your head!"

Everyone moved through the arch a bit faster and tried to sidestep as the rhyme came to an end.

"Chip chop, chip chop, the last man is dead!"

Amaryllis was caught. Thomas and Owen crashed their arms around her and swayed her back and forth before releasing her to join in their chant.

The line of boys and girls shuffled under their arms, grinning at Amaryllis, who had so easily fallen victim and now had to stand next to Thomas and Owen. Susan tried to push along the others so that she could be caught by Amaryllis and save her from disgrace. But the chorus came too late and Susan was past when "the last man is dead" rang out.

Amaryllis dropped her arms around Dennis Byrne, the Irish boy that smelled of cheese and sounded like he had a mouth full of marbles when he spoke. He looked down at the ground and then turned to the side to take his place. Amaryllis raised her arms high to grab the boy's hands, but he was so much taller that she had to lean forward to reach. Dennis smiled an apology and took her hands.

Amaryllis smiled back and sang the song with everyone else. She noticed Dennis only mouthed the words, sometimes not seeming to know what the verses were. She squeezed his hands as the chorus neared. They dropped their arms but caught no one.

"Dumb Irish. Don't even know how to play," Owen said and laughed. "Good luck, 'Ryllis. You'll be here the rest of break."

Dennis dropped his head. Amaryllis didn't say a word.

"Are you coming to the café?" Susan asked.

Amaryllis shook her head as she put on her coat. She pulled her long hair out of the back and over the collar.

"I have to check on the sheep. Lambing has begun. Allen has a new lamb in the house. You should come see it."

"Mm. Henry asked if he could walk me home after we finish." Susan turned pink and looked at her feet.

"Another time, then," Amaryllis said.

The girls walked down the hall and met Allen and Iris outside the school doors.

"Have fun." Amaryllis waved good-bye. "Come on, you two. We better hurry before Mum gets upset about that lamb."

The older students were headed toward the Italian café past the company store. Amaryllis heard a thud against the school wall. She turned to see three boys throwing rocks. Dennis ran past her and the little kids.

"Dennis," Amaryllis called. "What—"

"Go on with you then, stupid Irish!" came Thomas's voice.

A rock whizzed through the air near Iris.

"Thomas!" Amaryllis shouted. "Stop it! You're going to hit Iris." Amaryllis grabbed her sister and pulled her back. "What are you doing?"

Thomas stopped his arm in the air. His butties ran.

"Just teaching that Irish boy his place." Thomas heaved the last rock high in the air and turned. "We don't allow his kind at the café," he called over his shoulder.

———

"Why are they like that?" Amaryllis asked Ian Roi.

She watched the sheepdogs circling the flock above the tree line. She rested her head against the rod in her right hand.

"Fear." Ian Roi never said more than was needed.

"Why would they be afraid of Dennis? He's big but harmless. He can't even speak right."

"What can he do right?"

Ian Roi looked at Amaryllis. His eyebrows were raised. It was one of those looks she never knew how to read. Was he treating her like an adult and asking a genuine question, or was he trying to trap her in some juvenile logic that would make her squirm and turn red?

"I don't know." She looked away. The dogs were bringing the flock down the hillside now. "I've heard him whistle pretty well, I have."

Ian Roi whistled for the dogs to turn to the left toward the meadow gate. They flanked the sheep and turned them in a graceful sweep. Ian Roi started walking again, and Amaryllis fell in step.

"I don't know if he can whistle that good, though," she said.

Ian Roi chuckled. He was a lot like her father, never taking anything too seriously.

"You should keep looking for what he does well. In the meantime what are you going to do about your classmates who are attacking him?"

"Me?" Amaryllis looked over at the shepherd. "What can I do? The boys are bigger than I am. I can tell the teachers, but I don't think that'll make much difference."

They reached the gate where the dogs were waiting, sitting on their haunches. The sheep were grazing in the new field. Ian Roi latched the gate and patted the dogs' heads, then turned to watch the ewes.

"The other night," he said, "when your dad's ewe was lost by the river, how did he get her to safety?"

"You know. He sang a song and she followed him up."

"Why didn't he just hoist her up or beat her into charging up the bank?"

"She was too big to lift in that little space. And Dad would never beat one of his ewes. They trust him too much."

Ian Roi nodded. "Beating never seems to do much good for man nor beast in my experience. Those boys at school are too big for you to manhandle anyway. Maybe you could find a song?"

"What?" Amaryllis looked like she'd been thrown in a cold river. "I'm not singing to no boys. I'd never hear the end of it, I wouldn't."

"Not a real song." Ian Roi laughed. "But a gentle voice can often guide around sharp rocks."

Amaryllis looked at the bulky ewes, their heads lowered to the new spring grass. The darkness was growing, and her stomach was rumbling. Mum would have dinner on the table soon.

"Maybe. I don't know." She turned toward home. "Thanks for helping me move them, Ian Roi." She waved over her shoulder.

"My pleasure, Amaryllis."

If we had power over the ends of the Earth, it would not give us that fulfillment of existence which a quiet, devoted relationship to nearby life can give us.

Martin Buber

CHAPTER 6

RAIN SLAMMED AGAINST THE SIDE of the barn. The wind blew around the eaves, wishing one last winter blast. William breathed in the smell of manure and wet wool. The barn was warm and humid with the breath of ewes and the birth of lambs.

Spring was especially wet and cold this year. The ewes had to be corralled in small pens. While keeping five lambs behind the stove last night, lambing outdoors had proved too treacherous, with three dead lambs from exposure already. But the indoor pens had treachery of their own.

Several ewes in pen five refused to stand. William could smell the foot rot as soon as he pushed the first ewe aside. He sighed. Sheep needed to stand on dry ground or bacteria would begin to grow and infect the flock's feet. It was too painful for them to stand, so they would walk on their knees, or just refuse to move as these ewes were doing. Her lambs would starve if she wasn't treated quickly.

"Hello!"

The barn door slammed shut, and Ian Roi tipped

rainwater off his wide-brimmed hat. William exhaled and smiled. The cavalry had arrived.

"Just the man I need to see," William called as he closed the pen's gate behind him. "Have you got some time to help an old friend?"

"What's the problem?"

"Foot rot." William reached out his hand to welcome Ian Roi. "I've lost too many lambs in this cold rain. I had to bring the ewes in, but now …" He lifted his hands in resignation. "Do you have time to help me treat them?"

"I do. Have you got all you need? I can head back home and get some zinc."

"No, I'm good, I am." William turned, and Ian Roi followed. "So far the only pen infected is this one." He stopped in front of pen five. "I'll have to bathe these three pretty good, but we can just run the others through the standing pads."

"Right."

William mixed the chemical solution while Ian Roi turned the healthy ewes into an empty run. He dusted the area with zinc sulfate and ran them through it.

"Ready now," William called to Ian Roi as he walked from the other end of the barn.

Together they lifted the infected sheep and carried them one by one to the treatment stanchions.

"Hold still now, little lady," William said as he wrestled the ewe onto the raised stanchion. "It'll be over soon."

The ewes bawled and butted, trying to get away from the shepherds, but the men were more determined. The treatment left the sheep angry and achy, but they would survive.

Ian Roi wiped sweat off his forehead and leaned

against a pen. "You've lost some already this year?"

"Three lambs." William nodded. "They were born night before last. The mothers didn't have sense enough to get out of the elements. I brought the yearlings in for lambing, but I thought the others would be alright."

Ian Roi nodded his head. "That was the right thought. You just can't tell with sheep."

"I forget all sheep are stupid."

"Well now, I don't know as I'd say that. You haven't met all sheep." Ian Roi smiled.

"True. I guess I'd say they've all been dim, and some—poor souls—haven't lit the torch at all."

"William?" Eileen called from the door. "Lunch is ready."

"Got any extra? Ian Roi came to help me today. He's earned his lunch, yes he has."

———

"Turnips are all we've got left. Sorry we can't offer more," Eileen said. "It's been a rough year."

Ian Roi nodded. "Turnips are fine. The company makes them sweeter."

Eileen smiled and passed the plate of trout. "At least the fish are plentiful. I don't know what we'd do without Afon Tywi." She looked at her plate. "Thank goodness the river doesn't have a company store."

"What do you mean?" Ian Roi picked up his fork.

"Eileen sold fish to the colliers in town last year," William answered, "but this year the company put them under a thumb."

"I couldn't believe it," Eileen said. "A few people stood up to them and bought my fish, but most were too afraid." She twirled her fork in the pile of mashed turnips. "Bob was the one that made me maddest. He offered to buy the fish for half what they were worth!" She looked up at Ian Roi, fire in her eyes. "I gave him what for, don't think I didn't."

"Your dad shopped at the company store." Ian Roi looked across the table at William.

William nodded. "The company store's always been a nuisance, but it's the colliery what will kill you. Dad died while you and I were fighting in Africa, you know. He was in Pit Seventeen when it caved. When I returned from the war, some of the men who made it out told me they knew it wasn't safe, but they had to work. Dad never did stand up to the bosses." William took a drink. "When I left for the war, I knew I'd rather die a hero than a coward."

"Well, you managed half of it. You came home a hero." Ian Roi grinned. "I know a bunch of men who are glad you made it back."

"I know some other people that are grateful too." Eileen wiped her mouth. "Would you like a cup of coffee, Ian Roi?"

"No thanks. I need to head back home soon. I have a flock to care for myself, I do."

William ripped his bread in two and scooped up some mashed turnips. "I hope you have better luck than I do. Losing three lambs last night was tough. We'll be eating sheep food next winter too if this keeps up."

"You could always get some extra work at the colliery." Ian Roi looked William square in the eye.

"No." William shook his head. "I'm not as bad off as those colliers. I can breathe fresh air, and my barn roof isn't in much danger of falling on me."

"True, but who will be the leader that they need?" Ian Roi's blue eyes sparkled. "You were always good in a hole during the war."

If your right eye causes you to stumble, gouge it out and throw it away. It is better for you to lose one part of your body than for your whole body to be thrown into hell.

Matthew 5:29

CHAPTER 7

THE SECOND HARVEST OF FIGS was solely for the farmer. Amos would take them back to Tekoa with him to sell to the locals. The women would mix up fig cakes and other sweets, or simmer the figs into thick sauces to dry for use later, or dry the fruit whole to be eaten with nuts near a winter's fire. The second harvest was turning out as heavy as the first. Malaki would be happy.

Amos smiled thinking of his wife. It had been six weeks since he had left her in Tekoa. She was heavy with child again and couldn't make the annual trip. He took a deep breath of the warm autumn air and thought of her rounded belly, thick as a fat fig and twice as sweet.

"What are you thinking about, Master?" Kediah looked down from the top rung.

"Home." Amos shook the ladder. "Get on with it, man. I need to get back."

"You can go ahead of the others," Kediah said as he climbed down the ladder. "I have this under control."

"I know. I know." Amos picked up the ladder and

moved to the next tree. "A few more days and we'll be done anyway." He huffed as he set the ladder against the sycamore.

Kediah grabbed an empty bucket and climbed up. Amos started picking from the lower branches. A squirrel chattered at the intrusion.

"Go on now, this is my tree." Amos gave the branch a gentle shake. "You find another one. We've got work to do here."

The squirrel jumped from one branch to another until it disappeared into some bramble.

"Did you clear out the back pasture yet?" Amos called up to Kediah while he watched the squirrel's tail flicker warnings from its brush heap.

"No. I thought I'd get to it after third harvest. The undergrowth will be dying by then."

"Yes, of course." Amos couldn't see the squirrel now. "I'm going to go look it over; see how many seedlings I ought to get this winter."

"Great." Kediah's voice was muffled in the tree. "The more, the better. I'll clear as much as you want."

Amos set his bucket down and wandered to the edge of the western border of his land. A large pasture had gone to seed, and briers were taking over. He pushed through and ripped his shirtsleeve on the bramble. He rubbed the blood off his arm and walked into a clearing.

An Asherah pole stood in the middle of the clearing. It was ten feet tall, carved with tree leaves and flowers. Its narrow base rose out of the ground like a stick in an anthill that some naughty child had left behind. Amos was an indignant, angry ant.

"No!" Amos shouted. "No, this abomination will not stand."

He ran at the pole with all his might, but it didn't budge. He tore back through the briers to get a shovel.

"Kediah, get down here. Bring the others." Amos grabbed a shovel off the rear of the wagon and raced back where he had come from.

Kediah looked around the orchard. He couldn't see what had his master so worked up. He yelled for the other men to follow. They hurried through the brush, sending squirrels up trees and rabbits down holes.

"What is it, Master?" Kediah asked. He stopped short when he reached the clearing. "Oh no."

Amos was digging at the ground around the pole. It was beginning to shake and teeter as the earth loosened.

He looked up and glared at the men. "Did you know about this?"

"No, sir." Kediah felt sick. He knew his lord was a devout man. "I would never allow this. Never."

"Don't just stand there." Amos straightened up and took a breath. "Help me get this out of the ground. You!" Amos saw one of the Gileadite children hiding near the clearing. "Gather some kindling. We need to make a fire."

The boy gathered sticks and branches and set them in the middle of the clearing. The hired hands dug, pulled, and dragged the pole out of the ground.

"Have Leah bring some fire," Amos told Kediah. "The rest of you get back to work."

Kediah hurried to the house, and the men crept back to their work like naughty children caught with their hands in the cookie jar. Amos backed away from the Asherah and wiped his forehead. The boy's eyes darted from the pole to Amos to the trees beyond.

"Come." Amos motioned to the boy. "What's your

name?"

"Ben-Abel." The boy lowered his eyes but walked toward Amos.

"Ben-Abel, do you know where this pole came from?" Amos lifted the boy's chin.

The boy shook his head and kept his eyes down.

"Did your people place it here?"

Ben-Abel stepped back, his eyes big as summer melons. "No, sir. No." He looked at Amos now and shook his head furiously. "Papa Elelbet would flog us if we ever did that."

Amos smiled and sat on the ground. He patted the grass next to him. The child sat down.

"Elelbet is a good man, a godly man." Amos nodded. "A good boy will obey him. Do you miss your home?"

"I miss my parents. And I miss the green hills and the sheep." Ben-Abel spoke slowly. He picked a piece of grass and twirled it in his fingers. "But this is home now, with Papa Elelbet."

"And your parents? What happened to them?"

"Bad things." The boy stared at the ground.

Amos sighed and put his hand on the boy's shoulder. They were still sitting in silence when Kediah appeared with a bucket of hot coals.

———◆———

Amos blew out the lamp and sighed. It had been a long day. The Asherah pole had burned hot all afternoon and evening. He didn't leave until every chunk of it was charcoal. Leah sent dinner to him, but his stomach turned so much that he sent it back.

The men were quiet in the servants' quarters. The usual singing and games were replaced with hushed conversations and furtive glances. Everyone feared what Amos might do if he found out who was the pagan worshipper.

Amos couldn't sleep. The night wore on, the moon a waning crescent in the night sky. A few crickets chirped their autumn songs, and the scent of ripe fig drifted on the breeze. In the distance he could hear singing.

He sat up. Kediah and Leah were in the kitchen talking softly. Amos walked to his window and listened. It wasn't singing; it was chanting.

Amos looked for the merry-makers, but his body froze at what he saw. Light rose above the orchard.

"Kediah!" Amos threw his clothes on. "Get the men!"

Amos and Kediah flew from the house. Screams echoed through the orchard, and flames flickered above the treetops. Amos grabbed a shovel and bucket from the barn and ran toward the fire. The men were on his heels.

A large crowd of locals surrounded the Gileadites' compound. The children were crying, the women screaming, the men holding up clubs and torches. The tents were all ablaze.

"What's going on here?" Amos ran between the two groups. "What is this about? Put out the fires!" He motioned to his men to make haste.

"These foreigners tore down our Asherah, and they'll pay for it," said a local man in colorful robes as he raised his fist. Amos knew him; he was a blacksmith just over the hillside.

"Did they tell you they tore it down?" Amos asked.

"Who else would destroy our god?" the blacksmith said. "They're only here to take, rob, and destroy. We'll sell them to the Philistines. They'll bring a good price in Gaza."

The crowd hurrahed their agreement. Amos's men were struggling to put out the fire. The Gileadites still stood at Amos's back, guarding their women and children.

"It wasn't your god that was destroyed, and it wasn't them that destroyed it." Fire flashed in Amos's eyes. "You are Israelites. Yahweh is God, the only God. I destroyed your abomination. I burned it with fire—proving it was no god." Amos towered over them. He raised a fist in the air. "You had no right to put that on my land nor to attack my guests. The Lord will avenge! Now get away from here before I call the Lord to take his vengeance now."

The men in the crowd stood still until the blacksmith turned.

"Go on," the blacksmith said. "We'll take care of this later. We've a festival to attend."

The crowd grumbled, but they walked away. Several looked back to see Amos join the fire brigade.

It took half an hour to put the fire out. Smoke hung thick as a camel-skin blanket. Everyone rubbed their eyes and choked. One of the women passed around a dipper of water. Amos took a drink and handed it back.

"Come to the house. There's room for you in the barns. Leah will get you some clean things and blankets." Amos surveyed the total loss of the little encampment. "I'm sorry, Elelbet."

"It isn't your fault; people will believe what they will believe." The old man stared at the glowing embers of his home. "We'll go now."

"Where will you go?" Amos raised one eyebrow. "Come. It's late."

"It isn't safe." One of the younger men stood at Elelbet's shoulder. "We need to get out of here before they come back."

"You'll be safe with me. It's well past dark; we can discuss this in the morning." Amos held his arms toward the house.

The women took the children by the hand and waited for Elelbet to decide.

"Until morning, then." The old man was the last to leave the smoldering remains of his life.

*All the greatest things are simple, and many can be
expressed in a single word: freedom; justice;
honour; duty; mercy; hope.*

Winston Churchill

CHAPTER 8

HEAVY CLOUDS HUNG OVER THE meadow.
Wet grass squeaked under William's rubber Wellingtons as one of his dogs, Captain, trotted alongside him. He had walked the kids partway to school and then cut across the meadow to check on the ewes in the north field. Some neighbors had noticed badgers gaining ground, and he was worried about the lambs.

A beam of sunshine filtered through the dark sky. William stopped and raised his hand to shield his eyes. Captain sat on his haunches and waited. A couple men were walking along the border wall, pointing toward the field beyond.

"Hello!" William called, waving an arm above his head.

The two men stopped. William walked up the hillock to the wall. It was Granville Jones and his hired man.

"Mr. Jones." William extended a hand. "Didn't expect to see you out on a morning like this. Thought you'd need to be at the colliery."

"I'll be there soon enough, I will. How've you been,

Williams?"

"Fine. I was checking on my flock. Rumor is there are badgers stealing lambs at night."

"Might be what happened." The older man looked over at his hired man. "This here's Harvey. He's my head shepherd."

Harvey shook hands with William. It was a weak shake, the kind that one regretted touching.

"You lost some lambs?" William asked, looking back at Granville Jones.

"Yes. We've had a few stolen the last couple nights. Harvey didn't know what to make of it."

"Three ewes with twins each lost a lamb," Harvey explained.

William frowned. "Could be badgers. Might be they got caught in some bramble, though. You got some good dogs?"

Harvey shook his head.

"Have to get us some, will we?" Jones jumped in before Harvey could speak.

"Be a good idea," William answered. "Flock that size." He looked across the wall to the grazing sheep on the hillside.

"I've never worked dogs before," Harvey said.

"They're handy for the job," William said. "How long you been a shepherd?"

Harvey looked at Jones and back at William, then answered, "This is my first. I trained as a vet, and Mr. Jones talked me into coming here to care for his livestock."

"Nothing's too good for my animals." Jones smiled and clapped Harvey on the back. "Harvey's just a little green. He'll take off quick, he will."

William gave a nod. "Well, could be badgers, like

I say, but might be your ewes left their babes in the brambles. Sheep are pretty good at counting, but after they pass one, they get a bit confused." He smiled. "I'll help you look if you like. I can send Captain around the field."

Captain's ears perked up at the mention of his name. He loved a challenge.

"That'd be great," Jones said. "We've already looked by the river."

William sent Captain over the wall and whistled directions. Captain took off for the far corner of the field where briers were in abundance.

"Looks like you've been adding to your flock this year," William said.

"Yes, it's been a good year at the mine. Production is up, and prices are stable."

"There's been some bad too, I hear."

"Just dust on the windowsill." Jones shrugged. "What do you think? Did he catch a scent?" He pointed toward Captain slipping behind a rock outcropping.

William looked that way. "Could be. He's a good dog. If there's a lamb there, he'll find it." He glanced back at Jones. "The paper said five men died and seventeen were injured in that explosion in January. That's more than dust."

"Accidents are going to happen. Your mum must've told you that if you play with fire, you're going to get burned."

"Mm. My dad died in a colliery accident back in '16. He told me plenty of times the work was dangerous. He also told me that some dangers were needless."

"Careless, more like."

Captain appeared at the top of the rocks and looked toward the men. He sat down to wait.

"Did he find something?" Harvey asked.

"I'd say so,"William said.

The three men jumped the wall and headed up the hill. William used his staff on the incline. Jones and Harvey trailed behind. Captain turned in circles on top the rock, his tongue hanging out in excitement.

William was the first to hear the pathetic bleating of a nearly dead lamb. By the time Jones and Harvey joined him,William had spotted a tuft of wool deep in the briery brush.

"Where's your staff, Harvey?"William asked.

"I didn't bring it." Harvey bit his lip.

"Well, you're going to need a big stick to push aside all that." William pointed to the mass of bramble. "I'll hold it aside while you crawl in and pull it out. Careful of the legs. Looks like it might be in a hole."

William pushed aside the briers and Harvey got down on his knees. Soon he was on his belly sliding deeper under the bramble bushes. Captain barked directions as Harvey's head disappeared.

"Can you get it?"Jones asked.

Harvey's muffled response was lost in the barking and bleating. A crowd of yearlings was standing below them, watching the rescue.

The young man's pants slid up pale, thin legs as he backed out of the bushes. Red scratches and drops of blood appeared on his calves. Finally Harvey rolled over and handed the lamb to Jones. William offered a hand to pull him to his feet. Harvey's face was more scratched than his legs.

"Well, what do you know."The older man placed the lamb inside his coat. "Near to froze but I think she's going to be fine. Harvey, you do know how to raise a lamb, don't you?"

"Yes, sir. I took care of two at school."

Jones nodded toward Captain. "That's a fine dog you've got there, Williams. Care to sell him?"

"No, Captain is family." William stroked the dog's silky head. "Family's not for sale. Better get that lamb back to the barn. You might be able to get the ewe to mother up to it. If not, you'll need to feed it by hand. Watch it for scours. And don't worry if the mother won't take it; shepherds mother up quicker than sheep."

"I could use a man like you." Jones patted the tiny lamb under his heavy coat.

"You've got Harvey here. I'm sure he can handle it, being trained and all." William looked over at the young man wiping his face with his handkerchief.

"Thanks," Harvey said.

Jones shook his head. "No, not on the farm. At the colliery." He looked William in the eye.

"No way." William stuffed his hands in his pockets. "I was in enough holes in the war. I don't intend to do that ever again."

"I've heard some of the stories about you." Jones nodded. "A war hero, they say."

William blushed and patted Captain again. "Good luck with the lamb." He nodded to Harvey, then turned. "Good seeing you, Mr. Jones."

"Well, if you ever want to work for me, my door is open. We could use a smart guy like you. Some of those men are dumber than this here lamb."

William walked away with Captain at his side.

"Hurry up, Harvey," Jones said as he took off across the field. "This lamb's shivering like a kid in a cemetery."

"Hello!" Eileen swung the gate open. She could see Constance in the garden at the corner of the house. "Anyone to home?"

Constance looked over her shoulder. She stood and dusted her hands, then smoothed the hairs blowing in her eyes. "Hello, Eileen. How are you?"

"Just out for some air. Care to take a walk?"

Constance shook her head. "I'd love to, you know I would, but I've got to get these seedlings out while the sun shines. Doesn't seem to do that much these days."

"That's why I'm out for a walk." Eileen smiled at her friend. "How are the children? Amaryllis said Alice missed some school last week."

"Mm. Yeah, I needed her to help me. The wash got behind. The colliery started sending me some of the men's things. Every little bit helps." Her lips spread in a thin smile.

"You have the war pension, right?"

"Five mouths to feed and rent in town." Constance frowned. "Some of the colliers have been helping. They give me some food, and Silas passed along some shoes for James. That boy's feet are growing faster than my garden."

"That was nice of Silas. Where'd he get the idea James needed shoes? Men don't notice that sort of thing."

"He was by the other day." She shrugged her shoulders. "I guess some men notice. Been fishing lately?"

"A bit. The lambs are coming quick right now, they are. William's needed me more. Doesn't do much good to fish for long anyway. No one will buy them."

"I'm sorry about the store. Life is hard for everyone, I suppose."

"Not for Granville Jones. William said he's hired a veterinarian to take personal care of his livestock."

Eileen shook her head and huffed. "He should've hired William. That vet don't know head nor tail of a ewe. He lost lambs ... in the underbrush of all things."

"Well, enjoy your walk. I better get back to my planting." Constance squeezed Eileen's hand. "Thanks for stopping by."

"You sure you're alright?" Eileen asked.

"Quite right. Just busy, that's all."

"Well, don't work yourself to death. Make those children help you more. See you later, love." Eileen walked through the gate and back onto the path. "I'll come check on you again soon."

Constance waved and turned back to her garden.

No man chooses evil, because it is evil; he only mistakes it
for happiness, the good he seeks.

Mary Wollstonecraft

CHAPTER 9

"DENNIS BYRNE CAN'T EVEN LEARN."
The chant greeted Amaryllis and the younger children as they neared the school.

"Allen, you and Iris better go on in." Amaryllis pushed them in front of her. "You don't want to be late. Mum will hear of it."

Allen and Iris climbed the few steps to the front door. They turned to look at the crowd gathering, but Amaryllis shooed them inside.

"Get on in there. You'll be late, you will." She held the door open for them. "Don't forget the 's' in 'isle' today, Iris."

The younger two went in the school; Amaryllis shut the door on them. She spotted Susan near the tree. Susan waved and motioned her over. Amaryllis ran down the stairs.

"Why don't the teachers stop it?" Amaryllis asked.

She watched the group of boys grow around Dennis, who just stood there in the middle of them, his chin tucked to his chest.

"Why stop people from telling the truth? He's a dimwit that can't learn." Susan snorted. "He's not even smart enough to go to America like the other Irish."

"Susan, that isn't nice. We don't know why he didn't go to America. And I don't think he's dumb. I saw his history paper. He made good marks. He just can't talk right is all."

"Amaryllis! Are you soft on Dennis?" Susan's eyes grew wide. "Carol, Amaryllis likes Dennis Byrne!" she called to another girl standing nearby.

"I do not. I just don't think everybody ought to be picking on him is all. He can't help how he talks."

Susan looked at her. "I guess I know why I didn't get caught at Oranges and Lemons. You wanted to hold Dennis's hand." She clasped her hands in front of her and batted her eyes. "Hey, Thomas, Dennis has a girl-friend!"

"Shut up, Susan!" Amaryllis shouted. "Shut up right now, I tell you!"

Two upper-grade teachers came out on the stoop and called everyone to class.

Susan pulled Amaryllis's long braid and laughed. "You're soft on him for sure."

———————

Amaryllis stared out the window. She had always hated mathematics. She felt like that ewe on the path to the river. She could get down, but she could never find her way back up again.

A whisper caught her attention: "Psst. 'Ryllis, here."

Thomas handed her a scrap of paper. She looked at Thomas and saw Owen out of the corner of her eye. He was grinning ear to ear. She glanced at the paper and narrowed her eyes.

Amaryllis Byrne was written across it in smudged

pencil. She crinkled the paper in her fist and glared at the boys.

"Leave me alone," she hissed.

The boys snickered.

The teacher called them out. "Thomas. Owen. Do you have something to share with the class?"

"No, sir. But Amaryllis might." Owen laughed.

Amaryllis hid her fist under her desk and blushed.

"What's in your hand, Amaryllis? There'll be no note-passing in this class. Come here."

Amaryllis felt the heat race up her neck and out her ears. She stood up and walked to the front of the class. She handed the crumpled paper to the teacher.

He read the note and looked down at Amaryllis.

"School is not the place for love letters, Amaryllis Williams." He stressed her last name. "Return to your seat and finish your assignment."

"Yes, sir." She lowered her head and stared at the floor as she walked back to her seat.

———————

"What do you want a dumb Irish boy for?" Owen said. "He ain't going to take care of you."

"What do I need taking care of for?" Amaryllis punched Owen in the arm. "I don't need Dennis Byrne and I don't need you! Go and scratch, you … sheep fart."

Owen rubbed his arm and laughed. He started to cross the street when he saw Dennis at the corner of the company store.

"You're so dumb, you don't know when a girl's in love with you," Owen yelled across the street as he waved in dismissal.

Dennis ignored them and raced into the store.

William, Amaryllis, and Ian Roi watched as Captain and Lucy herded the flock to a new meadow. The spring rains were muddying up the fields and they had to be switched to new pasture every couple of days now.

"Don't be too upset about it, 'Ryllis," William said. "I had lots of sweethearts before I met your mum. Don't tell her I said that." He smiled and hugged his daughter.

Amaryllis frowned. "I'm not his sweetheart. I just don't understand why they have to be mean to him."

"Have you told them so?" Ian Roi asked.

"I tried, but all it did was get me in trouble with the teacher."

William whistled, and the dogs turned the flock. Lucy came around too quick, and several lambs shot out of the white sea of wool. They headed toward the edge of the field where the land dropped quickly to the river.

Lucy raced around the lambs and stood her ground. She bared her teeth and the lambs stopped short. They stood still, enchanted by the dog's eyes. The lambs' mothers called for their babes, and the little ones turned tail and joined the flock.

"It's not just that they say things," Amaryllis went on. "The other day they threw rocks at his head. That dumb Thomas nearly hit Iris with one of the rocks."

"And what did you do then?" Ian Roi asked.

"I held onto Iris. What more could I do, Ian Roi? I don't want to be mean like those boys."

"Mm. I can see that. But is it mean to keep someone

from doing something stupid?"

"Of course not. But no one is going to like it if I start telling them to behave."

Lucy and Captain stood at the gate as William closed it and locked the pin.

"Good job," William said as he tickled their ears.

Ian Roi nodded. "Your dad has some good dogs there, he does."

"Yeah, Lucy's pups ought to be here in another month. I hope they look like Captain." Amaryllis squatted next to Captain and held his head in her hands.

"As long as they don't act like Lucy," Ian Roi said, "I suppose they'll be alright."

"What?" William looked at Ian Roi. "Lucy's a great dog. Captain's good for finding lost ones. But it's Lucy keeps them in line."

Ian Roi shrugged. "She looked kind of mean back there, baring her teeth at those lambs like that. She might've torn their throats acting like that."

"Lucy would never do that," Amaryllis said, standing to face Ian Roi. "She was just saving them from going over the cliffs there, she was."

"What looks mean isn't necessarily mean is what Ian Roi's trying to tell you, 'Ryllis."

"What would have happened if Lucy hadn't warned those lambs?" Ian Roi asked.

"There's that, I suppose." Amaryllis looked down at the two sheepdogs. "I don't like it none, though."

It is easy to hate, and it is difficult to love. This is how the whole scheme of things works. All good things are difficult to achieve; and bad things are very easy to get.

Confucius

CHAPTER 10

"I'LL BE LEAVING TOMORROW; THE harvest is in." Amos sat at breakfast with Elelbet.

The old man nodded his head. He hadn't slept last night. There seemed to be nothing for them to do but to move on.

"Our father was a wandering Aramean," Elelbet said, then huffed. "We'll be like Father Abraham and wander to a new home God will show us."

"You're still welcome to the third harvest here." Amos sat back from the table and chewed his eggs. He watched the children through the door. They sat quietly under the trees.

"You're kind, Amos, but we can't stay here long enough for that." He looked at Amos. "The people here hold you in high regard, but you've made them angry. They may let you get away with destroying the Asherah, but they certainly won't let us stay. Your figs wouldn't be enough to get us through the winter."

Amos nodded and clasped his hands behind his head. He continued watching the children. They were cross-legged in the grass, the oldest child whispering stories to the smallest ones. A dark cloud gathered above their heads and covered the sun.

"How old are you, Elelbet?"

The old man raised an eyebrow. "Old enough to be your father, I'm sure. Eighty-nine winters have chilled my bones."

"Yet you were shepherding last winter." Amos stared at him.

"It was home. It was life. It was all I knew." This time he looked out the door. "Children and grandchildren and great-grandchildren. Everything I loved."

"Did you teach the children well? To shepherd, I mean." Amos leaned forward at the table.

"Yes, but we have no money to buy sheep and no land to graze them on." Elelbet turned back to Amos. "So we move on. Thank you again."

"Which direction will you head?"

"North, toward Jerusalem, I suppose. The men may find work on King Uzziah's progress works."

"Jerusalem is good." Amos lifted his shoulders and dropped them. "But Tekoa is better."

"Tekoa?"

"A land of hills and green pastures." Amos smiled. "Sheep with wool so thick you'd swear they have two coats."

"But—"

"I know a great shepherd there—name's Elroi. He'll keep your men safe, and I have plenty of sheep to keep them busy. What do you say?" Amos stuck his hand across the table.

"I say it sounds like home." The old man grabbed Amos's outstretched arm. "I'll tell the women to pack whatever they can find in the ashes."

"It's a boy, Amos! A boy." Malaki ran out to meet her husband on the road.

Amos jumped from the lead wagon and swung her around. "A boy! The Lord has heard my prayer." He kissed Malaki and then turned back to the wagon. "Elelbet, did you hear? I have a son."

The old man grinned and waved. The men behind the wagons cheered. Ben-Abel stood to the side and clapped.

"Amos, who are these people?" Malaki looked at the large group of strangers. She faced her husband. "Where did you meet so many along the way?"

"It's a long story … over dinner perhaps?" He kissed her again. "They'll be staying as well."

"Of course." Malaki straightened her head covering. "I'll let Cook know. How many?"

"Most are children. Tell Cook twelve men, several women, and an old man."

Two menservants came through the gate and took charge of the wagons. The children skipped and giggled, following the wagons of ripe figs. Amos led the Gileadites toward the barns to show them where they would bed down. There were two rooms for the women and children behind the house. Amos had built it for Malaki's parents, but they weren't ready to leave home yet. His own father stayed with his older brother in Jerusalem, but Amos couldn't live in the big city. He needed the soft earth and fresh air.

Amos walked into the bedroom. Malaki sat in a

cushioned chair feeding the baby. She smiled at Amos and took the child from her breast. He cried softly and then fell asleep licking his lips.

"He's so small," Amos said. "When did he arrive?"

"Five days ago," Malaki whispered, staring into the face of her newborn. "He came fast. He was in a hurry to see his papa, but you weren't here." She looked up at Amos, a question in her eyes.

"It took a little longer to get back with all of the children."

Malaki tipped her head. Her husband loved to tell stories. *This should be a really good one. How does a man pick up twelve men and their entourage on his way home?*

"They're Gileadites, our brothers from across the river." Amos leaned down to kiss her nose. "They were attacked by Damascus and Ammon. The children lost their families. They saw too much."

"But how do they come to be with you?" Malaki sat back against the cushion and gently rocked the babe.

Amos sat on the edge of the bed and told his story. He explained the horrors of why they were there, the helpfulness of the men and the generosity of the women. He told her about the children, especially Ben-Abel.

He became angry when he recounted the scene of the Asherah pole, and Malaki had to nurse the baby again to keep him quiet. Finally Amos ended with the dreadful fire and the loss of what little home they had.

"I was planning to let them stay the winter in their tents. Some of the men were going to help Kediah while the rest looked for work in Jerusalem." Amos leaned toward his wife. "But I was concerned that the Valley Grove locals wouldn't leave them alone once I was gone. They're good people, Malaki. They just need some help."

"Of course, Amos." She smiled.

"You're a good woman, an angel from God."

———— • ————

"Do you have everything you need?" Amos stuck his head in the front door of the little house.

The children ran to him and hugged his legs and waist. The women tried shooing them away, but Amos just laughed and hugged them all in his tanned arms.

"Thank you, yes, we're fine. A few of the men went into town to get some things." Elizabeth, the oldest of the young women, pulled the children back from the door. "They should be back soon."

"Good, good. We need to head to the winter fields to help with rutting season." Amos waved good-bye to the children and headed for the barns.

Ben-Abel joined him and asked, "Can I go to the winter fields with you?" The boy took double strides to keep up with Amos.

"What do you know about sheep?" Amos laughed down at the youngster.

"Lots!" Ben-Abel stuck out his chest. "I helped Papa Elelbet back in Gilead. Ask him."

"I'll do that." Amos ruffled the boy's hair.

———— • ————

The barn smelled of dried grass, oats, and barley mixed with animal manure and sweat. It was a sweet aroma that invigorated Amos. Elelbet sat on a bench under the leather straps and bridles.

"Papa Elelbet, tell Amos how good I am with the sheep." Ben-Abel ran to the patriarch.

"What?" Elelbet wrapped his arms around the boy. "Of course you are good with sheep. You'll be a fine shepherd in no time; it's in your blood."

"See?" Ben-Abel turned around to look at Amos as he neared. "Can I come with you to the fields?"

"Is he ready?" Amos looked at Elelbet. He wanted an honest answer, not the pride of an old man.

Elelbet sucked on his teeth and exhaled. "He's ready." He patted his great-grandson on the shoulder. "But are the other shepherds too rough for him? Will he be safe?" Fear stirred in his eyes.

Amos knew what Elelbet was asking: Would the others misuse him—abuse the foreigner?

"He'll be safe. I guarantee." Amos gave a firm nod. "If I'm not with him, Elroi will be there. I would trust Elroi with my own son."

Elelbet looked at Ben-Abel. "Then you may go, but I—"

Shouts sounded through the gate. Amos turned to see several townsmen pushing the Gileadite men ahead of them.

Amos hurried to the gate. "What's going on?" he asked.

"These men say they're staying with you," said Mattathias, the town's self-appointed governor. He knew everyone and their mother. He even knew what their mother ate for dinner last night.

"Yes, they're staying with me. They are brothers from Gilead." Amos was quiet. *Never engage a bear on its level. Stay in control.* "Was kind of you to help them home."

"Help them home? They were stealing in the market." Mattathias held up a basket of ripe figs. "Zechariah returned yesterday to sell his figs and these men took one of his baskets."

"We didn't—" Jacob started to explain.

Amos held up a hand. "Jacob and his brothers helped me with the harvest. I paid them in figs to sell at market. These are their figs, Mattathias."

"They stole them from Zechariah." The bear wouldn't give in. "How can we know these are the figs you gave them?"

Amos took a fig from the basket and sniffed it. He turned it in his hands and studied it. "This fig is from the Dead Sea valley. You can smell it in the flesh. Zechariah raises figs along the Mediterranean, near Gaza. Ask Zechariah and you will see." Amos eyed Mattathias. "Anyone who knows farming and the soil will tell you the same."

Mattathias fumed. Last year he had lost a competition to Amos and several other shepherds and farmers. King Uzziah, the judge of the contest, had spent the afternoon engrossed in conversation with Amos. It still burned in Mattathias's heart.

"Just the same, you better keep hold of these foreigners." Mattathias spit on the ground. "You can't trust everyone, Amos."

"I will remind them of that." Amos stood his ground.

Mattathias stood there a few seconds, then slowly turned. The crowd followed the mayor back to town.

Do something wonderful. People may imitate it.

Albert Schweitzer

CHAPTER 11

"I THINK SOMETHING'S WRONG WITH ALICE." Amaryllis looked at her mother over a plate of turnips and cabbage.

"Why? Was she out of school again today? Allen, close your mouth when you eat."

"How can I close my mouth if I'm eating? I'll never get nothing in my belly."

"Listen to your mother." William hid a smile. "Amaryllis, what about Alice?"

Amaryllis turned the cabbage over with her fork. She looked at Iris and then shook her head. "I don't know. I guess she's fine. She was in school today."

"Thomas punched a kid today for saying his mum was a whore," Allen said, then shoveled another pile of mashed turnips in his mouth.

Eileen's fork rattled against her dinner plate. "Allen Williams! Where in the world did you hear such language?"

"I just said at school. You always tell me to listen up and pay attention."

"What's a whore?" Iris asked.

"It's frost. You know that," Eileen said as she tucked hair behind her ear and looked at William.

"Why would they call Mrs. Davies 'frost'?" Iris asked. "Would you punch someone if they did that to Mum, Allen?" She cocked her head and looked at her brother.

"Heaven help us," Eileen said, then started clearing the table. "Allen, finish up your dinner and go help your father with the chores."

"I helped last night. It's Amaryllis's turn to help Dad."

"Amaryllis needs to help me with the kitchen. Get off with you now."

"Come on, Allen," William said. "I think we better hurry. Sounds like a wind blowing up to no good out there." He stood and grabbed his coat. "Coming from Shotton Cross, sounds like."

———◆———

"Iris is nearly asleep," Eileen said in a quiet voice.

She picked up the dish towel and started drying the dishes. Amaryllis said nothing and kept her head down, seemingly inspecting the wash water.

"Now what happened with Alice?" Eileen asked as she stacked dry plates on the sideboard.

Amaryllis sighed. "She just doesn't seem herself. She won't talk to me or any of the girls. Some of the boys have been asking her to the café, but you can tell they don't really want to buy her a coffee. It's like they're teasing or up to no good."

"And her brothers? James? Thomas?" Eileen stopped drying and stared at her daughter.

Amaryllis shrugged. "I don't know, Mum. They aren't in my class." She placed a teacup in the rinse water and glanced at her mother.

Eileen held her gaze. "But you've heard things."

Amaryllis nodded and looked back at the wash water.

April required a sweater, but fishing was pleasant now. Eileen threw out her line and sat on the bank. Thoughts of Constance flowed through her head like the waters of Afon Tywi.

Eileen and Constance had known each other since childhood. Their fathers were both colliers and their husbands were soldiers in the Great War. William came home; George didn't. It had been rough. Constance was pregnant when George left for the war. Baby Morgan was born half an orphan, never to know his father.

William had suffered in the war, Eileen knew. Time had eased some of the pain, and baby Iris had blessed them both with healing and new purpose. Constance didn't have many blessings as far as Eileen could see.

"Well, least ways you can be a blessing," she said to the bass she pulled from the river.

The road to Shotton Cross wound through the meadows of sheep and hedgerows. Eileen carried her pail of fresh fish. She would give some to Constance and try to sell the rest to the houses that had continued their commerce despite the company store threats.

Near the village the road crested a summit that was used by young lovers. The view of Shotton Cross on one side and Afon Tywi and the sweeping farmlands on the other lent itself to romance and daydreams. A spreading oak offered shade. Eileen dropped her bucket of fish and leaned against the trunk.

She could see Constance's little house near the river. The small garden at the side of the house was sprouting green in the warm spring sunshine. A man came out the back door and walked along the river toward town.

Eileen picked up her pail with purpose.

———•———

"Hello," Eileen called from the front gate.

She pushed it open and walked through to the front door. She and Constance had seldom knocked on each other's doors. Old friends were always welcome. But today she knocked.

Constance opened the door slightly and peeked out.

"Eileen." She smiled and opened the door farther. "Come in. Been fishing again, I see." She nodded toward the pail of fish. "Did you get Bob to ease up and let you sell in town?"

"No. There're a few that don't care about the threats. The fish money might be smaller, but every little bit helps. William's lost a few sheep, you know."

Constance closed the door with her shoulder. "Come on in the kitchen for a cup of tea. I'd buy some fish; you know I would." She smoothed her skirt and looked away. "Money's tight for all of us."

Eileen placed the pail on the kitchen counter and lifted four big bass into the sink. "I don't want money. They were free for me and the sunshine gave me back some sanity. I didn't clean them yet. Can James or Thomas manage when they get home?"

"Of course." Constance motioned toward the table. "Have a seat and I'll put the water on."

"How are the boys doing?" Eileen sat in the straight-backed chair.

"Growing like weeds." She opened the cookstove

door and turned the coals over with the metal poker. The teapot sat on the back of the stove, always ready. "There's biscuits in the pantry. Would you like some?"

"No thank you. ... Constance," Eileen said, then paused and looked at her hands. "Allen said Thomas got in a fight yesterday."

"He got my daddy's temper, that one." Constance busied herself with the teacups. "I spoke to the teacher and all's right again."

"Constance?" Eileen stood up and walked to the stove. She put her hand on the young woman's shoulder.

"Don't." Constance shook her head. "Let's just have a cup of tea." Her hands were shaking.

"Tea and teardrops?" Eileen put her arms around Constance and let her cry.

———◆———

The sun was heading west, and the children would be home in another hour or so. Eileen pulled the door shut and turned toward town. Francis Avenue was far enough from the colliery and company store that customers thought they could get away with fresh fish from Eileen. She nodded to some on the corner. They whispered and turned their backs.

Eileen knocked on the first door.

Mrs. Smith opened it. "We don't need no fish."

"They were fresh this morning." Eileen lifted her pail and let Mrs. Smith look at the slick, smooth skin glinting in the sunshine.

"I said we don't need no fish. Not from any whore-mongers, we don't."

"What?" Eileen took a step back.

"I'm not saying you're one yourself, I'm not. But you been friendly with that woman down the street."

"Well that's some Christian attitude. Sounds like gossip is for dinner at your house."

Eileen turned and stomped away. The door slammed behind her.

Her reception was the same at each company cottage.

*Our human compassion binds us the one to the other—
not in pity or patronisingly, but as human beings who
have learnt how to turn our common suffering into
hope for the future.*

Nelson Mandela

CHAPTER 12

WILLIAM WATCHED EILEEN LEANING AGAINST the oak. He used to meet her there when they were young. She looked tired now, her shoulders drooping. *She works so hard.*

He didn't consider himself much of a husband. He provided a house, but it wasn't always warm, and food wasn't often plentiful. The war had taken its toll. He'd been back eight years but doubted even a lifetime would make a difference.

One of the ewes had mastitis and refused to nurse the lambs. He'd bottle-fed them earlier, but they had scours and weren't looking promising. The weather was warm enough now to keep the flock outside. Outside or in didn't matter; he wasn't getting much sleep rising every two hours to check on the flock.

Eileen was taking the early-morning shift to check the sheep. She never complained, but he knew she was worried about the farm. It required money to keep a farm going, and there wasn't much of that around.

"What are you ruminating on?"

William turned quickly.

Ian Roi grinned and looked at the distant oak. "Mm. You still moon over her same as when you were young, don't you?"

William snorted and looked back at the tree. Eileen picked up her pail and headed over the ridge toward town.

"What are you doing over here?" William asked.

"Lambing is finished at my place. Thought I'd come check on you."

"I've lost another ewe. I tried singing, but it didn't work." He winked at Ian Roi.

"You must've used the wrong song," Ian Roi said and then began singing:

"Leading, follow paths of rock;
Follow, leading gentle flock.
Calling, hearing lamb's sharp cry;
Hearing, calling lest he die."

"I've heard that before somewhere." William looked off in the distance and scratched his cheek.

"In the hospital." Ian Roi sat on his haunches and looked at the horizon.

William's head crackled with memories. It hadn't been much of a hospital: a tent and a cot with a couple doctors to encourage him. It hadn't seemed like they did all that much. Probably thought he was a goner like George Davies. But he'd kept thinking of Eileen and the children, of the farm and the rolling meadows dotted with sheep. He had to get back home.

Nomadic shepherds had grazed their flocks in the hills around the compound. Once William was well enough, he'd watched them from the shade of a tall sycamore. Yes, now he remembered the song.

"How do you know the song? I mean, how do you

know it in English?"

"It's an old song. My father taught it to me a long time ago. Every good shepherd knows it." Ian Roi grinned at William and held an arm up to him. "Ready to learn?"

"Alright." William pulled Ian Roi to his feet.

The two men walked along the hedgerows, singing and searching for the missing sheep. Finally, desperate bleating found her trapped in a stone wall. She had found a hole big enough for her head to go in, but not big enough to come back out. Her ears were stuck, and she had scraped herself up trying to escape. Her lamb lay at her feet, trampled to death.

They sang to her. Ian Roi lifted the lamb out of the way while William extracted the simple sheep. Her legs and udder were nicked and bleeding from her own sharp hooves.

"Better get her treated with some goose grass and yarrow before infection sets in. Without the lamb on her she'll get mastitis quicker than a mouse can creep in the house." Ian Roi looked at the lamb. "You want me to take this one?"

"You sure?" William cocked his head. "I can dig a grave out back the barn. That's where the others sleep, you know."

"It's alright. I'll get this one, I will. You go on home and take care of her." He jerked his head toward the ewe already headed through the meadow, the safety of home her only thought.

William waved his thanks and followed her.

———

William cleaned up the ewe and put her in one of

the smaller pens. Maybe he could adopt the orphaned lambs onto her. He brought them in and set them under her. She skittered away and sidestepped, raising her hoof to brush off the offending lamb. But as fast as she got rid of one lamb, the other would jump on her udder. William watched her stamina lag and finally the defeat that meant the lambs were hers.

He sighed relief. It had been a bad month. His shepherding skills were considered good in the county, but bad luck seemed to be wearing him down like orphaned lambs on a tired sheep.

———◆———

Lucy and Captain barked from their pen. Eileen was coming home.

William met her at the barn door. She dropped the bucket of fish and threw herself in his arms. Silent sobs racked her thin frame, and her face stayed buried in his flannel work shirt.

"Eileen. Eileen. What is it? What's happened?"

She hugged him tighter, then stepped back from him. She took a deep breath and wiped her eyes with the back of her hand. "Cruel. They're just cruel, saying things they oughtn't to say. What's she supposed to do? If they would help her instead of standing around condemning …" Eileen bit her lip. "I can't say too much, though. I've thought things myself."

"Constance? It's true, then?" William searched her face.

Eileen nodded her head. "And then the bloody lot threw me out too." She huffed and lifted the bucket of fish. "Hope you like turnips and fish. Not even Bob will buy them for the store." She grimaced. "At least there's some onions ready in the garden for an extra hoorah."

Eileen turned and headed for the house.

"Think I'll go walk the children back from school," William called after her.

She lifted a hand in acknowledgment but never turned. Her posture said enough.

———◆———

William knocked on the wall. The door stood open.

"Yes?" A man in thick glasses raised his head.

"Is Mr. Jones in? I'd like to talk to him."

"He's showing an inspector round. You looking for work?"

"Yeah." William peered inside the room. "Should I wait outside?"

"Here, fill this out." The man pulled out some papers from his desk. "You a former soldier? We give them priority."

"Excuse me?"

"Do you need a pencil?" The man pulled one from behind his ear.

"No no. You don't understand." William put his hands up in front of himself. "I want to talk to Mr. Jones about a shepherding job. No, I could never work in a colliery." He shook his head.

"Not good enough for you, is that it?" The man's eyes flashed with anger.

William shook his head again. "I've got nothing but respect for hardworking men. My father was a collier, but I can't go underground. Had enough of that in the war."

"Williams!" came the voice of Granville Jones. "You

decided to take me up on the offer. This here's Mr. Collins, an inspector from the government offices." He motioned toward a man in a suit who had just walked in behind him. "Williams is a war hero. We only hire the best." He smiled broadly at Mr. Collins.

"Oh … no, sir," William said. "I'm sorry. I didn't come for a collier job. I was hoping you might need some day labor over on the farm. I could help Harvey get acclimated to the job."

Jones smacked his lips. "Harvey's doing just fine. Don't need any help out there. You want to come here and work, I can set you up." He motioned for the inspector to walk ahead into his office. "Always an open door for you." He shook William's hand and then walked into his office.

The solid wood thudded as it shut—like a hammer nailing a casket.

"Daddy!" Iris ran to her father. "What are you doing here?"

"Thought I'd walk my beautiful girls home," William said. He threw Iris up in the air and caught her. She wasn't much heavier than a three-month lamb. "Where's Allen?"

"He's talking to the Davies boys. They all got spankings today."

"Allen was spanked?" William put her down.

"No, just the Davies boys. They was fighting on the playground." Her eyes were big in her small face.

He saw Allen in a crowd of boys. Amaryllis was on the steps.

"Allen," he called over the boys' heads. "Time to go."

He took Iris's hand and headed down the walk.

Amaryllis caught up, and Allen and the Davies boys trailed a few steps behind.

When they passed Constance's house, William turned around. "You boys help your mother out. I don't want to hear about any more fights. You understand?"

"Yes, sir." They nodded and walked through the gate.

"Allen." William looked at his son. "I better not hear of any fighting from you either."

Allen dropped his head and fell in line.

If I have denied justice to any of my servants, whether male or female, when they had a grievance against me, what will I do when God confronts me? What will I answer when called to account? Did not he who made me in the womb make them? Did not the same one form us both within our mothers?

Job 31:13–15

CHAPTER 13

"WILL THERE EVER BE A place for us?" Elelbet prayed under the persimmon tree. "Will there be a green pasture and a quiet stream for us?"

Amos stood listening. Tekoa was his home. It had been a good place to grow up. He knew the people and buildings, the hills and valley passes like the back of his hand. Why did a few bad men have to ruin it for everyone else?

Elelbet leaned against the tree to raise his old bones. He was still able to work, but it was getting harder. He kissed the fringe on his prayer shawl and folded it away.

"A good man knows to pray. It eases his mind and turns him to the truth." Amos entered the shade of the tree. "You are a good man, Elelbet."

"Your friends don't see things as you do. We should leave; we'll only cause you more trouble."

"No." Amos shook his head and crossed his arms. "Your men will be with the sheep. No one will bother them there. And the women and children will stay here. They don't need to go to Tekoa. Malaki and the servants will take care of them." Amos looked up at the autumn sky through the branches. "And you will pray. A very important job."

"Yes." Elelbet sighed. "A very important job."

"Are Jacob and the men ready?"

"And me too." Ben-Abel came from behind.

"Yes, you too, Ben-Abel." Amos laughed. "I can't forget you."

———◆———

"This is Elroi, the best shepherd in the business." Amos hugged his friend. "If you have any problems, he's your man." He turned to face the twelve Gilead-ite men. "And these," Amos said as he threw his arms wide, "are your new recruits."

"Good to have you, and just in time. Rutting season has started." Elroi looked at the men. Ben-Abel hid behind them. "And who are you?" Elroi looked down at the boy.

"Ben-Abel—a shepherd, sir." The boy's voice quivered.

"Shepherd, huh? Let's see you round up those sheep on the eastern slope and pen them over here." Elroi smiled and pointed to the distant hill.

"Now?" Ben-Abel turned white.

"Yes."

The boy gauged the size of the flock and the distance to the pen. He took a staff from the pile Amos had gathered and headed toward the sheep. The men all watched, wishing the boy the best.

Ben-Abel walked through the flock and sat down

in the middle of them. The yearlings slowly walked toward him. He held out a hand and let them nuzzle him.

Like a whisper echoing through time, the men heard the boy singing.

"What's he doing?" Amos asked.

"Just what he should." Elroi started walking toward the flock.

———◆———

Elroi sat down next to Ben-Abel. He petted the sheep and watched the boy. The shepherd boy never stopped until the end of his song, and then, pink faced, he looked at Elroi.

"Papa Elelbet taught me to sing to the sheep." He licked his lips. "I didn't think they would follow me, being a stranger and all."

"You were right. They would have scattered if you had tried to bring them straightaway." He smiled at the boy. "They're used to singing, but they don't know your song. Let me teach you the song they'll obey." Elroi cleared his throat and sat up on his knees, then sang:

"Leading, follow paths of rock;
Follow, leading gentle flock.
Calling, hearing lamb's sharp cry;
Hearing, calling lest he die."

Elroi's bass vibrated across the hillside. The sheep gathered around, and he stood. They followed Elroi and Ben-Abel toward the pen, where Amos held the gate open. Ben-Abel was singing with the older shepherd by the time the gate was closed behind the last sheep.

"Good job." Amos tousled the boy's hair.

"That's the way," Jacob said. "Papa Elelbet will be so proud when he hears." His own cheeks were pink with pride.

"I told you I know sheep." Ben-Abel looked up at Amos.

"Yes, you did."

———◆———

Amos left the Gileadite men with Elroi. He had been away from Malaki too long and needed to get home. The baby would need to be presented at the Temple soon. Malaki was getting nervous about it. This was their first son.

Amos wandered down the highlands path toward home. Night frost melted in the morning sun, sparkling on clumps of grass. A cony skittered across the path and into the rocks. Amos took a deep breath.

All the earth was beautiful: the ocean, the river valleys, the village he knew and loved. But this ...

This was home.

———◆———

The days were shorter now. All the figs were processed or sold at markets throughout the hill country. The nights were colder, and Amos loved sitting by the fire watching Malaki nurse their son while the girls played on the floor at their feet.

"Did you hear?" Malaki whispered over the children's heads. "There's been some thieving in the neighborhood. The neighbors lost their chickens."

"Samuel's chickens?"

Malaki nodded and rocked Amuz.

"Were there feathers or signs of a struggle? Maybe it was a wild dog."

"Cook said there wasn't anything left, even the eggs were stolen."

"Samuel never locks up his animals the way he should. Anything could get to them." Amos picked up the youngest girl, Mariam, and started humming to her. She lay her head on his chest.

"Just seems strange if you ask me." Malaki looked at Amos through her lashes. "You don't think...? I mean, nothing like this has happened before."

"They are our guests and our workers. The Lord has given them to us for safekeeping." Amos put his head back on the chair. "Don't let idle gossip lead you from the truth."

———

"Snow will fly in a few more weeks," Amos said. "Are they headed down from the mountains yet?"

He sat at his desk going over the year's records. Twelve hundred ewes were roaming the hillsides with thirty rams to service them. Last year he had nearly a thousand sets of twins. He was doing well by all accounts.

"Yes, Master. The first of them started down as I was coming. The yearlings started going missing a week before that. Two a night, sir, sometimes three."

The shepherd standing in front of him pulled at the edge of his robe. Amos looked him over carefully. He'd known Simon since he was a young boy. He was good, responsible, and very careful.

"Bears getting ready for winter?" Amos bit his lip.

Simon shook his head. "Looked for tracks, sir. And weren't any bones or blood to be found." He shifted his weight and kept his head down. "The flock is mighty restless. The rams aren't doing well, but it don't matter; the ewes won't flag them."

"What does Elroi say?"

"He says we must be missing something." Simon blew out his lips. "What we're missing is sheep." He tried to chuckle at his own joke, but it wasn't in him. "It's just ... Well, sir ..."

"Speak freely, Simon."

"The men from Gilead. They don't mix with the rest of us shepherds. Sometimes I catch them watching us like they's up to something."

"Have you seen them do anything wrong?"

"No, Master Amos." Simon shook his head. "They're good shepherds. They know what they're doing for sure. Elroi has faith in them too."

"Alright, Simon." Amos stood up and shook the man's hand. "You go on home for the night, and we'll head up there together in the morning. Can't be losing sheep at that rate."

Simon's sandaled feet slapped down the wooden hall and out the back door. Amos watched him cross the barnyard and go around back to the servants' quarters. This would never do. He sat back down to study the numbers again.

———◆———

It took two nights in the open country to find Amos's flocks wandering down the hillsides. The shepherds were searching for the last of the grasses before making the final descent into Tekoa. Amos could hear the bleating and smell his precious sheep on the wind before he ever saw them.

"Master Amos!" one of the shepherds called from above them.

Amos looked up and waved. He leaned on his staff and waited for them to get to where he and Simon stood. The sheep looked healthy. Their coats were thick and long. The yearlings jumped from outcroppings of rocks. They were energetic, happy. *Why did Simon say they aren't doing well?*

Amos recognized the shepherds as they got closer. It was Jacob and his brothers.

"The sheep look good to me." He looked at Simon. "Have they improved so much in a week's time?"

"You'll see, sir."

The first of the sheep passed by, grazing and chewing their cud. Ben-Abel jumped from some rocks with a rowdy bunch of yearlings. He looked just like one of them, his hair a mass of unkempt curly locks.

"The women will have a fit when they see you," Amos called.

Ben-Abel waved and ran to him. He tackled Amos around the waist and nearly knocked him over.

"Amos! How's Papa Elelbet? Has he missed me?" The boy's eyes shone like king's pools, clear and pure.

"Everyone misses you, Ben-Abel. All of the children begged to come with me so they could see you." He took a fig cake from his pocket. "And Elelbet sent this specially for you."

"We should be to Tekoa by the end of the week, sir." Jacob stopped in front of Amos. "None too soon, either. Winter is setting in on the mountain."

"Simon here says there was some trouble on the mountain. Sheep going missing." He watched Jacob closely.

"None of our flock went missing, sir." Jacob shook

his head and raised his shoulders. "I know Elroi stayed behind with some of the other flocks because of some sort of trouble."

"Mm." Amos sighed and looked over the avalanche of white wool coming down the hillside. He missed being out with his flocks. Numbers and business dealings left little time for what he really loved: the sheep. "Well, you keep on heading back. Simon will help you get the rest of the way to Tekoa. You know which pens to keep them in?" He looked at Simon.

"Yes, of course." Simon nodded.

"Then I'll keep looking for the rest of them. See you soon, I hope." He hugged Ben-Abel, who was licking his sticky fingers. "Take care."

*The only thing necessary for the triumph of evil
is for good men to do nothing.*

Unknown

CHAPTER 14

"HURRY UP, IRIS! WE'RE GOING to be late." Amaryllis stood at the bottom of the stairs. "Mum, is it alright if I stay after school? Some of my classmates are reviewing for final examinations."

Eileen looked up from her cup of tea. Breakfast dishes still sat on the table.

"Yes, that's fine. Allen can make sure Iris gets back alright. I'll be helping your dad with the shearing."

"Thanks. Iris!"

Iris jumped the last three stairs. "You don't need to yell. I'm right here." She screwed her face up and stuck out her tongue.

"Enough of that. Your sister is right. You're late." Eileen gulped the last bit of tea. "Have a good day."

The girls ran out of the house and met Allen by the road.

"Why do girls have to take so long?" their brother asked.

"Because we're always cleaning up your messes. You didn't make your bed again today." Amaryllis smacked him in the back of the head.

"Bed-making is woman's work."

"I don't see much work that isn't woman's," Amaryllis said. "Hurry up or we'll be late."

———◆———

Fluffy white clouds pranced across the bright blue sky. The grassy meadows were deep green now with the promise of an early summer. There wouldn't be too many more mornings of walking to school. Amaryllis was thinking of getting a job this summer in town. A couple of the shops hired girls for odd jobs.

The Davies boys were coming out of their gate as the children passed. They waved but didn't say anything. It was better to keep some distance. Everyone thought so. Alice rarely came to school these days. She kept her head down and her hair loose. No one ever saw her face.

The schoolyard was loud. No one wanted to go in sooner than they had to. There were only a couple weeks left to play with friends. Then the long summer of separation would begin—for the country kids anyway.

The bell rang, and the teachers called them in.

"Aww. I didn't even get to throw ball," Allen said. "You girls always make me late."

Amaryllis shoved him up the stairs.

———◆———

"Take your seats."

Amaryllis's skirt swished as she sat down in the wooden desk. She pulled out her math book and paper. *Another day.* She sighed.

The school shook. Books fell off tables and desks. Children shrieked. Then the loud thunder of an explosion was heard.

"Is everyone safe?" The teacher looked around the room. "Good. Stay quiet while I go check on the other rooms."

No one stayed quiet:

"What do you suppose happened?"

"I hope it isn't Pit Nine. That's where my dad is today."

"It'll be alright. There aren't any sirens."

Just then the warning alarms blared. It was a bad explosion. All Shotton Cross would be at the mine. Wives and mothers looking for survivors. Children waiting in fear. Amaryllis had witnessed another explosion a few years back that affected nearly half her class. It was a constant dread that they all learned to live with. *I'm glad Dad is a shepherd.*

"School is dismissed," the teacher called from the door. "You should go home straightaway." He stayed in the hallway, directing stragglers and gossips.

The students gathered their books and left the room.

———

Outside, Amaryllis found a mass of running women. They were headed toward the colliery, a grey flock of scared geese.

Names were called. Children, summoned to their mothers' sides, ran in panic. Smoke was rising from the entry shaft.

Screams and gasps escaped as the large slag mound on the hillside began to shift and slide.

"Iris! Allen!" Amaryllis yelled when she caught sight of her siblings.

She waved her arms over her head until they spotted

her. Allen grabbed Iris's hand and they ran against the flow of human terror. Then Amaryllis clutched Allen's hand and dragged them both out of the stream. They stood back against the schoolhouse while others raced on, others who had family in the colliery—or, perhaps, no longer had family.

After a few minutes the crowds passed. Sirens still blared, and the acrid smoke of a colliery fire permeated the town.

Amaryllis looked at Allen. "You take Iris on home. Tell Mum and Dad what happened. They'll be in the pens shearing. Tell them I'm trying to help. They'll need people to dig out those houses where the slag slide is. Go on now." She pushed her brother and sister toward home. "Don't let Iris look back when you get to the ridge, Allen."

The boy nodded once. He took Iris by the hand and they headed home.

———◆———

Colliers surrounded the black sludge that buried houses and moved them from their foundations. They passed out shovels to any who offered to help. Amaryllis took one and started digging.

Most people should have been at work or school, so there was hope that there were no deaths; it was certain that no one could have survived if anybody had been in those houses.

Amaryllis's hands blistered and burned. The raw skin turned black from the slag. She kept digging.

"Amaryllis."

She turned and saw Alice and Mrs. Davies. Their faces were black from smoke and soot. Mrs. Davies had a shovel in her hand too.

"Come on back to the house and get a drink," Constance said. "I've some extra gloves there."

Amaryllis nodded, then followed them up the street. She saw Dennis at the edge of the black mountain of slag. He sat there, looking at nothing, his face streaked with soot and tears. His eyes were red, and his arms black to the elbow.

"Dennis, are you alright?" Amaryllis stopped beside him.

He never looked at her, didn't seem to hear her.

"Dennis?"

Constance stooped beside the boy. She put her hand on his head and looked him in the face. "Have you lost someone?" she asked.

He stared at her but said nothing.

"Come to the house. Come on." Constance wrapped her arms around the boy and pulled him up. "That's a good lad. It'll be alright, it will."

"Look it!" Owen pointed from the walkway. "He's so daft he don't know he's going with the town whore."

Amaryllis grabbed her shovel and ran for Owen. She smacked him twice between the shoulder blades before he moved out of the way.

"His dad's likely dead and you ain't got nothing to say but meanness!" Amaryllis shouted. "Get on down there and help the men." She looked at his clean hands and shirt. "If they even let you help ... you good-for-nothing child."

Owen stared at Amaryllis. His mouth hung open.

"And don't you be spreading lies about Alice and Mrs. Davies!" Amaryllis whacked him once more and turned.

She saw a group of women watching on the corner, so she ducked her head and hurried to catch up with the others.

When a train goes through a tunnel and it gets dark,
you don't throw away the ticket and jump off.
You sit still and trust the engineer.

Corrie Ten Boom

CHAPTER 15

O N A CLEAR JULY DAY a car pulled up in the barnyard of the Williams farm. William peered out the kitchen window.

"Who is it?" Eileen asked, smoothing her hair and looking in the mirror.

"I believe it's Mr. Granville Jones," William said. "Wonder what he's doing out here? I'll be back. Better put some tea on." He pulled the door shut behind him.

"Mr. Jones." William raised his hat. "Nice day, ain't it?"

Jones slammed the car door and looked up at the sunny sky. He took off his hat and extended his hand to William.

"Very nice day it is. July is my favorite month. No storms, long days, and lots of food. What could be better?" He laughed and shook William's hand like he was shaking the last apples off the tree.

"Come in for a cup of tea? My wife is inside."

"That sounds good. I've been out all afternoon." He waved his hat in front of his face.

William led the way to the house and held the door

open for Jones. He bent his head as he walked through the doorway. William followed, then glanced around for Eileen. She was busy arranging some biscuits on her grandmother's good plate.

"Eileen, this is Mr. Granville Jones. Mr. Jones, my wife, Eileen."

Eileen skittered across the floor, her face bright pink. She moved her hands quickly, unsure where to put them or whether to offer a handshake.

"Nice to meet you, Mrs. Williams." Jones put his hand out and took her fingers. "I didn't know William here had such a pretty wife or I would've come to visit sooner, I would." He smiled and looked her in the eyes.

Eileen blushed more and took back her hand. She flitted her eyes over at William and then turned back to the kitchen, saying, "I have some tea on and biscuits ready. Won't you have a seat?" She motioned to the best kitchen chair.

"Let me take your hat," William said. "Please, come on in." He waved toward the chair Eileen had offered.

Jones handed the hat to William and then took the seat. He looked around the sparse house. Two children could be heard arguing upstairs.

"You have children." Jones watched as Eileen poured the tea.

"Yes," she said, nodding.

"Two girls and a boy." William sat down across from the colliery owner. His home, once comfortable, now seemed insufficient. "You?"

"Mm." Jones sipped the tea and nodded. "Girl." He took a biscuit from the flowered pink plate and nibbled a biscuit. He smiled at Eileen. "Thank you."

"How's Harvey doing?" William asked. "He feeling more to home, is he?"

"Harvey's fine." Jones put down the teacup and looked at William. "Truth is, he needs a little help. I thought you might be able to come over for a day and show him how to separate the ewes and lambs. I got a new dog, but Harvey don't know what to do with it, he don't." He shook his head and took another sip of tea.

"Sure. I can come over tomorrow if that works. I'll bring Captain with me and help Harvey learn the signals. Maybe Ian Roi Bugail can come too. Separating a flock is tricky business if your dog doesn't know what's what."

"Oh, that'd be good. Thank you." Jones's face grew round and bright. His front teeth were large, like the rest of him. He stood and shook William's hand. "Sorry to rush out, Mrs. Williams, but I better get home and let Harvey know. Thanks again for the tea."

William pushed back his chair. He hadn't even sipped his own tea yet. "What time would you like me?"

———

Captain walked between William and Ian Roi. The dog always enjoyed a morning walk, and Ian Roi always had a treat in his pocket. It was a bit of biscuit today.

"Captain instead of Lucy today?" Ian Roi asked.

William nodded. He glanced down at Captain trotting along beside them. "He's good for today's work. He can outsmart a stray lamb better than any other dog. But Lucy, she's good for the lost ones."

"We each have a purpose. Humans and dogs are not so different." Ian Roi clapped William on the arm.

———

Harvey was sitting on the fence by the barn when they walked up.

"Morning, Harvey. This is Ian Roi Bugail." William shook the young man's hand and then turned toward his lifelong friend. "Ian Roi knows more about sheep than God himself."

"As much as, anyway." Ian Roi laughed. "Nice to meet you, Harvey. I hear you've studied animals."

Harvey nodded and shook the men's hands. His grip hadn't improved since the spring, still cold and limp.

"Mr. Jones said you're going to help with the new dog." Harvey turned toward the main house. "He keeps it up here."

The men followed Harvey up the drive and behind the house. A large lawn lay behind the house, overlooking a valley. A hedgerow marked the boundary, and flower beds bordered the house. *Eileen would love a place like this,* William thought.

Granville Jones was reading a newspaper and drinking tea on a patio near the back door. He folded the paper and set it beside him on the table. "Good morning, William." He stood and crossed the lawn. "This must be Ian Roi Bugail." He extended his hand, and Ian Roi grabbed it and nodded. "Major is ready for his training."

"Major?" William asked.

"Couldn't be outranked, now could we?" Jones tipped his head toward Captain sitting on his haunches next to William.

"No, sir. Quite right."

Harvey whistled, and a black-and-white Australian shepherd ran through the hedge. It spotted Captain and charged.

"Stay," William commanded.

Captain sat still and endured the sniffing, growling welcome. Major was too young to know better. Captain was used to pups; Lucy's litter had been crawling over him for more than a month now. Soon they would be culled and sold off to other Welsh shepherds. Captain and Lucy had reputations for smart whelps.

"Better get started," Ian Roi said. "The day won't get any longer."

Major jumped up on Ian Roi and started nipping his hands.

"It might," William warned.

———◆———

Granville Jones had a large flock for the local area, nearly two hundred ewes. William showed Harvey how to whistle and which calls to give for each turn or stop. Captain tore over the hillside culling the ewes and lambs. Major chased the lambs and Captain, bounding here and there, occasionally following orders.

"He's young yet. He knows what's expected, has a natural herding instinct, but he still thinks it a game." William ran his hand through his hair. "You'll need to practice with him every day, you will," he told Harvey.

"Mm." Harvey sighed.

"Don't you like dogs?" Ian Roi asked.

"Sure. Who doesn't like a dog? But I didn't come here to herd and shepherd. I came to tend and care. I'm a vet, not a shepherd." He looked up at the two shepherds. "Nothing wrong with shepherds, just …"

"Shepherds herd, but they tend and care too. No sheep will follow a shepherd who doesn't first take care of the flock." Ian Roi smiled. "Isn't that right, William?"

"Aye," William agreed.

Then he whistled for the dogs. Captain came straight-away. Major took a few more glances at the field of lambs, then followed behind the older dog.

"And no dog will listen to a master who doesn't want him," William said.

Harvey nodded.

———————

Granville Jones stood with his back against the barn wall. His car was parked near the gate.

"Thought I'd see how the morning went."

"Major has some learning to do, but he and Harvey will get it in time," William said.

"Thank you for the help today," Harvey said and shook hands with Ian Roi and William. "I'll be sure to work Major every day." He waved at Jones and walked into the barn.

"You have a nice flock, Mr. Jones." William wiped the back of his neck with a hanky.

"I hear you lost several of yours this year." Jones stared at William, then clasped his hands and pushed his thumbs against each other. "'Course things happen. Everyone knows you're a good shepherd; wouldn't have asked you to help if you weren't."

"You're right; it's been a rough year. Anytime Harvey needs a little help, I'd be happy to come over."

"I think Harvey can manage now, but I could still use some help over at the colliery office. Everyone knows you were a great soldier during the war. People would follow you as the supervisor."

William shoved the hanky back in his pocket and shook his head. "Mr. Jones, I thank you for the confidence and the offer, but shepherding is more to my liking."

Jones pulled out his wallet. William noticed its thickness.

The older man thumbed through the money and pulled out a few bills, then said, "Talk it over with your wife. Those children are going to need some shoes this fall." He handed the money over to William. "Thanks for helping out today."

While you are proclaiming peace with your lips, be careful to have it even more fully in your heart.

Saint Francis

CHAPTER 16

ICY SPLINTERS SLITHERED INTO AMOS'S toes and fingers as he walked the mountain. The wind had shifted overnight. He wasn't prepared for the bitter gusts that cut through him. His eyes watered as he stared into the distance. Perhaps those were his sheep.

A rocky canyon offered safe harbor from the cold whipping across them. Amos found the shepherds near a fire hidden under a rock ledge. The sheep huddled together for warmth; they seemed to be faring the weather for now. They would need water soon, though.

"Hello, boys." Amos entered the circle of warmth. "Did you get lost that you have taken my sheep so far from their home?"

The shepherds stood quickly, fear shining in their eyes.

"No, we were searching for lost sheep, sir," said Lamech, one of the older shepherds.

"And did you find them?" Amos held his hands to the fire.

"No, sir." Lamech shook his head. "It would appear that the men from Gilead stole them."

"Why is that?" Amos tipped his head.

"There was nothing left of the sheep, sir. They had to be stolen." Lamech held up his hands.

Amos looked around the circle at the other shepherds. They all nodded in agreement.

"Why must it be the Gileadites? Why not bandits … or even one of you?"

"We've never had problems before, Master Amos. It couldn't be one of us; we're brothers out here. You know that."

Amos nodded his head. Yes, there was a bond in the field that no blood could tie tighter. Shepherds fought wild dogs, bears, and lions. They needed each other to stay safe. They had to depend on each other.

"Did the new men give you trouble?" Amos asked. "Any reason to think it was them?"

"Trouble, no." Lamech pursed his lips and looked sideways at the other shepherds. "But they didn't join us. Kept to themselves the whole time."

Amos nodded. "I see." He rubbed his hands together. "And you asked them to join you at the evening fires, but they declined?"

"Well …" Lamech stroked his long beard. "I guess they built their own fires and stayed together. That would explain how they got away with the thieving."

"How so?"

"There weren't any traces of the missing sheep. They could've burned the skins and bones in their fire."

The other shepherds joined in:

"Mm-hm."

"That's right."

"I guess so," Amos said, then put his hands under his armpits. "The fire feels good, boys, but we better get those sheep off this mountain. They'll be caught in this canyon if snow starts flying."

Amos watched the flock gather around their shepherds and walk through the rocky pass. He stayed behind to make sure none were lost. It was exhilarating to see so many beasts follow their shepherd's voice.

But once they were out of the canyon, the howling winds tore the voice from their throats, riding wild, galloping fast over the mountain and far away. Keeping the sheep going in one direction was hard work. The shepherds used hand signals to guide each other and their sheep.

It took three more days to get off the mountain.

———

Rain poured straight down, drenching the sheep until they were too heavy to walk. They huddled together under trees and shelters in the winter pens. Amos loved being outside, but he was ready for the warmth and comfort of home.

"Where have you been?" Malaki came with a warm blanket and draped it over Amos's shoulders. "Naomi, tell Cook to get some hot soup for Master." She shooed the servant girl from the room. "Get out of those wet things. You'll catch your death, Amos."

Amos chuckled and let her make a fuss, clucking over him like a mother hen. He loved Malaki. She was a good woman, true and faithful. She wasn't just a wife; she was his friend.

Naomi knocked on the door and brought in the hot soup. Amos sat in his cushioned chair by the fire and drank. Yes, home was a good place to be.

"Did Simon make it back alright with the Gileadites?" he asked, then blew across the steaming broth.

"Yes. My goodness, they've been back five days or

more." Malaki took Amuz off her back and sat across from Amos. "I was getting very worried about you."

"No worries. We ran into some bad weather." He caressed her hand resting on his knee. "There was some mischief on the mountain, it seems."

"What kind of mischief?" Malaki readjusted the weight of the baby.

"The shepherds think our Gileadites stole sheep and ate them." He watched her eyes grow large. "What do you think? Would they do that?"

"I don't know them well. The men stay in the barns." She clicked a fingernail on her teeth, thinking. "The women and children have been helping with odds and ends. They seem honest, certainly grateful."

The baby stirred in her arms. Malaki wrapped the blanket tighter around him.

"The girls play with the other children all day," Malaki went on. "Sometimes at bedtime they tell me stories of what the children say." She sighed and shook her head. "They've been through a lot, Amos. I never want that for our children, for any children."

"Still, I have to talk to Jacob and the others." He sighed and finished off the broth. "But not till tomorrow."

———

"You wanted to see me?" Jacob knocked on the door.

Amos looked up from his paperwork. He wasn't looking forward to this.

"Come in." Amos motioned to a chair. "Have a seat."

Jacob came in, looking behind him to make sure his feet were clean. He sat on the edge of the chair.

"How are you and your brothers getting along?"

"Fine, sir." Jacob's voice betrayed him.

"I guess you've heard the accusations."

"We didn't take any sheep, Master Amos. We would never do that, especially not to you." He stood up, desperate to be believed.

"Sit back down, Jacob." Amos was calm. "I want to believe you." He took a deep breath and slowly exhaled. "Why did you not join the other shepherds at the evening fires when you were on the mountain?"

"It's hard, sir." Jacob paused. "Hard to say, see. They're your people." He looked at Amos.

"My people? You mean my shepherds?"

"Yes, your workers, but also your kind." Jacob looked away. "They talk like you, eat like you, worship like you. They know you and you know them."

"But you could know them better if you tried." Amos leaned forward.

Jacob looked back at his boss. Sadness painted shadows in the corners of his eyes.

"No." He shook his head. "They will always think we deserved what we got. That we were … *are* bad people." His shoulders drooped. "We'll never have a home again."

"Come on." Amos stood up. "Let's take care of this right now."

He led Jacob out to the barns. The bleating of sheep echoed against the walls. They found the other men playing Knuckles in the haymow. Jacob's brothers sat in a corner.

"Boys, this here is Jacob. He's a fellow Israelite, though from far away in Gilead. He comes from the shepherds of Gad and Reuben, a brother." Amos kept a hand on Jacob's shoulder. "Jacob, these men have worked for me for years. I trust them, and they say you stole sheep and ate them at night in the fields."

Jacob tried to back away, betrayal and anger heating the air around him.

The men in the haymow stood and faced Amos and Jacob.

"That's right." Lamech stood. "Wasn't any trace of those sheep and no bear tracks. Had to've been you."

"What do you say to that, Jacob?" Amos still held Jacob with a hand, but it was his gaze that captured the man.

"It isn't so, Master Amos." Jacob took a breath and stood up straighter. "We don't steal from anybody."

"So I have the word of a man I've known for years and the word of a near stranger." Amos looked at the group. "Who am I to believe?"

"How about believing the one who knows the truth?"

Everyone turned as Elroi entered the warmth of the barn. He held a bag high for everyone to see.

"What've you got there?" Amos asked.

"I followed some footloose yearlings that strayed from the flock." Elroi lowered the bag to his side. "They were ornery little critters, skipping over rocks faster than I could keep up." He smiled at the group and leaned on his staff. "I can see how they got away from you."

"Let Elroi sit down." Amos waved a few of the younger men aside.

"Thank you." Elroi walked to the bench and sat down. "Anyway, I followed those rascals till they got caught in a ravine. Some wild dogs were prowling nearby and heard them crying. By nightfall they were in real danger. I ran the dogs off and got back to the sheep. I sent them on ahead with your group, Lamech, before I went back for the dogs."

"You shouldn't have gone alone," Amos said.

"You think I can't handle some old dogs?" Elroi laughed. "I found their den and there were the missing sheep parts from your flock." He placed the bag on his lap and opened it for Amos to see.

Amos looked at the ears and hoofs lying in Elroi's bag. The ear notches matched Amos's sign. They were his sheep.

"Thank you, Elroi." Amos closed the bag. "Lamech, I think your boys owe our Gileadite friends an apology."

We must take sides. Neutrality helps the
oppressor, never the victim. Silence encourages
the tormentor, never the tormented.

Elie Wiesel

CHAPTER 17

"WHAT ARE YOU THINKING?" IAN Roi asked, breaking the silence.

Ian Roi looked over at William. Captain looked up at Ian Roi, then over at William. His master had stared at his feet while plodding the dusty road for the last fifteen minutes.

William sighed, then patted Captain's head. "Must be nice to be a dog. Go where you're told and get your dinner handed to you."

"Are you worried about eating?" Ian Roi asked.

"No. Aye, maybe. I feel bad about Eileen and the kids. They do without an awful lot."

"Has God failed to provide yet?" Ian Roi slowed his pace.

"No, the Lord's been good to us. To me, even more. You remember how it was in Egypt."

"No one could forget." Ian Roi sighed and reached out to touch William's arm. "Sometimes God takes care of you so you can take care of someone else."

"Yes, I was anxious to get back to Eileen and the kids. Now there's Iris too. Even more to take care of."

William shrugged his shoulders and kept walking.

"I wasn't thinking of them," Ian Roi said.

"Oh?" William returned his gaze to the road. The air felt heavy. It was hard to breathe.

"I've been hearing things." Ian Roi paused. "About the colliery."

William stayed silent.

"Those men need someone to take care of them, shepherd them."

"Now hold on," William said. "You know I can't go underground. I've had enough darkness and explosions." He quickened his pace, trying to outrun the shadow.

"Might not have to go down," Ian Roi said. "Mr. Jones mentioned it was in the office. Supervisor he said before, didn't he?"

William looked across the field toward his house. Clothes were hanging on the line. Iris was playing with the pups under a tree where Lucy dozed.

"I would miss the sheep too much. I was made to be a shepherd."

"Some sheep have two legs. See you later." Ian Roi waved and jumped the stone wall. He never looked back, but William felt his eyes.

———

"How'd it go?" Eileen looked up from the stove.

William could smell soda bread and new potatoes. He walked to her and wrapped his arms around her waist from behind. Her neck was soft against his cheek.

"Granville Jones has a nice-looking flock. He'll do well at market this year if he can keep the blowflies off in this heat."

"Your flock looks good too." Eileen kissed his head.

"Not two hundred strong like his, plus all the lambs."

"Two hundred? My goodness. That vet has his hands full, he does." Eileen moved away from the stove and William let go of her.

"That he does." William sat down at the table. "Amaryllis still at work?"

"Till two today. Bob told her he wouldn't need her much anymore. Doesn't want to buy my fish and now he doesn't want to pay my daughter."

Eileen poured a glass of water and took it to William. She sat down across from him and said, "A bill came from the animal supply. The sheep dip you ordered went up from last year." She pulled a letter out of her apron pocket. She unfolded the bill and handed it to William. "Can you hold them off until the first ones go to market this fall?"

William took the bill and glanced at it. He nodded. "I better go check on things." He stood up.

"But lunch is almost ready." Eileen looked up at her husband. His eyes were tired.

"This heat takes my appetite. Thanks, though." He bent to kiss her forehead. "It smells good."

He walked out the open door. Eileen watched his back bent in defeat.

———•———

A light breeze blew in through the open window. Everyone had been asleep for hours. William stared at the ceiling. He flipped the light sheet off himself and walked to the window. The barnyard glowed pale grey in the moonlight.

Eileen rolled over and asked, "Can't you sleep?"

"No." William turned to look at her lying there, strands of hair clinging to her sweaty face. "Been thinking."

Eileen sat up in bed and pulled her legs under herself. "What are you thinking?"

William looked out the window again. He knew what Eileen would say. It was up to him. She never pushed him to do anything he didn't want to do.

"Granville Jones offered me a job."

"What? That's wonderful. Finally realized that Harvey boy isn't cut out for it, did he?"

William looked over at her on the bed. He shook his head. "Not a job on the farm. A job in the colliery."

"Oh."

Her face was hard to read in the dim light. One of the kids rolled over in their room, and the bed squeaked. She looked toward the bedroom door. It was open to let the air move. Eileen stretched her legs and climbed out of bed. She stood beside William and stared at nothing out the window.

"What did you say?"

"I told him no."

Eileen nodded her head. She put her hands on the windowsill and leaned forward. Moonlight cast a shadow across her face.

"So why aren't you sleeping?"

"We could use the money. The bills keep piling up, and we lost so many lambs this spring. I don't have two hundred ewes. Small farms are having a harder time these days."

Eileen rested her head against the window frame. "Quite right on all of it, but shepherding is what you love."

"Mm." William looked out the window again. "It's a

supervisor's job. Ian Roi says the colliers need a shepherd." His eyes flickered to her face and back out the window.

"Maybe so. Maybe your dad wouldn't have died if he'd had a shepherd watching over him."

William put his arm around her shoulders.

———◆———

"Really, Dad," Amaryllis said. "You don't have to walk me."

"You don't need to be walking back in the dark."

"One of the boys would walk me home," Amaryllis said.

"That's why I'll walk you home." William grinned. "I know about the oak tree too."

Amaryllis turned red. "Dad! I would never stop there."

"You might want to with the right boy," Eileen said, walking by. She handed Amaryllis a couple of coins. "Have a good time." She kissed her daughter on the cheek and hugged her.

"Thanks, Mum. Come on, Dad. We're going to be late."

———◆———

"I'll come by in two hours and get you. Don't leave here." William opened the café door for his daughter and looked around the room. Young people were sitting around the tables, playing cards and talking. "Have fun."

"I will," Amaryllis said as she ducked her head to miss his kiss. "Dad."

"Alright." William pulled the door shut and walked

into the street. *When did she grow up?*

He walked to the Third Street Pub. There was a sing-along in progress, and he slipped in unnoticed. He ordered a beer and moved near an open window. He leaned against the wall as the song ended.

"Lights on the left side. Like that'll make any difference. We'll all go up like Keith's lot in Pit Five last year."

A table of men were talking. They were several beers into the night and getting loud.

"I heard they can't find a super for the day shift. No one wants that on their record. Be put in prison if they're found, they will."

"William. What are you doing out here on a Friday?" Ian Roi stood next to the table, a beer in one hand and a sandwich in the other. "Come sit. Move over, fellas." Ian Roi sat at the table with the men and elbowed them down the bench.

William moved to join them and put his beer on the table. He hadn't been here in years.

"So?" Ian Roi raised his eyebrows.

"Amaryllis was meeting some friends at the café," he said. "I didn't want her walking home alone, so I came in town with her."

"She'll be doing that more and more now. Maybe you'll become a regular here." Ian Roi smiled. "What do you think, boys? Should William join us every Friday?"

A chorus of hurrahs rang out. They all lifted their mugs.

"To Fridays!"

"William's thinking about working at the colliery," Ian Roi said as they slammed their glasses on the wooden table.

"Oh yeah? Giving up the sheep?" An older man, maybe fifty, eyed William with a crooked grin. "The colliery claims everyone. I knew your daddy. Johnson's my name." He stuck out a hand.

William shook his hand, then lifted his glass and took another drink.

"Have you decided? What did Eileen say?" Ian Roi asked.

"She left it up to me like I knew she would." He swished some beer around his mouth and then swallowed hard. "I still ain't decided. It haunts me, you know."

Ian Roi nodded. "Yes, but it's a supervisor in the office. You wouldn't be going under."

"What? They's asking you to be super?" Johnson asked.

William nodded and breathed deep. He blew his lips out and looked around the room. Colliers were packed like sheep in a pen. Their talking and laughter was just as loud.

"You going to take it?" Johnson asked.

William looked at Ian Roi and then at Johnson before saying, "Haven't decided. I like the sheep, but I need the money."

"Take it. We need a man like you on our side. There's some bloody bad business goes on over there."

William looked at him. Johnson's nails were black, his teeth yellowed, and his eyes red. What would it do to William to work for the colliery? What had it done to his dad?

"What kind of bad business?" William asked.

"Well, this week alone we had to go down when there was gas in the area. We all knowed it was bad air, but it was sticking to the right side of the wall, so they said keep our lights on the left and we'd be alright." Johnson shook his head. "I wouldn't have gone down, but I got a family to feed. Company raised rents again."

"They can't make you go down with gas in the shaft," William said. "It's against the law. Can't you report it to the inspectors?"

"Bloody inspectors are on the payroll, if you know what I mean."

"Some things never change." William gulped the last of his beer. "I've got to go, boys. Enjoy your beer." He stood up and shook hands with the men. "Good-bye, Ian Roi."

Ian Roi licked the beer off his lips and nodded good-bye.

*We should never forget that everything Adolph Hitler
did in Germany was "legal."*

Martin Luther King, Jr.

CHAPTER 18

"YOU'VE MADE A DECISION." EILEEN stood at the kitchen sink, her hands deep in dish-water.

William sat at the table staring into his teacup. The leaves were unreadable, but he didn't feel good about any of it. He looked up at his wife and gave one nod.

"So you're going." She turned back to the dishes and scrubbed furiously at a pot of dried oats.

"I spoke with some of the men last night. Things are still happening there. Maybe I can make it right." He shrugged his shoulders. "Maybe I'm meant for such a time as this. You know?"

"You're not meant to be your father, William." Eileen kept her head down. "You came back from the war. Too many didn't. Maybe you're meant to be safe in a field, shepherding."

"Others don't have that option. And it's coal what burns in that cookstove. Is it fair to ask someone else to get it if I'm not willing?"

"That's not fair, William. Others aren't willing to stay up all spring lambing and all summer waiting to see if blowflies kill off their flock. There's risk in being a shepherd too."

"True." William sighed. "Maybe it won't be for long. Amaryllis and Allen can keep the sheep going. Ian Roi will help too. I'll go talk to him this morning."

William found Ian Roi in the woods near the river. He was sitting in the shade with his feet in the water.

"Trying to cool off?" William waved his hat in front of his face.

"Something special about water. Cleansing. Refreshing. It takes away the sin and the grief." Ian Roi patted the ground next to him. "It takes what ails you and washes it downriver, far away."

"To the next poor bloke who has to deal with it." William chuckled as he sat down.

"Perhaps, but that poor bloke has troubles that wash down to the next poor bloke. And on it goes until it flows into the sea. We all have something to deal with. And what we can't handle, someone else can. Take your shoes off." Ian Roi smiled at William. "You have a lot to discuss, I think."

William took off his shoes and socks. He slipped his pale, bony feet into the cool water.

"I'm going to take the job at the colliery."

The two men sat in silence. Sunlight glinted off the surface of Afon Tywi. Sheep bleated in a nearby field.

"Aren't you going to say anything?" William asked.

"Like what?"

"Like, is that a good idea, with my fear of the mines and explosives?"

"You're a hero, William. Everyone knows that."

William huffed and looked down the river. A red

kite flew from the opposite shore, skirting the shade trees. Shadows played on the water like the demons in his mind.

"You know it wasn't like that. I did what had to be done to save them. I wasn't being a hero. They were my friends, my brothers."

"Not everyone would have done it, even for a brother."

William looked at Ian Roi. "You would have. You did. But no one knows the hero you are."

"Those who look for heroes find them." Ian Roi put his hand on William's arm. "Some are looking to you now. So you're taking on a new flock. What about your sheep at home?"

"Amaryllis and Allen can handle them, for now anyway. If you can help me get them shipped to market next month, I ought to be alright until tupping in October." William looked over at Ian Roi. "Maybe by then I'll know if I'm in for good."

"You know you can count on me." Ian Roi nodded. "Always."

———◆———

William walked to town in an early-morning fog. He could hear water dripping off the fences and trees along the way. A robin sang as the sun rose pink through the morning mist.

Eileen had packed a large lunch. The metal tommy box was about all he had left of his dad. It had been recovered along with his father's body in the mine. The weight of it in William's hand was a reminder that neither memories nor pain ever ended; they just softened with time.

The grey mining cottages of Shotton Cross were another reminder. His life had been defined by them at birth. His father was a collier, and his was a collier's life: accidents, coughing, dust, and fear. William had grown up in the huts, but he had breathed free in the country air of his grandfather's farm. Now he was back. He walked through the quiet town, shackles dragging his feet.

He stood in the courtyard of the colliery. Large machinery loomed in the mist, symbols of the immensity of his decision. Men walked out of the mist as the whistle blew for the next shift.

"Williams!" an older man called through the bustle. It was Johnson from the pub.

William raised his arm in salute. Johnson walked over with his hand out.

"You decided to come after all. Good. Good. We can use a man like you on the inside. Make them do right by us."

"I'll do my best." William shook his hand.

The office clerk that William had spoken with last spring passed by. He looked at William, pushed up his glasses, and walked on. The office was always unlocked. The men worked all shifts and a supervisor was always on hand.

The clerk waved for William to follow him in the office. "Mr. Jones thought you might be here today. He left me with orders to get you set up." He handed William some papers. "Fill these out. You can set your lunch here with ours." He pointed toward tommy boxes under the front counter. "The second desk is yours. You have the day shift. Not many start there." The young man sniffed.

"Thanks." William took the papers, set his lunch

with the others, and went to his desk. It was going to be a long day.

———

"Williams!" Granville Jones called from his office door.

William's body jerked at the shout, and he jumped to his feet. He hurried to Mr. Jones.

"Glad you're here. I knew your wife would help you see the light."

William shrugged his shoulders and smiled. *He doesn't know as much as he thinks he knows.* He stretched out his hand.

"She's a good woman, sir." He shook hands. "Glad to be here."

"Yes. Well, let's start here." He walked to the wall of filing cabinets. "Edward over there can give you the cataloging system, but everything you write up goes in one of these drawers."

Jones pulled out a filing drawer. It was filled to overflowing. Tags stood up every few files, giving order to the chaos. Jones shoved the drawer closed.

"You'll be managing the day shift in the West District. That's Pits Nine through Seventeen. Glenn is the night shift manager. You share a desk with him, so anything that happens the night before should be easy to access. He'll keep you informed."

William's ears rang. Pit Seventeen. His father's final breaths were taken there.

"Be back soon." Jones waved to Edward behind the desk and motioned William to follow.

They walked out the front door and down the steps. The mist was burning off in the summer sun.

"Let's check the ponies." Jones led the way to the stables. "Each shift has a supervisor; each super has a group of foremen. Each foreman has his trusted leads, and on it goes. The smart men are at the top. The ones that make mistakes are down the line. You have to control the mistakes and make sure they don't get too costly." Jones looked over at him. "You understand."

William wasn't sure he did. *Is he talking about profits or lives?*

"For the most part we can keep the losses under control. The inspectors come every couple of months. If the paperwork looks too daunting, they assume we've done what's required. Keep up with the papers." Jones winked. "Here we are."

The colliery ponies were stout and strong. They only saw the light of day on their way from the stable to the mine. They had hay and oats, lots of water. A stable boy was currying a brown mare; she chewed oats like Iris eating her favorite lemon biscuit.

Jones stroked the mare and cooed to her. He scratched her ear and gave the boy some instructions. Then they walked the line of stalls, stopping at each to admire the ponies.

"You're going to do just fine here," Jones said as they walked back to the office. "It's like the army. Report to your commander and do as you're told."

"Yes, sir."

It is justice, not charity, that is wanting in the world!

Mary Wollstonecraft

CHAPTER 19

"KEDIAH, WHAT ARE YOU DOING here?" Amos opened the door wide. "Leah sent you away?" He grinned at his arborist.

"She's expecting a baby." Kediah grinned like a ram at the start of tupping season. "She's more difficult than ever."

"Congratulations." Amos hugged Kediah. "Come in, come in." He held the door open wider to let the man in. "Join me in the front room by the fire. Malaki! Kediah is here," he yelled down the hallway.

The two men sat in front of the fire enjoying the warmth and catching up on the news. Malaki came in with the children to meet Kediah.

"We're glad to have you in our home." Malaki bowed as they entered. "How long will you stay?"

"Just a couple of days to go over things with Master Amos." Kediah stood. "There's work to do even in winter."

"Leah is having a baby," Amos said, knowing Malaki would want news of the young woman. They were fast friends on their last visit.

"That's wonderful." Malaki looked down at the babe in her own arms. "May the Lord bless her with a son as perfect as our Amuz."

"Or a daughter, Mama." Jemima pulled on her mother's skirt.

"A daughter is just what Kediah needs to keep him straight." Amos picked up his daughter and threw her in the air. She squealed and laughed as he set her back down.

"I'll go arrange the room for you and let Cook know we have a guest for dinner." Malaki shuffled the children from the room. "Congratulations, Kediah, to you and Leah."

"Thank you," Kediah said as he sat back down across from Amos.

"How are things in the valley? Any trouble since I left?" Amos spoke low until Malaki was out of the room. He didn't want to alarm her.

"Fine. Fine." Kediah waved the past away. "It's the trees I'm here about."

Amos raised an eyebrow.

"They really must be replaced, sir. We've lost an acre at least from this last ice storm. The winter has been colder than usual, and the trees aren't vigorous enough to withstand it."

"Ashdod. I see." Amos sighed. "If it must be, it must be."

"I've heard the Moabites talking."

"Still making Leah feed them?" Amos leaned back and clasped his hands behind his head.

"She likes hearing how good her cooking is." Kediah laughed. "I did get her a couple of new dresses and some bracelets. Good advice, sir."

"She works hard like you. Good move." Amos nodded approval. "Now what about these Moabites?"

"They've been getting some new trees up from

Egypt. They're hardier and mingle well with the valley trees. I think they'll be a good addition to your orchard, sir."

"Getting them in Gaza, then, I suppose?" Amos scratched his head and rubbed his face.

"Mostly, yes."

"Mm. Malaki won't hear of that." He half smiled at Kediah. "I'll go to Ashdod and bring you what I can find. You need an acre's worth?"

"At least, sir. We've lost an acre so far and there were some to replace before that." Kediah sat forward. "Whatever you can get, I can plant."

———◆———

"Why couldn't Kediah go?" Malaki sat on the bed with a blanket draped around her shoulders. She shivered in the night air.

"We've been through this, Malaki. You know I must go away on business sometimes. I can't hire everything done. The sycamore figs are part of our livelihood." He threw the nightshirt over his head and climbed under the covers. "It's only to Ashdod. Kediah wanted me to get the trees from Gaza."

"Well thank the Lord you had enough sense to say no to that." She huffed and flopped down onto the feather mattress. "How long will you be gone?"

"I think I'll take several of the men with me. Kediah said a shipment is expected at the end of the month. If I can get four wagonfuls, we can go straight from Ashdod to Valley Grove. The men can help Kediah get them into the ground before spring." Amos smoothed Malaki's hair from her face.

"You didn't say how long." She stared him down.

"A month. No more if I can help it." He kissed her nose. "Will I come home to another announcement?" He moved his hand down her throat and cupped her breast. "Another boy to play with Amuz?"

"You should be so lucky." She kissed him back and then bit his nose. "Don't be late."

———◆———

Amos pulled the donkeys up short. Ashdod lay below him, shining white in the winter sun. The city had been a Philistine outpost when Amos was a child. It was conquered by King Uzziah and now had a strong Israelite presence. Its proximity to the port city of Gaza made it valuable to Judah and Israel.

The other wagons stopped behind Amos. Jacob climbed out of his wagon and approached.

"Everything alright, my lord?" Jacob put a hand on the seat. He gazed over the city below to see what Amos was looking at.

"Yes, fine." Amos took a deep breath. "I haven't been here in a while. Keep your wits about you, Jacob; they are hostile still."

"Yes, sir."

Amos clucked to the team of donkeys and they headed down the slope toward the city. Jacob climbed back into his wagon and followed. He'd never been to the Mediterranean Sea. It spread before him like a great shining obelisk, greater than the sea that he had always admired back in Gilead.

The city was walled. A wide road curved around the countryside and through the gates of the city. It was a busy place; people selling products from around the world lined the streets with open-air handcarts or small donkey carts. The smell of animal and human waste turned Jacob's stomach. He didn't like cities.

Amos led the way through the entire city and out the western gate toward the city port. He pulled alongside a hitching post and stopped. He filled the grain bag for the donkeys and gave instructions to the other men.

"I'll see if I can find the harbor master. If the shipment hasn't arrived yet, we'll camp back in the hills. You stay here; don't talk to anyone." Amos looked each man in the eye. "Not to anyone."

They all nodded, shepherds guarding their sheep.

———————

Amos walked the wooden docks to the harbor master's quarters. Several large ships from Cyprus were anchored on the northern side of the harbor. Their figureheads of Aphrodite were painted with garish embellishment. *She's nothing compared to my Malaki.*

Smaller ships were anchored throughout the harbor, waiting their turn to dock and unload. Some Egyptian ships were unloading horses, and Tyrian ships were riding low in the water loaded down with lumber.

Amos knocked on the master's door.

"Enter," a deep voice bellowed.

Amos opened the door and found a giant of a man standing behind a long counter. He was weighing silver while other men watched.

"Take your place," the man said, not lifting an eye to see who had entered.

Amos walked to the end of the line and waited. The line moved slowly as captains and businessmen took care of payments, orders, and shipments. Amos watched with interest as the man in front of him unwrapped a bundle of coins from around the world.

Finally it was his turn.

"I'm looking for a shipment of fig trees from Egypt." Amos tipped his head back to look the man in the eye. "I heard there was to be one arriving at the end of the month."

"Figs from Egypt? This isn't the time for figs." He curled his lip.

"No, of course it isn't. I'm looking for trees—fig trees. Should be here anytime from what I hear." Amos tried to smile, but it melted in the man's glare.

"I don't know what's coming, just what's come. No trees from Egypt. Next."

I want to live my life so that my nights
are not full of regrets.

D. H. Lawrence

CHAPTER 20

IRIS HELD A DAISY CHAIN as long as she was tall. She had been ordered to stay quiet while Eileen fished along the riverbank. Now the last fish was in the bucket.

"Can you make it into a crown, Mummy?" Her blue eyes pleaded.

"Certainly. I think that's long enough for a double crown, m'lady." Eileen laughed and sat in the thick grass. "You were a good girl, Iris. You have to be good just a little longer and go to town with me." She wound the chain into a crown around the girl's head.

"Will we see Daddy there?" Iris threw some dirt in the river.

"Maybe. Depends how well the fish sales go. With Daddy working at the colliery too, maybe people will be a little more inclined to buy our fish."

She finished winding the daisy chain and tied it off. She squeezed Iris's shoulders and kissed her cheek.

"All done. We should get going, we should."

———◆———

The shades were drawn at Constance's house. Eileen

could see the boys running races from the back door to the river. *I'll check on her on the way home.*

They walked down Francis Street and turned left. Eileen was pleased that two more houses opened their doors to her. William's new job might help in more ways than one. Amaryllis and Allen seemed to be holding their own with the sheep. Amaryllis would finish school in another year. If Eileen could help through the lambing next spring, then they might be able to keep up both the colliery and the shepherding. A little fishing on the side, which Allen could easily start doing on his own, and Eileen's mind reeled. She wouldn't have to eat turnips once if she didn't want to.

"Mrs. Williams." A woman on the street interrupted Eileen's thoughts. "I see you're selling fish again."

It was an old school friend, Catherine Smith. Eileen stopped to let her peer in the bucket.

"Yes. Would you like some? I have some paper with me; I can wrap them up right here."

"No thank you." The woman shuddered. "I just thought you should know that your friend, *Mrs. Davies*, has been going in and out of the doctor's office a lot lately."

"Oh? Has she been ill?"

"Hmph. Just thought you'd want to keep your little ones away from her. Reputations can be quite catchy." She looked down at Iris. "I'd keep the older one away too. Who knows but that her girl helps her out in the business."

Catherine crossed the street and went into the company store.

"Does reputations hurt, Mummy?" Iris looked up at her mother. "Does it make you throw up?"

"Sometimes." Eileen watched the woman's back.

"But most of the time they just need some tea and toast." She took Iris's hand and walked on.

———◆———

The store was dark after the bright summer sun. Eileen stood still a moment. Amaryllis had been let go just as William went to work at the colliery. Bob's wife, Eleanor, had taken Amaryllis's place.

"Mrs. Williams." Eleanor's voice was shrill, like lambs separated from their mothers. Eileen never liked dealing with her. "How are you today?"

"Fine, thank you. I was wondering if Bob would be ready to pay for his fish instead of robbing me." Eileen smiled to soften the words. "We're on our way to the colliery to see William, and I have a few fish left."

She had not planned to stop in the store, but Catherine's remarks had baited her.

"I'll have to ask him if we need any fish. Be right back," Eleanor said. She went into the back room and shut the door behind her.

Eileen and Iris looked at the candy jars on the counter, but Eileen's attention was on the group of women surrounding Catherine near the canned goods. They whispered and chattered together, glancing at Eileen every now and then.

Leaving her bucket on the counter, Eileen smiled and walked over to them. "Good morning, ladies. Can I interest you in some fish? You know Bob is going to double the price as soon as it goes behind his counter."

"Good morning, Eileen," Catherine said. "I was just telling the ladies about the sad business of Mrs. Davies' condition." She tipped her head and clucked her tongue.

"Yes, it is a sad condition when the country doesn't take care of a soldier's family." Eileen crossed her arms. "You and I were very blessed to get our husbands back from the war. Of course, I could always depend on the farm, but what would you have done, Catherine?"

"The war pension takes care of those who know how to live right." Catherine shot back. "I would learn to scrimp and save like all the other widows."

"Scrimping and saving doesn't feed three growing boys and a girl besides, it doesn't. And I haven't seen Constance in new shoes since before the war." Eileen looked at Catherine's feet. "I don't know but you might find it difficult, Catherine. Good day, ladies."

Eileen walked down the aisle and took Iris by the hand.

Eleanor came out the backroom door. "Bob says he'll take the fish for a shilling a pound."

"I have better people in mind to eat these fish." Eleanor looked over her shoulder, then grabbed the pail off the counter.

She stomped out the door and let it slam behind her.

———•———

"I thought we were going to see Daddy," Iris complained. "I want to see his big desk."

"Daddy's busy, Iris. We'll stop and see Mrs. Davies and you can play with the boys by the river."

Iris sighed and fell in line.

———•———

Eileen didn't knock this time but pushed the door open.

"Constance? Are you in the kitchen?"

Alice came around the corner of the hallway and held her finger to her lips. "She's asleep."

"Iris, you go on out back with the boys." Eileen shoved Iris toward the kitchen and back door, then looked at Alice. "Is your mum not feeling well?"

Alice shook her head and her eyes swam. Eileen put her arm around Alice and held her close. Iris stood by the door.

"Go on, Iris. Go play with the boys." Eileen watched her daughter close the door quietly. "What's going on?" she asked the top of Alice's head.

Alice shook with quiet sobs. "She … She gets bad headaches. The doctor gave her some medicine, but it just makes her sleep all day. When she wakes up, she still has the headache." Alice pulled away from Eileen and wiped her face on her apron. "People are saying things. I've heard them. No one will come near us."

"People who don't know how to stay busy doing good find other ways to occupy their time." Eileen looked around the kitchen. The table was still full of breakfast's dishes, and the stove was covered in grease and crumbs. "Looks like you could use some help."

Alice sighed, and her shoulders drooped as she followed Eileen's gaze.

"Come on," Eileen said. "Get the water hot while I straighten up the table." She turned in that direction. "Has your mum had anything this morning? Tea?"

"No."

Eileen took her bucket out back and started the boys cleaning fish. Then she cleared the table and poured Alice's hot water in the sink.

"Go raise the shades and straighten the front room," she told Alice. "I'll get the dishes done up and make some lunch."

Alice gave her a hug and left the kitchen.

It didn't take long to set the room right. There were some garden vegetables on the sideboard, and she called Iris in to clean and cut them. The boys brought the fish in, and soon the smell of lunch was drifting through the house.

"Alice?" Constance called from the bedroom.

Eileen met Alice in the hallway. "I'll check on her, Alice. You watch the fish." She motioned toward the kitchen.

Constance was catacorner on top of the sheets, her eyes covered with a damp cloth.

"Just lying around all day, are you?" Eileen laughed softly and nudged Constance's foot. "Must be a lady of leisure, I see."

Constance moved aside the cloth and looked at Eileen. Her eyes filled with defeat, like the fall pig on butchering day.

"Oh, Eileen." A tear trickled out the corner of her eye. "I ... I ..." She tried to sit up.

"Shh. The boys cleaned some fish and Alice is helping cook. I even have Iris slicing vegetables. You'll be feeling better in no time, you will." Eileen sat on the edge of the bed and held her friend's hand. "Alice says the medicine isn't working. Your headaches won't go away?"

Constance looked at the ceiling. She shook her head. "They aren't headaches. I had to ... I had to take care of it."

"Oh. ... Love." Eileen's voice caught in her throat. She stroked Constance's arm, stood up, and fluffed the pillow. "Straighten yourself up and get under the covers." She helped Constance turn in the bed. "You need rest. I'll take Thomas and Morgan home with me. They can help Allen in the sheep field. Alice and James can stay and take care of you and the house and garden."

Constance grabbed Eileen's hand. "You can't do that. You shouldn't be here. People are talking."

"You're my friend, and you need help. What you've done isn't right, Constance, but I don't know that I would have done any different in your shoes. George didn't leave you a farm like my William would have left me. We'll figure this out. You just rest."

A tear slid down the broken woman's cheek.

———◆———

"Quiet down in there!" William yelled from the bedroom.

Three boys made more noise than Eileen had expected. Allen was thrilled to finally outrank the girls in number. He, Thomas, and Morgan spent the whole afternoon traipsing across the sheep field, throwing rocks in the river, racing Captain, and playing with the pups.

"How can they have any energy left?" Eileen asked William.

He turned his head on the pillow. "It was your idea. What were you thinking?" His lip curled in a smirk.

"I wasn't thinking. She just looked so pathetic; I had to do something." Eileen raised up on her elbow. Her hair fell across her face. "All I could think of was me and Amaryllis and Allen when we got the telegram that you'd been injured. It was a bad day."

William tucked her hair behind her ear. He rolled over and kissed her fingers.

"It's not right what she did, but it's not right what people are doing to her either." Eileen put her head on his chest. "I just wanted to slap Catherine."

"I know how you feel. There are some people I'd like to slap at the colliery." He stroked her head. "They act like the workers aren't people with lives and families. I swear Mr. Jones thinks more of those ponies than he does his own men."

Animal noises and laughter burst out from the next room. William pounded on the wall over the headboard. It was quiet immediately.

Eileen breathed deeply and sighed. "There's got to be a way to help her." She rolled over and looked at the ceiling. "What about starting a benefit society? We could have a fair. Baked goods, a singing contest, races."

She sat up in bed and looked at William, then continued, "Like we used to have when we raised money for the war effort. Now we can raise money for the war widows. We'll call it the Shotton Cross Benefit Society."

"Good idea. It's about time people started helping others instead of just looking out for themselves." William smiled up at her. "You're a good woman, Eileen Williams."

"It's why you love me like you do." She laughed and planted a kiss on his mouth.

*Mankind has to get out of violence only through
non-violence. Hatred can be overcome only by
love. Counter-hatred only increases the surface
as well as the depth of hatred.*

Gandhi

CHAPTER 21

THE SHEEP WERE CROWDED IN the far corner
of the pen. The wooden frame narrowed at one
end and forced the sheep to descend into a small canal
for plunging them in the dip. Amaryllis looked scared,
but the three boys were excited.

"There's very little a sheep can remember," William
said. "You can take them through the same pasture five
days a week, and on the sixth day they still won't know
where they're going. But the smell of dip is unfor-
gettable." He reached for the staff he used to guide
the sheep through the dipping. "You've got to go slow,
boys. Don't make it worse than it has to be."

The boys wrestled sheep all morning. Captain did
his part negotiating the narrowing run with expertise.
He didn't get butted or kicked once. The boys couldn't
say the same.

Amaryllis opened the gate at the end of the canal and
let Lucy guide the soaked sheep to their new meadow.
It was a long morning. They were ready when Iris
appeared announcing lunch.

"I thought a picnic would be a good idea." Eileen stood at the kitchen door, noting how the boys were covered in sweat and dirt. "I put everything under the tree." She motioned toward the elm in the front.

The boys washed in the pan of water by the back door and ran for the tree. Bread, cheese, fried bass, and fresh berries were piled in the middle of an old quilt there. The boys jumped on it like a pack of wild dogs.

"Good thinking." William laughed as he watched the boys from the back door. "They should go swimming after we finish this afternoon."

He stuck his head in the pan of water and splashed his face. Eileen handed him a towel. He dried his face and gave her a kiss.

"Are we all outdoors?" William asked.

"Yes, but I made a separate blanket for the girls here by the house. Would you like to join us or eat with the heathen?" Eileen kissed him back.

"I'll take you over heathens any day."

Amaryllis and Iris were already on the other quilt in the shade of the house corner. Two big rhubarb pies sat on top of a basket.

"A beautiful woman and pie as well. Yes, I'll take this over the heathens, thank you." William sat down next to his wife.

"Dad, can I go swimming?" Amaryllis asked. "Some of the kids from town were talking about going to the river in the afternoon."

"Boys?" William took a bite of bread and eyed his daughter.

She nodded and picked at a piece of fish. She glanced up at her dad and then back at the fish.

William looked at Eileen. She tipped her head and

raised her eyebrows.

"Who's going?" William asked.

"Susan, Carol, probably Amy." She shrugged her shoulders.

"And the boys? Who will be looking at my daughter?"

"Daddy!" Amaryllis turned red and her eyes grew large and round.

"Oh, 'Daddy,' is it? I'm not a sheep, Amaryllis. I remember things quite well."

Eileen giggled and popped a berry in her mouth. Iris leaned over in her mother's lap and watched an ant crawl across her hand.

"I don't know what boys will be there, but I'm sure none are going to be looking at me. Susan is the one who flirts. Maybe Owen and Frank will be there. I haven't heard anything about Dennis Byrne since the explosion. Maybe he'll go, but I don't know if he's even in town anymore."

"He is." William tore another piece of thick bread with his teeth. "He's working at the mine. I saw his papers last week."

Amaryllis licked her fingers and looked at her father. "Do you think he'll come back to school this fall?"

"Doubt it." William shook his head. "He's sixteen and needs to work. No mother or father left for him to count on."

Amaryllis gazed across the yard. Two pups were pulling on a rope with the boys.

"So can I go swimming?" She looked back at her father.

He smiled and nodded.

"And if you ever see Dennis at work, will you tell him I said hello? He needs a friend."

"I will." William swallowed something that tasted like pride. "Eileen, cut me a piece of pie."

———◆———

The noise of the lift hauling men up in the middle of a shift caught William's attention. He walked outside to meet Clarence, the foreman for the Number Ten Pit.

"What's going on?" William asked.

"Air's bad." Clarence was shaking his head. "We've got the men working on the ventilators, but it's too dangerous down there. They've got to come up till the air clears."

"Send them over to help at the Number Twelve. They're short a few men today."

The foreman nodded and gathered the men. William headed back to the stack of paperwork on his desk. He could hear the foreman giving directions.

"After your heads clear, you four go over to the Number Twelve. The rest of you can take lunch early. Maybe the ventilators will get fixed and we can make up time this afternoon."

"What's going on here?" Granville Jones stormed into the office. "Why are your men sitting around aboveground?"

William looked up from his work. "The ventilators on Ten went down. The air was bad on the right side of the shaft and they had to come up. We're working on getting it fixed."

"Working on it doesn't get coal in the chute. Get those men down there!" Jones's face was red. He started for the door.

"But, sir, the air is bad. Clarence said the whole right wall of the pit is foul."

"Then stay on the left!" He blustered and slammed the door behind him.

William jumped from his desk and followed on his heels. "Mr. Jones! Mr. Jones." He caught up to the boss. "Sir, we can't send them down in bad air. They'll light up the shaft and get killed."

"Didn't you say the air was only bad on the right?" The older man turned on William.

"Yes."

"Then they ought to carry their lights on the left and stay away from the gas." He blew air out his nose. "You're still new. I'll let it go this time, but you have to think how to keep the coal moving."

"I sent some of the men to cover Number Twelve, and Clarence had the men take an early lunch, so they can work through once the fans are working again. The coal is moving, sir, but the men must be kept safe." William stared Jones in the eye.

"We wouldn't have beat the Germans with an attitude like that. I thought you were a war hero." Jones looked William up and down. "I expect workers to work."

Jones turned and walked toward Clarence and the other men finishing their lunches. Their tommy boxes were empty.

"Clarence," Jones said, "get these men back to work."

"Mr. Jones," William said, "I can't let you—"

"It's alright," Clarence said, putting his hand up to stop William. "The fans are working again. We ought to be able to go down as soon as the lift can get back up."

"Glad to hear it," Jones said. "I'm going to check on the ponies, Williams. Make sure these men are on the next lift."

"Yes, sir," William said as Jones strode off.

"He'll check the ponies but let us blow to kingdom come. I told you we needed a man like you." It was Johnson, from the Third Street Pub. "You better have our backs or that man will kill us all."

"The air should be fine now." William looked at Johnson. "But I'll check it myself."

William climbed onto the lift with Clarence, then said, "You men stay here until we come back."

As they descended, William watched the light disappear above him. The darkness below was deeper than the mine.

All the victories are won in battles.
Smith Wigglesworth

CHAPTER 22

A MOS WALKED OUT OF THE harbor master's hut into the afternoon sunshine. He held a hand up to shield his eyes and looked across the harbor. *Who would know when to expect the shipment?* He turned to look around the dock and then back toward the city.

Amos spotted a grove of fig trees on the hillside above the city. He strode back to the donkeys with purpose.

"Well?" Jacob waited at his wagon.

"None yet. But I might know where to get some information." He climbed into the wagon and headed east.

The small caravan of donkeys lumbered up the slope in single file. A large house nestled inside the grove of trees near the base of the hills. It looked like no one was home. Amos reined in the donkey and climbed down.

"Stay where you are until I see if anyone's home." Amos held a hand up to the other men.

He tapped on the door and waited. When no one came, he walked behind the house. Two young women were cleaning out animal stalls, throwing manure into handcarts.

"Shalom." Amos waved.

The girls startled and then giggled.

"Shalom." The smaller girl put her shovel down and walked to him. "Can I help you?"

"Yes. I'm Amos, a dresser of figs in the east. I heard some saplings were being shipped up from Egypt, but the harbor master didn't know anything about it. I wondered if the owner here might know something." Amos gave the smile he reserved for his daughters. It worked.

"There is a shipment coming. My lord has gone to Egypt to bring them back. We expect him any day. You aren't a Moabite?" She furrowed her brow.

"No." Amos shook his head. "I live in Tekoa."

"Master has been selling to Moabites. I thought you might be one of them. I don't trust their kind. Are you alone?"

"I have four wagons and six men."

"Well, dark will be falling soon. You're welcome to stay in the barn. There's grain for your donkeys, and Deborah and I can fix some dinner." She looked to the other girl and then back to Amos. "It will be good to have some fellow Israelites around. We're overrun with Philistines and foreigners. I haven't felt safe since my master left."

"That's very kind of you." Amos bowed his head.

———◆———

The barn was comfortable, but Amos was up early. Ships sailed through the night and he intended to be there as soon as they arrived. He scanned the harbor below as the rising sun cast long shadows across the landscape.

"Come on, men. Let's get a move on," Amos called from outside. "Those trees won't grow in your dreams."

"We're ready, sir," Jacob said.

Amos turned to see Jacob and the others appear in the barn doorway. They held their bedrolls on their shoulders. Several chewed fruit cakes and nuts for their breakfast.

"There's a bucket of water near the house. The girls left it there for us. Get a drink and wash up before we head out." He held the door wide for them to leave.

———————

The city was just getting busy as Amos and the others entered. Beggars lined the street near the open-air market. Children were the main panhandlers. Their empty eyes watched Amos and the others pass.

"Some food, sir?" A boy, maybe twelve years old, held the hand of a little girl.

Amos threw a bag of dried fruit to the children.

"Thank you, sir," the boy called as he knelt beside the girl.

Amos saluted and watched the little girl pop a few raisins in her mouth. Then, out of the corner of his eye, he saw Jacob throw some nuts. He was glad he had decided to help the Gileadites.

The morning sun warmed Amos's back as he neared the hitch at the dock. New ships lay at anchor in the harbor. Yesterday's ships had been unloaded and were moored away from the dock to let others disembark. Amos jumped from the seat and tied up the team.

"I'll walk the dock before I check with the master," he called to Jacob.

Jacob waved and nodded. He pulled up beside Amos's

team and hitched his own donkeys. The others were getting out buckets to fetch water for the donkeys.

Salt hung heavy in the morning air. Amos breathed deeply and headed across the docks. Dockhands were unloading incense from Sheba and sweet calamus from a distant land. He stepped out of the way of some huge crates of fabric from Cush. Men yelled to each other from aboard ship, giving directions to the men below.

Amos smelled it before he saw it. Earth. Damp, pungent, clean, and pure: dirt. He walked faster and saw the first of the fig trees being unloaded. A bearded man was giving orders from the edge of the gangplank. Amos stopped and watched until he caught the man's eye.

"Shalom!" Amos waved. "You have fig saplings, yes?"

The man nodded and held up a hand for Amos to wait. He talked with some of the crew and then joined Amos on the dock.

"Elias." The man held out his hand. "Of Ashdod."

"Amos of Tekoa." They shook hands. "I think I may have spent the night in your barn. Your servant girls said you were expected anytime."

"And why does a man from Tekoa want to know about fig trees?" Elias scratched his head.

"I'm a shepherd in Tekoa but a dresser of figs in the Dead Sea valley." Amos stepped back to let a handcart through. "My man in Valley Grove said you would be bringing a shipment from Egypt at the end of the month, and so I headed over. My orchard is aging, and the winter has been hard on them."

"I might have some for sale … for the right price."

"Of course. Can I treat you to a hot breakfast while you wait for the crew to settle matters with the harbor master?"

"That sounds perfect." Elias shook Amos's hand again. "Give me just a minute."

Amos nodded as Elias climbed the narrow plank and left instructions. One of the Egyptian crew passed by with an armful of fig saplings. He was humming a familiar tune.

"Calling, hearing lamb's sharp cry."

Amos picked up the words as the man passed. *How does this Egyptian know Elroi's shepherding song?*

The tavern was filled with sailors just off the ships. The place smelled of sweat, beer, and salty sea air. Amos and Elias sat at a table near the door and talked about figs and fertilizers. Elias had some new ideas about crossbreeding figs from the Mediterranean and Egypt.

A band of children sat outside the door taking crusts of bread that were offered as people left the tavern. Amos watched while he and Elias talked. Some young women, barely past marrying age and thin as new grass in springtime, approached the children with some bits of fish from the dock.

"What are they doing?" Amos peeled his boiled egg and watched the children and women.

"That's Mehellah's lot." Elias leaned forward to look out the door better. "Mehellah, here."

Amos watched as Elias held two eggs out toward the oldest of the women. She took the eggs, bowed, and gave them to the children.

"She's a good woman," Elias said, looking toward Amos again.

"She's not old enough for all those kids." Amos kept staring at them.

"They aren't hers." Elias laughed like he'd heard a bad joke. "No, those kids were left after the king of Ashdod sold off their people to Edom."

"What?" Amos looked back at the man.

Elias twisted his lips, nodded his head, and went back to the last egg.

"Why would he separate families?" Amos glanced at the children and back at Elias. "That's bad policy ... for everyone."

"Don't I know it. Little children running around with no one to take care of them. Old men, too feeble to work, separated from their sons. There was no mercy; people were cast out and sold off." Elias snapped his fingers. "City's overrun with leftovers."

"So who's this Mehellah?" Amos asked.

"Just a good soul who was raised right."

———◆———

Amos and Elias came to an agreement about the figs. Amos could have the saplings and several larger trees that should produce two years after transplant. They shook on it, and Amos headed back to the wagons.

"Good news. We'll be on our way today." Amos greeted the men. "I got a good bargain." He smiled and clapped his hands twice. "Jacob, you can drive down to the loading area, and Elias will meet you there—long beard, older. You'll know him. He's the only one with trees."

Jacob untied the donkeys and climbed onto the wagon seat. The loading area was near the harbor master's quarters. Amos walked down to pay the tax.

An old man, stooped from age and hard work, leaned on a cane. He walked, trembling down the dock, and stopped in front of the harbor master.

"Get off the dock, you old fool, before you get hurt." The giant pushed the aged man toward the edge of the wooden walkway.

The old man stumbled and fell. His cane rolled off the edge and floated in the surf below. He cried out like a lamb caught in a brier patch. Amos helped him up and held his arm to steady him.

"What good did that do?" Amos looked up at the harbor master. He felt like David facing Goliath. "Now he can't get off the dock without some help."

"Then you help him." He spit a wad of phlegm at Amos's feet. "The king should have sold them all and been done with it."

"This won't go unpunished, and neither will the king." Amos pulled himself up taller. The old man kept his head down. "The gates of Gaza and Ashdod will burn with fire for this disregard of life."

"Oh yeah? You and whose army will light it?" The large frame of the man cast a shadow over Amos.

"The army of the Lord always conquers." Amos stepped forward.

"Get off my dock." He spit again and looked at the crowd that had gathered. "Everyone back to work!" He threw his arms in the air and the crowd dispersed, heads down and mouths shut.

———◆———

"Pull the next one around," Amos called as Jacob's wagon tail was roped off.

The next wagon stopped in front of the loading area, and the men jumped out, ready to help. Amos directed the crew about which trees were to go on this wagon and then watched as the men followed orders.

"Hey! Leave those alone!" Jacob yelled at some men who were feeling the root balls of his load. He jumped off the cart and walked to the back.

"What you going to do with these? They won't grow where you're from." A middle-aged Moabite man eyed him up and down.

Amos heard the commotion and went over. "Can I help you with something?" He stepped between the wagon and the men.

"This your man? He has our trees."

"No, he doesn't; I purchased them from Elias of Ashdod." Amos crossed his arms. "If you're in the market for some, he still has a few."

"Those trees are ours." The man stepped forward. "We ordered them from Elias last fall."

"You'll have to take that up with Elias. He sold them to me this morning." Amos didn't back down.

"You're that troublemaker on the dock. Harbor master will knock you to Tyre when he hears about this."

The men started to leave.

"What should I do, Master Amos?" Jacob stood at his elbow.

"Master Amos, is it?" the Moabite man said, turning back. "No wonder you didn't have sense to leave the harbor master alone. You're a rich slave owner. Bet you own a lot of slaves. Is that how your army works?" The man towered over Amos.

"I don't own anyone. And I certainly don't rip open pregnant women to watch their babies die." Amos burned with his own fire. "Moab will pay just like the Philistines." The veins in his neck throbbed as he thought about Elelbet's granddaughter.

"Master Amos, please," Jacob spoke up from behind.

"Let's just go. The Lord will bring justice without us."

"Yes." The Moabite grinned. "Let's see what justice the Lord exacts. Chemosh, the Destroyer, will conquer your weak god. He has no softness for women." He sneered and walked toward the harbor master's hut.

"I bought the trees fair and square, but we better go." Amos turned to the wagons. "Let's get on the road."

The filled wagons swayed through town and up the hillside like an army of trees on the march, their branches raised with prayers for mercy and justice.

*None are more unjust in their judgments of others than
those who have a high opinion of themselves.*

Charles Spurgeon

CHAPTER 23

"COME TO LUNCH SUNDAY."

William looked up from his paperwork. Granville Jones stood over him.

"Excuse me?" William asked.

"Sunday lunch. Bring your family too. You have three children, right?"

"Yes, sir." William was confused. "You want all of us to come for lunch?"

"Of course. I got some new dogs. They're already trained. Paid big money for them too. I thought you might like to see them in action. Come by at eleven and we'll eat at noon."

"Yes, sir. Thank you." William blinked a few times as Jones walked away. *Maybe he doesn't hate me after all.*

"What?" Eileen said. "I don't have a dress for lunch at the Joneses'." She stared at her husband in horror. "And the kids too? Allen's shoes don't fit anymore, and we can't buy new ones until you get paid again."

"I already said we would go. He'll have to squeeze into them, and you look good in anything. You're still as beautiful as when I met you." William grinned.

"I know your tricks, William Williams. Don't you try to sweet talk me." Eileen punched him in the chest but laughed. "I suppose I can wear the blue dress I wore to your mum's funeral."

"Mr. Jones will be jealous. I hear Mrs. Jones is uglier than a camel's behind." He pulled her close in a bear hug.

"And how ugly is that?" Eileen laughed.

"Ugly, trust me. I saw plenty of them in Egypt. They don't compare to you; not even close, they aren't." He smacked her backside. "What's for dinner?"

"Nothing as fancy as you'll get at your boss's house. You can be sure of that. But I hear the cook is good-looking." She laughed and pushed him away. "You better go check on everything while I finish up. Allen's been gone a long time."

———

William could hear the sheep in the far meadow. He looked across the horizon at the sun still high in the sky. He missed being in the fields, but the summer days were long. He followed the worn path through the gate and along the stone wall, enjoying the fresh air.

"William!" Ian Roi called from the tree line.

William stopped and waved. Ian Roi walked toward the border wall between them. He shook William's hand, then leaned on the wall.

"How've you been?" Ian Roi asked.

"Good, good." William leaned against the wall and took a deep breath. He exhaled slowly and stared across the field. "I miss this, though; I don't mind telling you."

"Nothing like fresh air and green grass, is there?" Ian

Roi followed William's gaze.

"And quiet."

The two men sat on the wall in comfortable silence. The sheep were getting closer, and then Allen's small figure appeared over the hill.

"I don't mind the colliery; I don't want you to think that. But sheep … I once had a mare that would be meaner than a badger if she thought she could get away with it." William crossed his arms. "But you always know where you stand with sheep."

"What's bothering you?" Ian Roi looked at him.

William glanced at his old friend, then looked away. Allen was near now, and Captain and Lucy were herding the sheep toward the men.

William shook his head and said, "Got invited to Granville Jones's place for lunch Sunday. The whole family is invited to see his new dogs." He massaged the back of his neck.

"Probably have something good to eat there." Ian Roi shooed a yearling with his staff.

"Mm. It's not the food that concerns me." William sighed and rested his hands in his lap. "I'm afraid I've not been invited to open my mouth but to shut it."

"You've found something, then?"

"Maybe."

"Just remember, some dogs bite the sheep. A good shepherd never lets bad behavior continue. It's too dangerous for the sheep."

Allen ran up to William and hugged him on the wall. William kissed his son on the head and tousled his hair.

"The sheep look good, son. You're a great shepherd." He looked in his son's eyes.

"Just like his dad," Ian Roi said.

———————

"Are you sure I look alright? How's my hair?" Eileen smoothed her hair again as William approached the front door of the Jones home.

"You look great, Mum." Amaryllis smiled at her mother.

Eileen fussed with Iris's braids while William knocked on the door. The heavy brass knocker thudded on the oak paneling.

"My feet hurt." Allen shifted his weight from one foot to another.

"Maybe they're out back," William said. "Last time I was here, Mr. Jones was having tea in the back on his patio." He peered down the front of the house as if he should go have a look.

"Don't go poking your head around. Just knock again," Eileen said.

William raised his hand to the knocker as the door swung open, revealing a man in a butler's uniform.

"Come in," the man said, waving them forward. "They're expecting you."

The house seemed dark after the bright sunshine. They stood blinking in a grand foyer of marble and mahogany. Three arches framed the foyer.

The butler motioned them toward the one on the left. "Mr. and Mrs. Jones are in the library."

William stood back for Eileen to walk in front. He and the children followed in line. Their shoes clicked on the marble floor.

"Here they are, sir." The butler nodded his head to Granville Jones and then left.

"Mrs. Williams." Jones stood up to greet everyone.

"You look lovely."

Eileen blushed.

Jones went on, "This is my wife, Evelyn."

Eileen shook hands with them both. She took the children by the shoulder and introduced each of them. Evelyn Jones was actually shorter than Allen—and twice as wide. She wasn't obese, but she wouldn't blow over in a Welsh wind.

"This is Mr. Williams," Jones said, looking at Evelyn. "He's an expert with sheep." He clapped William on the back. "And he's becoming a good colliery supervisor."

"You'll be taking Granville's job from him, no doubt." Evelyn smiled and shook William's hand. "It's nice to meet you."

"Hello," said a young woman with upswept hair as she clicked into the library. "You must be the Williams family."

"You're late," Granville Jones said, frowning at the young lady. "Everyone, this is my daughter, Etta."

Etta shook hands with Eileen and William, ignoring her father's reprimand. William introduced his children to her.

"Amaryllis ... what a beautiful name," Etta said. "I hope you don't let them shorten it." She held the younger girl's hand. "No one ever calls me Marietta. Mother named me, but Father says it's too cumbersome."

"Some boys call me 'Ryllis, but most know better. Daddy named me for the shepherd's flower." Amaryllis smiled.

"Shall we go see those dogs?" Granville Jones turned to the younger children. "They're professionally trained."

"I bet they can't beat our dogs," Allen said, throwing out his chest.

Evelyn Jones excused herself to check on lunch while everyone tramped out the back door and followed the path to the barns.

———————

Three black border collies were barking in a pen near the barn. They jumped at the gate. William saw the younger pup, Major, cowering in a corner.

"Beautiful, aren't they?" Granville Jones smiled ear to ear. "They're out of Old Hemp, they are." Jones looked at William to make sure this information was received with proper respect.

"Where's Old Hemp?" Iris asked, twirling her braid around a finger.

William smiled. "It's not a place, Iris. Old Hemp is the granddaddy of all border collies."

"That's right." Jones raised his eyebrows. "You know your dogs, then."

"I know a dog can be bred for good but turn bad." William pointed to the pup in the corner. "And a good pup can be ruined by a bossy bitch."

"That pup didn't have what it takes to herd sheep. Harvey couldn't get him to follow commands." Jones shook his head. "I'll give him to some farmer. Maybe he'll be a good watchdog."

"You're just going to give him away?" Allen asked, then looked up at William. "If he is, Dad, can I have him?"

But Jones nodded and said, "Sure, you can have him." He shook Allen's hand. "Every boy needs a dog."

"Can I, Dad?" Allen turned to William with pleading eyes. "I can teach him to herd good as Lucy and Captain."

"Are you sure you want to just give him away?" William looked from Jones to the dog and back again.

"Yes, yes. He's all yours, Alton."

"Allen," the boy said, never taking his eyes off his father.

William looked at Eileen. She bit her lip. She knew animals—and that pup was in a bad spot. She nodded slightly, giving permission.

William turned back to Jones. "If you want to give him to Allen, it's fine by me."

He stuck out his hand toward his boss. The two men shook on it.

"Looks like you have a dog, Allen," William said.

"Now let's see what these real dogs can do." Jones hollered for Harvey. "I told him to have the sheep ready in the north field."

Harvey came around the corner of the barn. He was drying his hands on an old rag. Dark circles ringed his red eyes.

"I'm ready to show Williams here what real dogs can do. You moved the sheep into the north field, didn't you?" Jones shoved his hands in his trouser pockets.

"This morning, sir. I was just treating the heifer that skinned a leg." Harvey nodded his head in greeting to William. "The dogs should be ready for you too. I didn't have time to run them today."

Jones huffed and opened the gate for the dogs. They tore out like demons on the loose. The young pup stayed in the corner.

"Can I stay with my dog?" Allen stepped toward the dog pen. "I'd like to get to know him."

The dog raised his eyes. His tail thumped slowly

against the dirt.

William patted his son on the back. He grabbed Iris's hand and followed Jones. Eileen and Amaryllis fell in behind Etta.

———————

The dogs ran well, herding the small flock toward the pen. They had been trained for trials and knew the signals. The yearlings filed into the pen, watching every move. The dogs sat by the gate eyeing the ewes, holding their positions.

"Well done." William and the girls clapped. "You'll have a good team by the end of the year."

"Hmph." Jones blew out his lips. "They're a good team now. They'll be great by the end of the year."

"I need to go check on that heifer now, sir," Harvey interrupted. "She needs more antiseptic on that cut."

Jones waved the vet on. He raised his eyebrows at Eileen and smirked. "He should take so much time with all the animals. He leaves the sheep in the closest pasture so he can watch over the cows. The sheep need more time in the other meadows."

"Shepherding is a full-time job," William said as he watched Harvey walking to the barns. "He needs some help. You've got too much to do for one man."

"He ought to be glad to be working here. I have pure-bred dogs, the best sheep in the UK, and prize-winning cattle. Where else could he get such experience?"

"He looks tired to me," Eileen said from behind.

Jones peered over his shoulder. He looked Eileen up and down, then faced forward again, saying, "He's lazy. Says he sleeps in the field some nights because of the badgers. I think he's trying to pull the wool over my eyes." He pointed to a large area recently filled with footers. "This is where the new lambing barn will be. My sheep won't have to worry about the wet and wind when lambing time comes next year."

William winced. Eileen and Amaryllis would be in the cold and rain next season.

"You could have nice barns like this, you know." Jones was watching William out of the corner of his eye. "The right man for the job gets paid right, he does."

William stood up straighter. He was ready: "But what does it cost everyone else?"

Jones faced William. A knowing look passed over his face; the shadow changed in a flash to innocence. He tipped his head and lifted his hands in a question. He didn't say a word.

"Sheep are important, and lambing barns are convenient." William was treading carefully. "But when men are sent home wet from the colliery, they fall to pneumonia. A bathhouse at the colliery would save workers' lives and make life better for the women at home."

Jones stopped walking and turned to Eileen. "Have you had difficulty cleaning up after William?"

Eileen shook her head, not backing down. "William isn't in the pits. He comes home dry, but other men in town aren't so lucky. Bathhouses are common now in many collieries."

"Yes, well, the funding isn't as much as the unions want you to think. I would have to pay for half of it myself, I would." Jones pushed his hat back on his head, a willing fighter too.

William said, "Half a bathhouse wouldn't cost as much as that new lambing barn. You have room enough to bring in the ewes in the barn you already have." He spoke quickly, excitement ringing in his voice. "And the money left over could add some stanchions for new shearing tables. They were all the talk at the auction last year."

"Were they? You know all about them?" Jones put his hands in his coat pockets.

William nodded.

"Good. Talk to Harvey about them and I'll add some while the barn's being built. The men can buy themselves heavier coats to walk home in. I pay them plenty enough for that." He jerked his head toward the house. "Now let's get some lunch. Herding sheep makes me hungry."

Eileen couldn't help herself: "Will Harvey be joining us too, then?"

Jones kept walking up the hill to the house. He never acknowledged Eileen—or Harvey.

*Returning hate for hate multiplies hate, adding
deeper darkness to a night already devoid
of stars. Darkness cannot drive out darkness;
only light can do that.*

Martin Luther King, Jr.

CHAPTER 24

SWEAT WAS ROLLING DOWN AMARYLLIS'S back. She had looked forward to Sunday all week; her mother had promised she could go swimming in Afon Tywi with the town kids. She missed her friends and the customers at the store. Shepherding was fine for Allen. He could have a brilliant conversation with ewes, but she needed people to talk to.

Laughter and chatter rose from the scrubby treetops that lined the riverbank. Amaryllis climbed over the stone wall covered in lichen and moss. A few pebbles broke off in her hand. She pocketed them and slipped behind the trees.

"Where's Amaryllis?" Susan's voice carried on the water.

"Said she was coming last I talked to her." Carol sat on a half-submerged log and splashed her feet. "She'll be here."

Amaryllis pulled the pebbles out of her pocket and tossed them in the water next to the girls. They jumped and looked up the bank. Amaryllis slipped forward from behind the trees.

"Anyone could sneak up on you girls, they could." She laughed and slid down the grassy slope. "Why aren't you swimming? I'm burning up in this heat."

"We're waiting on the boys. They're bringing their coracles this time." Susan shook her head. "It's always a contest with them."

Amaryllis bit her lip and looked at the girls.

"They had a swimming race last week," Carol explained. "Owen won all the races, so they said they'd have a boat race this week. You know Owen's going to win that too. He makes sure of winning, even if he don't."

"Well I'm not waiting on any old boys' boat race. I'm hot." Amaryllis pulled off her dress. The blue bathing suit underneath highlighted the curves that had appeared over the summer. "Come on!"

The girls jumped off the log and into the cool river. The water was shallow in most areas, but there were a few deep recesses good for treading. Amaryllis ducked her head under and let the river carry her heavy hair in the current. She popped her head up just as the boys' coracles appeared.

"Here they come," Susan said. "Better swim for shore."

"I'm not going anywhere. I've waited all week for this." Amaryllis circled back around to the top end of the deep, then drifted on her back in the current. She spotted Dennis coming down the opposite bank with a fishing line.

"Hello, Dennis!" Amaryllis waved her arm high and went back to a doggy paddle. "Coming swimming or just fishing?"

Frowning, Carol and Susan slit their eyes at her.

Dennis stopped at the water's edge and lifted a hand in greeting. "Fishing."

Amaryllis swam for shore. The boys were getting closer now. Several whistled as Amaryllis walked into the shallows. She paid no attention.

"I heard you're working at the colliery," she said.

Dennis nodded his head and glanced at the three girls. "I'll go farther down so you can swim. Won't catch much this time of day, but thought I'd try." He turned to climb up the embankment.

"Stay and swim with us," Amaryllis said. "You're right you won't catch anything this late. It's too hot for fish. You got to go fishing early."

"I was working." Dennis turned back to her. "Took an extra shift."

"Well if it ain't dumb Dennis Byrne," Owen said from his boat. "You can't go fishing in this heat, boy. Don't you know nothing?"

Amaryllis turned on Owen. "Boy? Dennis is a man. He's got a job at the colliery. Took an extra shift today. What'd you do today besides eat your daddy's food and let your mum wipe your butt?"

It was out before she could stop it. Carol and Susan gasped.

"Amaryllis!" Susan took her friend by the hand. "Hush."

Owen called out, "Learn that kind of talk from your whore friend Alice? Is Dennis one of your customers?"

Dennis dropped his fishing line and ran through the water. He ducked under Owen's coracle and stood up, turning the boat over with Owen inside. Owen came splashing and spluttering to the surface. His boat drifted downstream.

"I'll get you for that, you lousy Irishman." Owen

took a swing at Dennis, but he slipped on the rocks and fell to his knees. Water ran down his face, and long strands of hair clung to his neck and forehead.

"Alice and Amaryllis are ladies," Dennis said. "Too good for you and me both." He lifted Owen out of the water and set him on his feet. The colliery had already made him stronger. "Now you tell Amaryllis you're sorry."

"My coracle's getting away." Owen started to turn, but Dennis grabbed him by the shirt collar.

"Then you better apologize quick-like." Dennis kept his hold on Owen's shirt.

The other boys dug their oars in the rocks and sat still.

"It's alright, Dennis," Amaryllis said. "I didn't act like a lady." She stared at the young man.

Dennis shook his head, never taking his eyes from Owen.

"I'm sorry, 'Ryllis," Owen finally said. "You're not like those Davies women."

Dennis pulled back and punched Owen square in the jaw, then let him drop. Carol and Susan screamed as blood darkened the water.

Amaryllis grabbed Dennis by the elbow. "Maybe we better go." She pulled on his arm. "Come on, Dennis."

Dennis shook his arm free of her and kicked water in Owen's face. He turned and stomped out of the water. "Good-bye, Amaryllis." He charged up the hill like a ram looking for a fight.

"Dennis!" she called after him, but he never looked back. "I'm going home." She picked up her dress and threw it over her shoulder. "See you later," she said to Susan and Carol.

"Bye," they both murmured.

The sun burned Amaryllis's shoulders and back as she walked through the fields toward home. She took her time. She didn't want her parents to ask why she was back so soon. A crumbling wall from some ancient hut offered shade. Amaryllis pulled the dress over her head and sat down on the grass.

She closed her eyes and leaned her head against the wall. Everything was quiet in the heat. Amaryllis breathed out her nose and let her shoulders droop.

"Nice place to rest, yes?"

Amaryllis startled and then laughed a little. "You scared me, Ian Roi." She looked at him and sat up straighter. "Yes, it's a good spot."

"Thought you'd be swimming with your friends today. I heard them over at Afon Tywi earlier." Ian Roi sat beside her and stared across the valley. The river glinted in the sunshine.

"I was." Amaryllis didn't look at him. "I'm on my way home now."

"Still plenty of day and heat for swimming." Ian Roi looked over at her. "You not feeling well?"

"Some of the boys got in a fight." Amaryllis pulled her heels to her thighs and wrapped her arms around her knees. "I didn't feel like swimming anymore."

"Mm."

A group of sheep walked at the edge of the woods, keeping in the shade of the trees. Two lambs butted each other. A third one jumped from a rock and landed in the middle of them.

"I didn't sing a very good song, Ian Roi." She glanced at him, half smiled, and watched the lambs again.

"How's that?"

"I was trying to get Dennis to join us swimming. Then Owen came by and said something mean about him and I just couldn't help it. Mum would've yanked me good if she'd heard me." Amaryllis rubbed her head just thinking about it. "But then Owen said something even meaner and Dennis went crazy."

She crossed her legs and looked over at the shepherd, continuing, "He stormed out in the water and turned Owen right over in his coracle. You should've seen it. We were all stunned." She smiled at Ian Roi. "Who knew he was that strong?"

Amaryllis pulled a long piece of grass and chewed on it. The lambs were fighting over a patch of wild rose now. The older sheep had moved on into the cool darkness of the woods.

"There's a butting order among sheep," Ian Roi said. "The old ones know their place in the flock. They give the good grass to the old ewe with the split ear. She's tough, that one." He pulled a wildflower and twiddled it in his fingers. "Sometimes they get to fighting, just to see if things have changed, and I have to walk among them."

"Ours do that too." Amaryllis nodded. "They stop if Allen or I get close."

"A shepherd has to learn to be quiet during a fight. You have to know when to walk in and when to leave it alone." He grinned at her. "Maybe you need some more time shepherding."

"I don't think I'll ever know whether to keep my mouth shut or to open it."

"You'll know when it's important." Ian Roi put the flower stem in his mouth and chewed.

Above all else, guard your heart,
for everything you do flows from it.

Proverbs 4:23

CHAPTER 25

"TELL IT AGAIN."

The children were begging for their favorite story of how Master Amos stood up for them. He didn't back down from a giant and he defended their mothers and fathers to the Moabite.

"You've heard it all winter." Jacob laughed. "You should be in bed by now. Tomorrow's a busy day."

"Can we all watch?" one of the little boys said as he tugged on Jacob's sleeve.

"Yes," Jacob said, "you can all watch if you stay out of the way. Shearing isn't fun for sheep. They kick and thrash like a boy in a tickling match." He grabbed the boy and threw him into the air. He caught him under the arms and tickled him on the cold ground near the fire.

"That's enough," one of the aunts spoke up. "You'll be too wound up for sleep."

She took the boy's hand and dragged him toward their place near the main house. It had become familiar to them this winter. Now they were preparing gardens and planting vegetables in the side yard. It looked like there might be a home for them here. She smiled and picked up the sleepy boy.

———◆———

The bleating of sheep could be heard all the way to Tekoa. The first batch of sheep to change their winter woolens for summer's bare skin was already out to pasture. The men from Gilead were proving their worth.

"You taught them well, Elelbet," Amos said, leaning on the corral gate.

"It's in our blood." Elelbet grinned and watched his boys. He stood a little taller. "The land here is harsher than Gilead, but you have a good flock. Jacob and his brothers are happy to be here, to be with sheep again."

"And you? Are you happy, Elelbet?"

The old man was quiet, staring across the corral and into distant time. His hand shook as he ran it through his thinning hair.

"It is not for me to be happy," he finally said. "I can't forget what was done to my children, the way we were forsaken." He shook his head and took a deep breath. "But I'm content, and I know that the Lord is good."

"The Lord is my shepherd. I want for nothing. He makes me lie down in green pastures, he leads me by the quiet waters, he refreshes my soul." Amos looked into Elelbet's eyes. "The Lord is a good shepherd, and he led you to me. We need each other."

Elelbet silently agreed.

———◆———

"The wool will be cleaned quicker than you can sing the Shema." Malaki stood over the table delivering bowls full of spring vegetables, grains, and meat to the workers. "Your women are as clever as your men,

Elelbet."

"They were taught by the best: my wife." The old man smiled and winked at her.

Amos nodded. "I can take the taxed wool to Jerusalem next week." He spooned some sweet peas on his plate. "Will you have it ready by then?" He looked up at Malaki.

"Yes." She glanced at Elroi. "Will you be going with him this year?"

"He goes with God." He smiled at her. "What are you worried about?"

"Just wanted to make sure that he holds his tongue after his trip to Ashdod. He needs someone to look after him."

———◆———

"Have you been into Tekoa lately?" Elroi asked.

He sat down beside Amos outside the barn. There were several hundred more sheep to shear in the next few days. He leaned back against the barn wall.

"Yes, last week. Why?" Amos's eyes were closed. It had been a long day.

"There's a new altar outside the city wall and an Asherah pole nearby." Elroi stretched his legs and crossed his ankles.

"I know, but I don't own that property." Amos opened his eyes and looked at his old friend.

"King Uzziah's father and grandfather were good rulers for most of their reigns. They removed the other gods from Jerusalem and the Temple. But their influence isn't as strong as it once was. People forget."

"What are you saying?" Amos leaned his elbow on his knee and watched Elroi.

"You spoke for God in Ashdod. Jacob has talked about nothing else all winter." Elroi sat up straight and put a hand on Amos's knee. "You know the king. It's time to speak up in Jerusalem."

"Why me?" Amos's eyes were big. "There are priests and rabbis all over Jerusalem."

"Yes, and there are prophets in Judah." Elroi held Amos's gaze. "God called a shepherd to be a king. He can call one to be a prophet too. See you in the morning, Amos."

Elroi stood and stretched, then walked away singing:
"Leading, follow paths of rock;
Follow, leading gentle flock."

———————

"Don't forget to bring back something for the children." Malaki lay wide awake in bed. "The carpenter near the king's garden makes wonderful toys."

"Mm-hm." Amos stared at the ceiling.

"What are you thinking?" Malaki rolled over on her side. Baby Amuz rustled in his cradle.

Amos didn't answer. Malaki put her hand on his chest. He held her hand and turned his head to her.

"What are you thinking?" she asked again.

"Our children. You teach the girls of God's grace and wisdom, yes?" He held her hand tighter.

"Of course." She wrinkled her forehead.

"Do the servants worship other gods? Do they talk to the girls about them?"

"Some of the servants." Malaki raised up on her elbow. "What's wrong, Amos?"

"Jacob's sheep."

"Jacob's sheep? What are you talking about?" Malaki

flipped her long braid over her shoulder.

"Jacob ... Isaac's son. He had the sheep look at striped wood and they came out striped. What we look at—what we hear—comes out in our behavior." He sighed. "I don't know." Amos stared back at the ceiling. "I think ... I think I might need to say something in Jerusalem."

"Is this about Ashdod? Because there aren't any families ripped apart in Jerusalem." Malaki whispered the words, but her eyes raged. "You better keep your wits about you, Amos. You'll get more than yourself in trouble. Think of me and the children."

"I do, Malaki. I do." He squeezed her hand and closed his eyes.

It is certain, in any case, that ignorance, allied with power,
is the most ferocious enemy justice can have.

James Baldwin

CHAPTER 26

ILEEN CROSSED THE CORNER TO the Third
Street Pub. No one was buying beer this early in
the morning. She looked around, then tacked a piece
of paper to the community board. It felt exciting and
risky, even devious, to post the advertisement. Eileen
giggled.

A door banged shut down the street, and she turned.
No one had seen her. She skipped two steps at the end
of the sidewalk and hurried across the street.

"It must have been the vicar. Who else would've
done it?"

Eileen peered around the corner of the school building. Several women were standing under the shade
tree, talking. Catherine Smith was in the center directing the conversation.

"I heard it was Mrs. Jones—Mrs. *Granville* Jones. It'll
be quite the event. The chairwomen will meet in her
house." Catherine smoothed her hair. She was wearing
white gloves. "All the big cities have a benefit society."

The women twittered about who would be there,

and one of them said, "What does one even wear to a society meeting?"

Eileen smiled and headed home.

———•———

"You should have heard them going on." Eileen glowed. She set a plate of biscuits in front of William. "Catherine was wearing gloves. In this heat! You would have thought the prince invited her to Caernarfon Castle for tea."

"What's the first order of business?" William fingered through the shortbread for the one he wanted. He picked it up and took a bite.

"Well …" Eileen poured a cup of tea and turned back to the cookstove. "We'll need money to help the widows, so we'll have to have fundraisers. I was thinking a dance and sing-along on the green, but when Catherine mentioned Mrs. Granville Jones …"

Eileen set the teakettle on the stove and came back to the table. She sat across from William and smiled ear to ear. William took another bite of shortbread and sipped his tea.

"What do you think?" Eileen asked. Her own tea sat untouched.

"A dance on the green's a good idea."

"But what about at the Joneses'? Do you think they'll do it?"

"The Joneses' place? Wouldn't a town party be better in town?" William shifted in his chair.

"Well sure, if what you want is ragtag and bobtail, but a party at the Joneses' house would bring in some money. Everyone would want to be there." Eileen picked up a biscuit and nibbled on it.

"Sounds like Catherine Smith is sitting with me." William dodged the biscuit that came flying across the table. "You asked." He laughed and picked the biscuit from his lap.

"You're right. It's not just about the rich people helping the poor. It's about all of us helping each other." She broke off another bite. "I'll get Amaryllis to help me make a list of ideas. She'll know what the young people like."

———

The tenth-grade schoolteacher let Eileen and Amaryllis into the main hall.

"You can use the eighth-grade room on the left," the teacher said as she pointed down the hall. "It's the biggest one. I've heard several of the women talking about coming."

"You didn't tell them it was us, did you?" Eileen asked, dismayed. Surprise was part of the fun.

"No." The teacher shook her head. She grinned and winked at Eileen. "Just listened."

"Thanks."

Amaryllis led her mother down the hall and turned into the classroom. Coal dust lay thick on the desks.

"I'll wash down the table, and you dust the desks and chairs." Eileen handed Amaryllis an old rag from her basket. "I came prepared."

They washed and dusted the room. Eileen threw a cloth over the table, and Amaryllis pulled out trays of shortbread, raisin cakes, and ginger snaps from their basket.

"I hate we don't have any tea." Eileen twisted her skirt.

"No one will expect it, Mum. It's nice that you brought biscuits." Amaryllis kissed her mother on the cheek. "It looks great."

A creak echoed in the hallway.

"Here they come," Eileen whispered.

———

"Is it alright if I come in?" Etta Jones poked her head in the room. She glanced around and then walked in. "Are we the first ones here? I thought the vicar would be here by now."

"No, just us." Eileen smiled and motioned for Etta to come over. "Would you like a snap or a biscuit?"

"These are the best," Amaryllis said, then nibbled a raisin cake. "You should have one."

Etta walked to the table as several other women came in the classroom, including Catherine Smith. Soon the room sounded like a gaggle of geese with everyone talking, catching up on news, eating, and having a good time. When the flow of new arrivals had trickled to a stop, Eileen went to the front of the room and knocked on the teacher's desk.

"Ladies. Ladies." She paused while the chatter died down. "If you will please have a seat, we will begin discussing the possibility of a benefit society here in Shotton Cross."

The room grew quiet. Women sat in the students' desks and looked at one another. Several ladies whispered comments across the aisles and rows.

Eileen knew she had to take control quickly, so she said, "Some of you were under the impression that this meeting was instigated by the vicar. I'm sure both he and the priest would be willing to help us get started, but since this would be a ladies' society, I thought it might be best if the ladies initiated it." She smiled at Etta Jones in the front row. "I'm so glad we have young ladies here like Ms. Jones and my own daughter, Amaryllis. It makes me happy, it does, to see our young people showing concern for the disadvantaged in our community."

"Always willing to help out," Etta said.

"Hear! Hear!" several women agreed.

"Wonderful." Eileen took a deep breath through her nose and exhaled through her mouth. It was going well. "The first step is to determine who needs help. We have a lot of widows in Shotton Cross. Perhaps that would be a good place to start?"

"Our men are miners; of course we have widows," someone in the back said.

The room became a busy hive of comments, snide remarks about the colliery, and titters from those sitting behind Etta. She turned pink and looked at the floor.

"We also have war widows," Eileen spoke above the buzzing.

The women quieted and looked up at her.

Eileen went on, "Several women I went to school with lost their husbands in the war. There's Freida Walton, Maggie Lewis, and Constance Davies."

"So that's what you're at," Catherine Smith said from the middle of the room. She stood up. "I'll not be a part of paying for a prostitute." She put her hands on her hips.

"What on earth are you talking about?" Eileen was astonished. Catherine was rude in small groups, but she was always a lady in public. "We aren't going to be paying for prostitutes. Why would a widow want a prostitute anyway?"

A few women caught the humor and chuckled, but Catherine was not to be swayed: "We all know men visit Constance. There's a steady stream of them every day going and coming after each shift. You can time them with the colliery whistle."

"I can't say that I've seen that." Eileen glared at Catherine. "But I also can't say what I would do if I had four children and had to survive on a widow's pension. I do know Constance takes in laundry from the miners, and her daughter works hard to help her. The boys do their best to help with the garden and odd jobs they can pick up." She stopped to look at each face. "If Constance has had to do other kinds of work, well, if they were my babies, I would do what I had to do."

She reached for Amaryllis and squeezed her hand. "I was blessed to have my William return from the war; Constance and others, too, weren't so blessed. Isn't it up to us to make sure that they don't have need to worry?"

"There's the church," Catherine said. "Let her look there for help." She nodded and sat down with a thump of the desk. "She could use some church."

"And some of us could use some Jesus." Eileen's nostrils flared as she said it.

Etta raised her hand. Eileen crossed her arms and nodded to the young woman.

"What would a widows fund be used for?" Etta's voice was a green field of softness.

"House repairs, clothes and shoes for the children, medicine ... whatever pensions don't cover." Eileen lifted her shoulders and half smiled. "I know Freida needs some plumbing work done, and the Davies boys need shoes."

"How would the benefit get money?" Etta asked.

"That's where I'm hoping you and our other young women can help." Eileen raised her eyebrows in optimism. "Maybe you have some ideas of what would draw a crowd. I was thinking about a dance and sing-along."

Two girls turned to each other, their cheeks pink with excitement. The buzzing began again.

Catherine stood up. "I think we need some rules before we—"

The building shook, and Catherine grabbed the chair in front of her. Women screamed and started running for the door.

"I left the babies with Joanne!" a young redhead cried and raced out.

"Explosion! Get to the mine, quick." Older women who had been through this too many times before knew the drill.

"Not again." Women fell to their knees in prayer.

Eileen was in the group headed for the mine. Women were always needed in a crisis.

At his best, man is the noblest of all animals;
separated from law and justice he is the worst.

Aristotle

CHAPTER 27

WILLIAM WAS WATCHING A FALCON circle the colliery, its black wings spread in silent flight. He shaded his eyes from the afternoon sun. The bird dived in the field nearby and then lifted a rabbit into the air. The ground shook, and the bird's piercing shriek was the beginning of chaos.

Smoke and flames shot out of the pit. The pump house roof caught on fire. Men came running out, dragging whatever equipment they could get their hands on.

William sprang into action. "Over here, boys!" he yelled to the firemen. "Send the lift down fast as you can. I'll check with the ventilation crew."

Clarence had checked in an hour ago. The men had finished lunch and were working on the longwall of Pit Sixteen. Production was up, and the men were in good spirits. There were some fumes, but nothing out of the ordinary.

Granville Jones came running up from the stables. "What have those stupid sheep farts done now? The horses are crazy with terror."

William replied, "Explosion is all we know. Sixteen

reported some fumes earlier this afternoon but thought they were good." He met Jones and turned to follow him back to the main pit entrance. "I was headed to the ventilation fans. Should I stay with you?"

"No no." Jones waved him off. "Take care of ventilation. I'll get Edward to start the paperwork."

"Sir, we don't know how many are down there, let alone how many are hurt. It's too soon to start paperwork."

"Ventilation, Williams!" Jones roared and struck the air. Another blast of flames and smoke bellowed out of the shaft. "Now!"

Eileen and the other women circled the edge of the slag drifts. They hadn't been properly piled up after the last accident. Some reckless people climbed on top the slag to get a better vantage point.

"Too much fire and smoke." An old man shielded his eyes with his hand. He squinted toward the pit. "Looks like the pump house is on fire. Maybe it's aboveground."

A chorus of hopeful whispers flowed through the crowd. Shotton Cross had already had plenty of misery. There were enough widows and orphans to last a lifetime. A few held hands and prayed aloud.

Eileen felt Amaryllis's hand slip into her own. She squeezed her daughter's hand, an unspoken comfort that William—Daddy—would be alright. Eileen's mind raced over the events of the last hour. How quickly she could become one of the widows and her children the orphaned.

"Fans are still on," one of the ventilation engineers assured William. "Whatever blew up in there wasn't bad enough to knock us out."

"Thank God." William sighed.

He ran back to the main shaft. The cage was coming up, the chain sounding off like a trumpet. Was it a call of defeat or triumph? He stood with the other men, waiting.

Nearly a dozen men, black and choking, rose to the surface. A cheer went up, echoed by the groups waiting at the edge of the colliery. William spotted Eileen standing near the slag heaps. She seemed a world away. He waved, but she didn't see him. Her face was searching the men; he knew who she was looking for, but he couldn't leave the workers.

A blast of rock and smoke belched out of the shaft behind the pump house. William ducked his head and ran for cover behind a coal cart. Shrapnel and bits of rock landed around him. He had to get to his men. It seemed so familiar. What was the first step?

"Williams?" A man shook his shoulder. "You alright? You get hurt?"

William turned. It was Johnson.

"My men," William whispered. "I've got to get my men out of there. The Germans ..." He couldn't breathe.

"There're no Germans in there. That Irish kid you gave us is down there, though." Johnson helped William stand. "He went down just before the blast."

"Dennis. Yes. Dennis. Thanks." He patted Johnson's hand. *The boy Amaryllis asked me to watch out for.* He nodded his head.

The colliers were off the lift now, and rescue workers were headed down. William helped the men find places to lie down. He needed to talk to them, but they wouldn't be any good to him if they didn't get some good air and rest from the shock.

"Floyd is gone." Soot choked one of the men as he spoke to William. "He didn't have a chance. The explosion knocked him off his feet." Tears leaked out of his eyes and rolled down his cheeks, leaving black smudges of fear and grief.

"What about you?" William held the man's hand. "Are you hurt? Cuts? Breaks?"

"I'm fine." The man patted William. "Seen worse. It was his own fault, it was. Floyd knowed better than to set his light low when the damp was cat-creeping."

"What about the others?" The sound of chaos receded in William's conscience. Only this man existed. "Anyone else shot?"

"Shot? No. No one was shot." The man looked up at William. "It was the gas what exploded."

"Quite right. Here come the docs. You'll be fit as a fiddle in no time. Just lie still."

William stood and ran a hand through his hair. He had to think straight. He took a deep breath and headed toward the next victim.

———◆———

"Are you all right?" Eileen stood in the kitchen, a plate of dinner warming behind her on the stove. "I saw it all, but I couldn't find you." Her voice caught in her throat.

"Yes." William pulled off his black clothes and dropped them onto the floor. "The kids in bed?"

She nodded. Her eyes were as full as Carmarthen Bay at high tide. William crossed the kitchen and held her. She was so small and fragile. The heat of her skin pressed through the thin dress and warmed him. How could he be chilled in August?

"I kept dinner for you and I've got water on the stove. Sit down and eat. I'll get the bath ready." She held his face in her arms and looked into his eyes. "I love you, William Williams."

———•———

"One minute I'm talking about helping widows and orphans, and the next I wonder if I am one." Eileen looked up at the ceiling. The quilt was pulled tight against her shoulders. "I think you should come back home, William. It'll be hard, I know, but we can make do."

William closed his eyes. He wanted nothing more. Today's accident had put him back on the front lines. He was afraid to fall asleep. It had taken years for the nightmares to subside. Now what would meet him in the blackness of his mind?

Eileen rolled over and stroked his chest. She couldn't look him in the eye or the tears would start again.

"It was a bad start this year," she said, "but we got worried for nothing. The sheep are doing well. The lambs are sure to bring a good price at market. And with the babes going back to school ..."

William took her hand in his and squeezed its soft-ness. "There are other sheep in danger, Eileen."

"What do you mean?" Her hand tensed.

"There are things going on at the colliery. It isn't safe and there's no one willing to make it right. I can't leave my sheep alone in the field while the dogs are prowl-ing." He turned his head on the pillow. "I'm not sure what's going to happen, but today was just another step toward the slaughterhouse."

"It isn't your job to fix the world, William." She sat up on an elbow. "You have a family and a farm to take care of."

"But if I leave now and something else happens, I'll know that I deserted my men. I won't be able to live with that, Eileen."

She sat up and stared at him. How many nights she had lain awake during the war wondering if he was coming home?

"This is not the army, William. These men have choices. They can leave or refuse to go in the pits if it's too dangerous. They have to make decisions for them- selves." Fire flashed in her eyes. "You aren't responsible for them."

"Sheep do a lot of dumb things, Eileen. You know they do." He looked her full in the face. "They ought to know not to cross that wall by the river, but every time they get the chance, over they go. Then they get bloated from the grass and end up cast on the hillside." He put her hand to his face. "All these men see is the paycheck that feeds them green grass. I'm their shep- herd checking the fences."

Eileen stared into his eyes and blinked back tears. She had known as a girl that William was for her. He was compassionate and gentle, always seeing the good in people.

"I know." She tried to smile. "Just make sure you get back to the fold yourself."

"I promise." He kissed her fingertips. "That's where my favorite ewe is kept."

She laughed and swatted at him, but he pulled her close.

A note lay on William's desk a few days later: *It was Floyd Samson*. Glenn had left the message along with notes from the engineers and witnesses. The colliers were always quick to blame the men in charge. To blame one of their own could only mean he was in the wrong.

William exhaled and sat down. He glanced through the notes. Everything seemed to have been done by the book this time. He looked across the office. Jones's door was still closed.

"When do you expect Mr. Jones today?" he asked Edward across the room.

The nervous office secretary glanced up. He shook his head and looked at his watch. "Can't say that I expect him at all. He called late last night and said to send the inspector over to his house in the morning. Said they would go over the details of the accident at his house." Edward looked back down at his papers and mumbled something.

"What's that?" William said.

"Nothing. 'Don't lift your petticoat after you've peed,' my mother always said."

"I'm heading over to Mr. Jones's place. I want to talk to him about some sheep."

William waved to Harvey as he passed the barns. A truck was parked in front of the house. He stood on the front step, shook out his arms, and rolled his neck. Confrontation always made him nervous.

The door opened before he could knock, and he saw

Granville Jones and another man.

"Thanks for coming by the house," Jones said to the man. "I'll have to show you my sheep next time you're around." As Jones shook hands with the man, he looked up and saw William. "Good morning, Williams. What are you doing out here?"

"I got the report back on the accident and thought you would want to hear about it. Thought I'd check on the dogs while I was at it." He looked at the stranger. "How do you do?"

"This is Mr. Hughes, Charles Hughes," Jones said. "He's an inspector with the office in Cardiff." Jones then motioned the inspector out the door.

William shook the man's hand as he passed by.

Jones nodded toward the door and said, "Williams, go on in. I'll be with you in a minute."

William stepped up into the house, and the door shut behind him. He stood alone in the marble entryway. The men's voices outside were muffled. An engine started, and then the truck pulled away from the house.

A moment later Granville Jones walked in. He was as quiet as a London fog—and just as dangerous, William was sure. Jones led the way to the library. William followed.

"What did you find out?" Jones pulled a cigar out of his desk and lit it.

"Good news for the mine." William wrinkled his nose. "Not so good for Floyd Samson's widow."

Jones smiled with all his teeth. He pulled another cigar out of his desk and handed it to William.

But William shook his head and held up a hand. "No thank you. I just thought you would want to know. Thought you might want to break it to his wife."

"Yes. Quite right." Jones took a long draught on the

cigar and held it in. "You know this woman?"

William nodded.

Jones walked to the tall window and looked out. He exhaled the smoke and turned back to William. "Might be best if you talk to her, then. She'll find you more of a comfort."

"But, sir, you should be the one. Maybe you can offer some money to help her through for a while."

"Thought you said it was his fault." Jones's eyes were dark. "Why would I pay for his mistake?"

"Floyd worked for you all his life. His widow deserves some sort of recognition."

"For being married to a fool?" Jones sucked long on his cigar.

"He was a good worker, and he lost his life, sir."

"You better head back to the office, Williams. I don't think I'll be showing you any dogs today."

———◆———

Harvey met William by the front gate.

"Heard you had quite a time the other day," Harvey said, shaking hands with William.

William nodded and grasped the young man's hand. He smiled at Harvey. He felt sorry for the poor man. It couldn't be easy to work for and live with Granville Jones. *At least I get to go home.*

"I'm alright. How about you? How's the shepherd business treating you?"

"I like it. The air is clear, the customers pleasant, and I'm the boss. Well, most the time." He looked up to the house. "Wish I could talk Mr. Jones into a couple more rams, though. I don't think we have enough for rutting season. He's added so many ewes this summer." Harvey shook his head.

"Hmm. I might be able to help there. I held some back last year thinking my old rams were about used up."

Harvey's eyes brightened. "I think Mr. Jones would appreciate it if you could spare any. They'd be well-fed and cared for."

"Better than a collier's widow, I bet."

"How's that?"

William shook his head. "Come over and see what I have whenever you want. My boy, Allen, can help you."

*Ethics and equity and the principles of justice
do not change with the calendar.*

D. H. Lawrence

CHAPTER 28

A MOS LEFT THE WOOL AT the weavers to be weighed and recorded. It was a good shearing this year. The Gileadites were the best shearers Amos had ever seen. There would be plenty of money left after the tax.

Amos always stayed at his older brother's house with his father when he visited the city. The conversation was pleasant, but the noises and smells of the big city were not. Amos breathed through his mouth as he walked through the streets of Jerusalem.

A sleek, young goat trotted at his side. The rope was clenched tightly in his hand, but the goat didn't resist. He seemed interested in all the activity of the city.

Amos entered the outer court of the Temple and found one of the priests ready to offer the sacrifice.

"You should have bought the ram here. It's easier for everyone," the young priest complained as he sharpened his knives.

"I can only give the best to the Lord." Amos looked over at the herd of cattle, goats, and sheep waiting for slaughter. "I wanted to be sure of what I was giving."

The young man looked up at Amos but didn't say

anything.

"How long will it be until you're ready for me?" Amos asked.

"An hour or so." The priest never looked up. "There are several ahead of you."

Amos tied the ram to a metal ring in the wall and went into the Temple. Vendors and animal cries echoed off the walls, turning the morning prayers into a dissonant undercurrent. *God must have good hearing,* Amos thought. He offered a prayer and hurried back out.

Several booths stood near the steps. He stopped to see if there was anything the children might like. There were tiny scrolls rolled into boxes that would fit in a child's pocket or string bag. He bought one for each of the girls and for Amuz. He liked thinking about the day that he and Amuz would talk together about God. Amos slipped them into his own pocket and then wandered into the street.

A row of houses nearby stood with their doors and windows wide open. They begged for a fresh spring breeze to bring them relief. Several statues stood on the windowsill of the corner house. Amos slowed his pace to stare in the window.

A golden statue of a man with a pointy hat was in mid-stride across the sill. It was Baal, the Canaanite god of rain. He strutted toward a clay statue of a woman sitting on a throne surrounded by two sphinxes. She held a bowl under her breasts to collect milk for the wooden babies strewn across the sill.

Amos paled, and his stomach lurched. It wasn't the smell of waste that turned his breakfast onto the walkway.

"Stay away." An old woman stood at the door of the house. "Don't be bringing your sickness round here."

She held up a hand to stop Amos from coming farther.

He looked up and wiped his mouth. "What have you done, woman?" Amos said, almost shouting. Malaki's earlier warning barely controlled the anger boiling inside him. "Is this your house?"

"Yes. And who are you?" The woman looked him up and down, her lips curling.

"I'm Amos of Tekoa, and you are a danger to us all."

A young woman stopped at the door. She held a covered basket over her arm and looked up at the old woman. "It didn't work." The young lady peeped inside the house. "Can we try again? I brought the incense."

"Go on, dear." The old woman pulled her cloak tighter and motioned the girl inside before looking back at Amos. "And off with you." She waved her fingers toward Amos, then went in the house and slammed the door.

Amos backed away from the house, praying.

———◆———

"You're next." The priest jerked his head toward Amos. "Get your goat ready."

Amos untied his offering and pulled on the reluctant goat. The smell of blood hung heavy in the midmorning air, and the ram was frightened. Amos tackled it around the neck and led it toward the slaughtering table.

It was a sin offering for Amos and his family. For whatever sins he and Malaki and the children committed, whether knowingly or not, the goat would pay the price. For the Asherah that had stood on his land, the yearling would die.

Amos placed his hand on the head of the ram and

prayed as its throat was slit and the blood drained into the collection bowl. The priest handed the body over to another to be skinned and the fat burned on the altar.

"Next." The priest didn't wait for Amos to move out of the way.

Amos followed the priest with his offering to the altar and watched as the blood was dripped onto the altar's horns before the fat was burned. His sins were forgiven, but his thoughts were singed with the image of Baal and Ashtoreth on a windowsill across the street.

———•———

"Why isn't anything done?" Amos banged his fist on the table where he sat with his father and brother.

"The Lord is God of Judah." His father patted the table, trying to soothe his son. "Uzziah follows in the footsteps of his father and grandfather in doing good. If some old woman looks for help to increase our numbers, how does that hurt? More babies are born for the Lord."

"How does that hurt?" Amos stared bug-eyed at his father. "'You shall have no other gods' means everyone … in the city and in the country."

"The king makes sure that we are true to God. And look how he prospers. God can't be angry with us." Amos's father spread his arms wide over the table filled with food.

Amos shook his head. "Moab rips babies from the womb. Damascus runs people over with threshing irons. And the Philistines sell their own people off to the Edomites." He felt his eyes fill. "But this … this is adultery against our own Lord. It will mean death."

His brother rolled his eyes. "You're so dramatic, Amos. You spend too much time out in the fields with those sheep." He took a drink of wine. "Better you should move your family to Tekoa where you can have a little company."

"Better we should all live in the fields. The sheep know who the shepherd is." Amos stood up. "I have an early appointment at the weaver's tomorrow. Good night."

Shall I acquit someone with dishonest scales, with a
bag of false weights? Your rich people are violent; your
inhabitants are liars and their tongues speak deceitfully.
Therefore, I have begun to destroy you,
to ruin you because of your sins.

Micah 6:11–13

Chapter 29

"A LLEN SAID HE THOUGHT YOU were over here, Ian Roi," William said. "What's got you all gloomy-eyed?"

William followed Ian Roi's gaze across the stone wall to his neighbor's field. Even in the failing light, William could see it was full of dock and thistle.

"I've given advice, I have," Ian Roi said. "Even offered to come help clear it out, but he says, 'No, all's well.'" He sighed and turned to William. "You should have seen his flock staring after mine today. They know things are better over here, but they're stuck until they get a better shepherd."

William pursed his lips. He felt the same as Ian Roi. There was no excuse for letting sheep graze in bad fields. He and Taid Williams had spent many a spring-time clearing out weeds and winters burning off briers.

Ian Roi took a deep breath and smiled. "What brings you out here? Allen's doing a good job with the sheep. Amaryllis won't let him get away with anything." His eyes twinkled.

"Thought you might like a walk to the pub. My treat, old buttie."

"I never pass up a drink with a friend, especially a paying friend." Ian Roi laughed and turned toward town. "How are things at the mine?"

"Recovering."

They walked in silence. A crescent moon hung on the horizon as the last of the sun's rays waved farewell. Frogs and crickets chirped near the river.

"I trust your judgment, Ian Roi."

William fell silent again. Ian Roi stayed at his side, saying nothing.

"I'm concerned," William finally said.

"Mm." Ian Roi kept his eyes down, focused on their steps in the gloaming light.

William cleared his throat and continued, "The investigation on this last accident showed the fault lay with the men. Floyd Samson, to be blunt."

William stopped walking. He looked up at the sky and took a deep breath. His thoughts swirled like Afon Tywi's spring waters. He couldn't make supported accusations, but he felt them nonetheless. He glanced at Ian Roi, now resting his chin on the staff in his hands.

"You know when you feel down in your gut that a lamb is hanging over the cliff, but you can't see it? You just have to trust that your staff will find it and pull it to safety?"

Ian Roi nodded once.

"Well, I feel like there's a lamb in terrible danger and all I've got is a staff poking around the edge of a cliff." William shook his head. "I don't know what to do."

"What would you do if it was a lamb?" Ian Roi stood

up straight and looked William in the eye.

William only bit his lip.

"Quite right. You know what to do."

———•———

The tavern sing-along was over, and the men were packed into the pub like turnips in a gunnysack. William tried to walk to the bar, but he couldn't find a clear path.

"Williams! Come on over here and join us," Clarence, his tall foreman, called from a nearby table. "Move over, boys. The boss man's here."

"No no." William shook his head as the men moved down on the bench. "I was just bringing Ian Roi over for a drink. We won't interrupt."

"Ian Roi's a good buttie of ours. Come on, settle your bones."

William looked at Ian Roi. They both shrugged and sat down with the others.

Clarence clapped Ian on the back and laughed. "Ian Roi's a regular here. We all owe him a round, don't we, boys?"

The men raised their ales and tipped them toward Ian Roi. "Hear! Hear!" they chorused and then threw back their beers.

"Bring us a couple glasses," Clarence called to the barkeeper. "And another pitcher of this fine ale." He winked at the men, then looked at William. "What brings you to town this time of night?"

"Well …" William looked at Clarence and then all his men. "Well …"

Ian Roi jumped in. "We were just coming to chew the fat. What's news, boys?"

"Some talk there might be a bathhouse coming to Shotton Cross Colliery." One of the younger men spoke up as the barkeeper set down glasses and a full pitcher. "Ida will be glad of it. She gets so pinched when I come in soaked in the winter."

"Mrs. Williams is heading it up, I hear." Clarence filled the men's glasses. "That's a good woman."

"To good women," Ian Roi said.

All the men raised their drinks, and William joined them. Their heavy glasses thumped the table. Clarence topped them off again.

"Is a bathhouse the thing you need the most?" William asked.

"It's a start," Johnson said, leaning forward at the end of the table. "I told you we needed a man like you in the office. You got to watch over us, Williams—keep us safe."

William nodded. "Doing my best. It might take a strike, you know. Jones covers his backside like a badger."

"No." The young man shook his head. "Can't be striking. Ida's got another bun in the oven. I've got mouths to feed."

The others joined him. They had notes to pay off at the company store, kids to feed, and empty coal scuttles that reminded them how cold it would be in a few more months. They weren't willing to take the next step.

William took a deep breath and exhaled. "Floyd Samson was the cause of the last accident, but I know you men aren't always at fault. Jones is dirty. It takes work to get rid of dirt; you should know that." He took Clarence by the wrist and shook his coal-stained hand to get their attention. "And the time to do that is before there's another accident, before it's too late."

———•———

The moon was high now, the land glowing in its white light. The frogs and crickets were in bed. Silence whispered in William's ear. He walked with his hands in his pockets, dejected.

"What did you think would happen?" Ian Roi walked beside William.

"I thought they would understand the danger, understand the necessity." William shook his head. "How many will die before they put a stop to it?"

"My neighbor was chasing his sheep up the hillock today. One of the ewes collapsed." Ian Roi looked straight ahead. "They got into that field of clover I've been saving."

"I'm sorry to hear that." William crinkled his brow. He knew Ian Roi was a fastidious farmer and shepherd, but couldn't he focus for a few minutes?

"Oh, the field will recover quick enough; it's the sheep what concern me. A good shepherd would've left them alone once they headed up the hill. He could've saved that sheep."

"Mm." William nodded. "If you leave 'em standing on the hillside, they'll belch it up and be right as rain in no time."

"Why do you suppose he chased those sheep all over the field?"

"Leaving them alone is one of the hardest things to do; it takes a lot of nerve. I remember the first time I did it. I was sweating thinking how it might go."

Ian Roi stopped walking and looked at William. His eyes were a bottomless sea, deep and calm.

William took a breath. "I can't do nothing, Ian Roi. Something bad is going to happen. I feel it."

"You aren't doing nothing, William. You've got the sheep facing uphill. Now you must wait for them to work it up—the courage, the faith, the desire. Waiting is never doing nothing."

William nodded and looked across the fields. Lights glimmered in a few windows over in Shotton Cross. They reminded him of the lights shimmering in the African desert. He had learned a lot about waiting in the war.

"You're right; you always are." William smiled and looked at Ian Roi. "I better get home before Eileen gets everything ruminated. She's not so good at waiting."

They laughed and turned toward home.

———————

"Good morning, Edward. Have a good weekend?" William asked as he hung his hat on the wall and then dropped his tommy box on the shelf under the counter.

Edward half nodded and went on with his typing.

"Mr. Jones isn't in yet, is he?"

"No." Edward looked up from his typewriter. "He's meeting some people out at his house today."

"Oh?" William raised an eyebrow.

Edward looked around. "Some bigwigs from Cardiff," he whispered.

"Why are they here? Did something happen?" William rubbed his chin.

"The boss man likes to entertain. They came in yesterday and will be over today for a tour. It's usually afternoon before they make it here." Edward pursed his lips. It was obvious how he felt about it all.

"Do you think Jones pays them off?" William low-ered his voice.

Edward shrugged and turned his attention back to his typewriter. "Haven't seen it myself, but it smells like Aberystwyth at low tide."

William smiled and walked to his desk. He pulled out a piece of carbon paper and put it behind the night's logs that he had to update. He knew that doing noth-ing to bloated sheep on the hillside involved watching and calculating.

There's more than one way to do nothing.

*Can both fresh water and salt water flow from the same
spring? My brothers and sisters, can a fig tree bear
olives, or a grapevine bear figs? Neither can a
salt spring produce fresh water.*

James 3:11-12

CHAPTER 30

WILLIAM WATCHED TWO CARS PULL up in front of the office. The front one was Granville Jones's car. Three men stepped out of the second car. William recognized Inspector Hughes as one of the men. They stood outside talking. Jones pointed to each building like a proud father.

William shoved the carbon copies in his desk drawer and stood. He rolled his neck and lifted his shoulders. He had forgotten to eat lunch.

The bigwigs, according to Edward, would only stay an hour. They needed a cursory look over the equipment to report to the Mines Department back in Cardiff. William brushed his hair back with his fingers and strode out of the office.

"Good afternoon, Mr. Jones … Mr. Hughes." William stuck his hand out to greet the inspector. "We met at Mr. Jones's house a few months ago."

"This is my day supervisor, William Williams," Jones jumped in. "A fine man. A war hero. We only employ the best of Wales." Though he smiled broadly, his eyes were shooting darts.

"Where did you serve?" one of the men asked. "You look familiar."

"Two years in North Africa. Came back in '17." William looked the man up and down. "Actually I think we met here. I was looking for Mr. Jones last spring and you were here."

"Yes, that's it. Quite right. So Granville hired you after all. He's hard to say no to for very long, like a rock you can't go around." The man winked at William.

"Have I finally won you over, Inspector Collins?" Jones said to the man, raising his brows.

"There's still some paperwork to look over," Inspector Collins said. "Good to see you again." He nodded to William and then the men walked to the office.

William turned to look for Clarence before the shift change. He made mental notes while singing under his breath: *"Leading, Follow paths of rock. Follow, Leading gentle flock."*

"Williams, come in here," Jones's voice called from his office.

William glanced at Edward, but he was busy shuffling papers. William pushed his chair back and checked that the drawer to his desk was closed. He stood and walked to the door.

"You need me?" He stuck his head inside the room.

"Sit down." Jones motioned toward the chair across from his desk.

William rubbed his hands on his pants as he sat down. He hoped his nervous behavior wasn't noticed. The last couple weeks of copying records and finding discrepancies were beginning to wear on him.

"I know you've got something on your mind, Williams, and I think I know what it is." Jones clasped his hands together on the desk.

Has he found my papers?

"Sir?"

"Etta told me she went to a meeting your wife commissioned, a sort of benefit from what I gather." He looked straight at William. "Mrs. Williams has good intentions, but she's softhearted like you. I can't help every widow, but maybe I can help your wife get started on the fund for a bathhouse."

William stayed silent, letting little spurts of air out his nose to keep from sighing in relief. He was safe. Jones thought he was sore about the Samson widow.

"Of course, I can only put up a third of the money. Etta was hoping for half, but she also wants a big wedding. She thinks I'm made of money." He chuckled. "Between her and Mrs. Jones it's a wonder I have any money left." He slapped his hands on the desk. "What do you say, Williams? Does a bathhouse sound good to you?"

"Quite." William smiled. "Should I tell Eileen to start raising money or will you be waiting until after the wedding to put up the money?"

"I think the Miners' Union in Cardiff can spare the money. I talked to the inspectors about it when they were here. Go ahead and tell Mrs. Williams to lead the way."

"Thank you, sir." William stood and shook hands with Jones. "I'll let her know when I get home." He pulled at his pants leg. "Mr. Jones, since we're talking about changes, maybe we could discuss safety in the tunnels."

"Yes, I've been thinking on that too." Jones sat back in his chair. "I was thinking about a dog rescue team. I saw some special breeds at the last dog trials—thought they might be good for sniffing out men when there's a collapse."

"Well, there're some possibilities in that, I suppose. But I was thinking more—"

"I could put a kennel in down by the stables. They'd be good for the ponies too. I'll have to see about a trainer. You think you could work with them?" He sat forward in his excitement. "No, better stick to a professional. We'll be the talk of the collieries."

"Maybe we should talk about safety," William tried again, sitting back down.

"Quite right. People might try to steal good dogs like that." Jones stood up and shook William's hand. "You talk to Mrs. Williams and get things rolling on the bathhouse. I'll take care of the dogs."

William was on his feet. "Speaking of animals, last time I was out to your place, I talked to Harvey about a ram. He said you might like to borrow one for the rutting this year."

"Have you got a good one?" Jones still held William's hand in a strong grasp.

"I have a few. Thought I'd sell off my old fellas last year, but the market wasn't high enough. Should I bring one by?"

"Yes, of course. I knew hiring you was a good idea." Jones cupped his other hand around William's shoulder.

"I'm not sure how a man can be so blind." William

held Eileen's hand as she jumped over the stone wall. "Thinking about dogs and bathhouses when two of the pits can't pass a simple safety test."

"It's a start." Eileen squeezed his hand and smiled at him. "Rome wasn't built in a day."

"No, but it fell pretty quick, it did." William tried to laugh and then put his arm around her.

"Is it really so bad?"

"The records are changed after the foremen make their rounds. It isn't good, that's for certain."

They stood at the top of the meadow and looked at the sheep lying in the field while Captain and Lucy sat nearby. Fireflies flickered in the dusky light. Summer was fading like wash too long on the line. There wouldn't be many more warm evening walks.

"I worry about you." Eileen lay her head against his chest. "You take as many risks staying in the office as the men who go down the pit."

"My risks don't mean I get injured or die. Soon I'll have enough proof to save those men. I just hope it's not too late."

Captain and Lucy stretched out beside them and watched the moon rise.

"It's never too late to do the right thing." Eileen looked up at her husband.

William kissed her, and then they stood for a long time, wrapped in each other's arms and the darkness.

*Even the king may not override the immutable,
unwritten laws of heaven.*

Paraphrase of Sophocles by Michael
Yankoski

CHAPTER 31

AMOS ROSE EARLY AND WANDERED through
the morning mist. He couldn't enjoy the city
even at this quiet hour. He felt a dark presence blowing in the alleys, and a cold ache burned in his chest.
He hated fighting with his father and brother, but he
couldn't get the Asherah pole in Valley Grove out of his
head. How long until it showed up here in the capital?

He was the first at the weaver's hall. The chief manager complimented the fine wool. Amos signed all the
papers and collected his money; it had been a very
good year. Malaki would be happy. She had worked
just as hard as he.

Amos remembered his wife's request for toys from
the carpenter. He meandered through the streets, the
mist now turning to warm spring sunshine. A large
building project caught his eye. Amos stopped to watch
the masons placing stones on a wall watchtower. Some
soldiers were hoisting a new catapult up the side of
the wall.

"Amos of Tekoa." Amos turned—and bowed.

King Uzziah stood next to him. "Stand up, man.

How are the sheep doing?"

"It's been a good year." Amos stood and smiled at the king. "You'll be pleased with your tax this season."

"My own sheep have fared well. Ten thousand lambs were born this spring. I just dug new wells, but they will run dry at that rate." The king thumped his chest. "Judah is a rich nation. Have you seen my new contraptions? They throw heavy rocks and burning oil on attackers."

Amos turned to marvel again at the catapult now lifted onto the wall. "You've strengthened many of the towns and cities in Judah, even Tekoa." Amos nodded and watched the workers. "The Lord has been kind to you and us—just as your father said he would be."

The two men stood in silence for a moment.

"And your ... figs, isn't it?" the king continued.

Amos nodded. "Also a good year. I'm sure your servants ate well all winter from my grove." He looked at the ground, but it seemed that heaven was whispering, urging him to speak. "I had a problem in Valley Grove last fall, though. I might be in trouble when I return."

"What kind of trouble? You're a good man. I'm sure we can work it out." The king spread his legs, leaned back, and crossed his arms.

"Some of the locals put up an Asherah pole on my land." Amos looked the king in the eye, determined to see this through. "I found it during the second harvest. I pulled it down and burned it to a crisp."

"You're a priest at heart, Amos."

"But, sir ..." Amos licked his lips. "It shouldn't be overlooked."

"What am I to do? That happened on your little heathen acre, not here in the civilized part of the country." The king shrugged his shoulders.

"Tekoa is ten miles away, and Asherah has raised an ugly branch there as well. It won't take long before the people bring her back to the city." Amos held his hands open to the king, begging him to see the danger.

"Tekoa is an important stronghold, yes. But it's hardly a major metropolis. How can I watch an entire nation?"

"Your father and grandfather didn't think themselves so small." Amos tried to control his voice. "Have you forgotten how your grandfather restored the Temple and demolished all the foreign gods—and how your father walked in the ways of God?" He lowered his gaze, thinking of Malaki and the children.

"My father and grandfather were great men." Uzziah cleared his throat. "They would be proud of the improvements I've made to the country."

"Yes, Your Majesty. They would be very proud to see the way Judah prospers and Jerusalem shines." Amos turned to watch the construction. "They would also warn you to learn from their mistakes."

"Mistakes?" The king's voice was low, simmering on a fire of bitter rumors. "What have you heard?"

"Not heard, my lord." Amos shook his head. "No, it is fact known throughout the land. Your grandfather eventually worshiped Asherah, and your father turned to the gods of Edom and Seir when it was the Lord who kept him safe in battle." He looked straight at the king. "Don't think that you will be innocent when payment for this adultery is due."

"I remember a prophet who spoke to my father this way." Uzziah's face was red, the veins in his neck throbbing. "Death would have been too good for him."

"The sheep must know their shepherd, or they'll climb out on every ledge and fall into every ravine."

Amos looked back at the wall. "Catapults and burning oil won't save you then. Excuse me, my lord. My wife requested some things before I return home."

Amos bowed and backed away from the king.

———◆———

The carpenter was easy to find. A group of children gathered around to look at the toys hanging from the beams of his shop. Toy horses and soldiers seemed to gallop across the air of the workshop, chased by an army of elephants and giraffes.

The carpenter sat at his bench whittling curves into the ear of a donkey while a child leaned on his knee to watch. Amos pushed closer to look over the children's shoulders. There was no doubt the man had skill.

"Can I help you?" The carpenter looked up from the donkey forming in his hand.

"You're very talented." Amos smiled and nodded at the miniature. "You have a gift for bringing the wood to life."

"The wood lives even in death. It breathes life into what I make." His curly beard and mustache were filled with wood shavings. "Are you looking for something in particular?"

"Sheep." Amos looked up at the menagerie of animals gliding on a spring breeze above his head. "Do you have any sheep?"

The man slipped the donkey into the waiting child's hand and stood. He scoured the ceiling until he found what he was looking for.

"There." He pointed toward a flock of fluffy sheep. "How many do you need?"

"I'll take the entire flock. Do you have any shep-

herds? I need three shepherdesses and one shepherd."
He winked at the man. "The girls may take after their
daddy too, you know."

"Right." He started pulling sheep from the rafters.
"The shepherds are over there with the other people
and gods." He jerked his head toward the wall at the
back of the shop.

Amos's eyes grew large. Surely this man wasn't wast-
ing his talent in idol making! Amos followed the man's
nod toward the back wall. Tiny shepherdesses stood
ready to fight bears and lions. Shepherd boys wielded
slingshots and clubs to fight off enemies. And facing
them were not wild beasts but images of Chemosh,
Baal, and Molech. Tiny Asherahs and Ashtoreths, just
big enough to slip into a young girl's pocket, bowed
at their feet.

Amos backed away from the wall and knocked into
the carpenter. Sheep spilled onto the sawdust floor.

"Forget it. I don't want anything here." Amos trembled.

"You alright?" The carpenter bent down to pick up
the sheep.

"You've called a curse on yourself." Amos ran his
hands through his hair. "How could you make those?"
He turned and ran out of the shop.

"Fire and death! Fire and death!" Amos shouted as
he ran into the street. He knocked into a priest. "Have
you seen what's in there?" He pointed toward the shop,
where children now stood in the doorway and stared
out at the crazy shepherd in the street.

"What's wrong, man?" The priest held onto Amos's
arm. "What's your name?"

"Amos. Amos of Tekoa."

"There's no fire." He craned his neck, looking for

smoke or flames. "You must be mistaken."

"Are you blind? Your sheep are running wild." Amos grabbed the priest's shoulders. "He's making idols and selling them. Right there. With children watching."

"Come on now. He's selling toys to children." The priest smiled.

"Children who play with toy gods grow up to follow those gods." Amos threw his arms in the air. "Your time is coming, Jerusalem. Judah will fall because of this. Mark my words."

———

Amos threw his bags into the back of the wagon and started for the front seat.

"Why such a hurry?" His father followed behind him.

"I can't be here any longer." Amos turned on his father and the two men bumped into each other. "You have to know what's been going on here."

"The gods aren't in the Temple or the public places." His father spoke low, looking side to side. "King Uzziah has made sure of that."

"It isn't enough." Amos threw his hands in the air.

"Shalom." An older man came up the short path to the house. "Is there a problem?"

Amos's father spun around. "Azariah, so good of you to come." Amos's father let out a little huff of air as he composed himself in front of the high priest. "Amos is upset about the carpenter over near the wall."

"Yes, I heard." Azariah nodded.

The other men looked at him, their lips parted in astonished silence.

"Amos attacked one of the priests earlier today," Azariah said.

"I attacked no one," Amos said. "I was rushing out of that pit of destruction and ran into a priest. I tried to warn him of what was going on, but he laughed as if it's not a problem."

Amos felt the heat rising in his neck and face. The men—shepherds—whose purpose was to guide the flock of God were instead letting wolves and lions pick them off one by one.

"Surely your son knows that King Uzziah is a man after God's heart, like his father, King David." Azariah looked at Amos's father and smiled calm waters and courage.

"Yes, he loves God," Amos said, "but he loves his place in the world more. King Uzziah is a rich man. It will be his ruin. He'll forget where it all came from, just wait and see." He jumped into the wagon and picked up the reins. "Judah is lost. Good-bye, Father."

It is the duty of a good shepherd to
shear his sheep, not to skin them.

Tiberius

CHAPTER 32

"I WISH DAD COULD STAY AT home, but I'm happy to have a few new dresses." Amaryllis twirled in the kitchen. She smiled ear to ear. "Can I stop by the colliery and show him my dress before school?"

"He would love that." Eileen grinned, remembering what it was like to be a young girl. "You go on and Allen can walk Iris to school. He's old enough now … and much more responsible after this summer." She winked at her daughter.

Amaryllis ran to give her a quick hug. "Thanks, Mum. I'll come home straight after school." She turned and ran out the door.

Eileen poured another cup of tea and stood in the door frame watching Amaryllis skip down the lane. The morning dew sparkled as the sun rose higher. Song birds in the oak twittered their good-mornings, and the sheep called back their own greeting.

The sound of new shoes on the stairs made Eileen turn. Iris stood at the bottom of the steps, large tears rolling down her cheeks.

"What's the matter, Iris?" Eileen crossed the room

and set her teacup on the table.

Iris ran to Eileen and buried her face in her mother's apron. Eileen sat down and pulled the little girl onto her lap.

"Allen called me a pig with two butts." She wiped her nose with the back of her hand.

"What?" Eileen stifled a giggle. "Are you sure that's what he said?"

The little girl nodded and sniffled, then dug her face in Eileen's shoulder. Allen jumped down the last three stairs and landed with a thud that shook the dishes on the shelf.

"What did you say to your sister?"

"Nothing." Allen shrugged his shoulders.

"Yes, you did." Iris twisted in her mother's lap. "You said I'm a pig with two butts."

"I just said you have two pigtails." Allen smirked.

"I see where this is headed. Apologize to your sister." Eileen shook her head.

"Sorry, Iris."

"And?" Eileen set the girl down.

"Do I have to?" Allen asked. "I'm getting awful big, don't you think?"

"You're never too big for a proper apology."

Allen dragged himself to his sister and looked her in the eye. "Will you forgive me?"

Iris nodded and sniffled again. Eileen wiped her face with the apron.

"Now hurry along or you'll be late for your first day of school. Amaryllis already left. You'll have to keep an eye on Iris today, Allen."

"This day smells like sheep fart." Allen took his sister's hand. "Come on, Iris. Summer's over; no more fun."

Amaryllis was still beaming from her father's compliments. She waved to Susan and Carol under the tree, but they didn't see her. She ran up the steps to catch them just as Allen and Iris arrived.

"Amaryllis, Mum said you have to take Iris to her class." Allen tugged on her sleeve and then took off down the hall with some friends.

"Alright." Amaryllis sighed. "Ready for the first day of school?" She smiled at her baby sister.

Iris's eyes were big in her face and the plaits on her head bobbled. She smelled of fear.

"What's the matter, Iris? You aren't afraid of Bottom Junior, are you?"

"I don't know mulkiplation. Allen said I have to know it." Her bottom lip quivered.

"Allen's just showing off because he's Top Junior this year. You don't need to know multiplication. You're going to be just fine, and Miss Lewis is a wonderful teacher. I had her when I was a Bottom Junior."

"Are you sure?" The quiver stopped, and she looked at her grown-up sister.

"Quite sure. Come on." Amaryllis took Iris by the hand and led her to the classroom.

Everyone was seated by the time Amaryllis made it to her classroom. It was a smaller room since many of the students didn't need to go any farther in their lessons. They would work in the colliery or farm the land like their parents and grandparents. There was only one seat left in the front of the class.

Susan and Carol looked at Amaryllis, but they didn't wave or smile. Susan hinted at a nod and then looked away when Carol whispered something. Amaryllis slipped into the chair as the teacher started roll call.

It seemed like this year would be no different than the last few—English compositions, a few literature studies, dry history lectures, and too much math. Amaryllis wondered how much she really needed to know if she was just going to be a shepherdess until she became a collier's wife. Heat rose up her neck and ears as she looked around the room considering which boy might make a husband in a few years.

The teacher soon dismissed them for lunch. Books slammed closed on the desks, and a murmur rose as they were finally allowed to speak. Amaryllis slid out of her seat and looked back for Susan and Carol. They were huddled with some other students around a desk.

"She's not like that," Susan said as Amaryllis edged into the group.

"Hello." Amaryllis smiled at everyone. "It's good to be back in town."

"Really? Since when, last Friday?" Owen snickered.

"What do you mean?" Amaryllis furrowed her brow.

Susan looked at the floor, but Carol maintained a steely gaze.

"Did something happen Friday?" Amaryllis asked.

Owen smiled. "Just figured that was your regular night. ... Nice dress, 'Ryllis. How'd you pay for it?" He rocked on his heels. "Or did that Irish boy give it to you?"

Amaryllis eyed him. "Are you still sore about being dumped in the water?" It was beginning to make sense. "You know you had it coming. How could you be so mean toward Alice after you've known her all your life?"

"You're really taking up for her when you know what her mother is?" Carol crossed her arms. "Talk is your mum's been by her house an awful lot."

"What's that supposed to mean?" Amaryllis put her hands on her hips.

"Just haven't seen you in such fancy clothes before. Some wonder how you afford them."

"Some? You mean you?" Amaryllis clenched her jaw. "I've had enough of you. They say every flock has its black sheep, but I'm thinking this flock has more than one."

Amaryllis turned on her heel and marched out of the room. She was so angry that she left her lunch on her desk. She was in no mood for the loud schoolyard, so she walked a couple of times around the block until it was time to return to class.

———

The afternoon was worse than the morning. Amaryllis felt darts stinging her back. She heard whispers and snickers. Out of the corner of her eye she watched a note being passed around the entire room. The teacher didn't seem to notice.

When class was dismissed, Amaryllis gathered her books and held her head high. She resolved not to let them know how hurt she was, but she blinked back tears as she walked to Iris's classroom.

"How was your first day?" Amaryllis asked as Iris skipped out of the room.

"You were right. Miss Lewis is nice, and she said I can be classroom helper this week, and we didn't do any mulkiplation." She grasped Amaryllis's hand. "How was your first day?"

"We had mulkiplation." She pursed her lips and then laughed.

Allen met them at the bottom of the front steps.

"Come on," Amaryllis said, "let's go home."

———————

Allen dragged his feet and kicked at pebbles. Iris pulled on Amaryllis to hurry.

"You run ahead and wait at the tree." Amaryllis let go of her sister's hand. "What's wrong with you, Allen? Mulkiplation?" She smiled.

"Dumb Elmer Brewer said Dad's a thief and crook like all the other colliery office men." Allen struck his fist into his palm. "I ought to give him what for."

"It wouldn't do any good. They'd just talk behind your back." Amaryllis sighed and joined Allen in the kicking. "I never thought I'd say this, but I missed the sheep field today."

"Me too." Allen's stomach growled. "And Mum's meat pasty."

"I didn't finish my lunch. You want it?" Amaryllis handed him her lunch pail.

"Didn't finish? How much did she send you?" His big eyes peered into the pail. "This was all I got!"

"Go ahead and eat it." She waved at Ian Roi across the field. Iris was waiting under the tree ahead. "Can you walk Iris home? I'm going to see Ian Roi."

"Sure," he said, stuffing the last of a thick slice of bread in his mouth.

"Tell Mum I won't be long." She waved good-bye and turned across the meadow.

———————

"How is the shepherdess scholar?" Ian Roi leaned on his staff.

Amaryllis shrugged. "It was a long day. I missed the sheep." She stroked a yearling behind the ears. "Sheep aren't cruel."

"Not usually, though sometimes they can be mean in their greed."

He slipped a few grains of roasted barley from his pocket. The sheep watched his hands and butted each other to be closest to him. Amaryllis and Ian Roi laughed as the sheep started climbing up his leg. When the barley was nibbled away, they lost interest.

"So what happened at school?"

Amaryllis looked at her father's best friend. How could she talk about this to him? She wasn't comfortable speaking to her own mother about it. She shrugged again.

"Was it about the Irish boy, Dennis?"

Amaryllis looked up quickly. *How does he know?*

"A little." She blushed. "But there was more."

"Mm. I imagine Mrs. Davies was part of it. Some people around here talk too much." He put a hand on her shoulder. "And some people don't talk enough. It's alright to talk to me if you like, Amaryllis."

She half smiled and took a deep breath. The words bounded out like spring lambs in a fresh field. "Owen is mad at Dennis for dumping him in the water when we went swimming. But Dennis didn't do anything I didn't want to do. Owen was saying mean things about Alice and Mrs. Davies. And maybe they're true, but they don't have to say it." She took a deep breath.

"*Gorau prinder, prinder geiriau*—the best shortage is a shortage of words."

"Quite right." Amaryllis gave one sharp nod with

her head. She could feel the anger bubbling up. "But they didn't stop there. They said things about my mum … and me!" Tears wet her cheeks.

Ian shook his head and sighed.

"And that's not all! Allen said the boys in his class were saying things about Dad—that he's a crook and thief. Bunch of *cŵn melynog*. They don't know what they're talking about."

"Smelly dogs or no, they might have reason to feel that way."

Amaryllis stepped back. She blinked and swiped at the streams flowing down her face.

Ian Roi held up his hands. "Feelings aren't always truth, but they still matter." He tipped his head. "Your dad has a difficult job, Amaryllis. He must keep the men safe without them losing any work. They have families to feed and clothe. That's what they see clearest, and likely what they talk about the most. The boys are just reacting to what they feel—fear."

"Maybe you're right, but that doesn't change anything." The anger still simmered like a pot of stew. "Dad isn't a thief or a crook. And Mrs. Davies is just trying to take care of her family like their dads are doing."

"Quite right." Ian placed an arm around her shoulders and pulled her tight. "Dennis is just trying to feed himself. Mrs. Davies is trying to care for her family. Your dad is trying to take care of the men, and your mum is trying to care for everyone. Love is what we all have in common."

Amaryllis hugged the shepherd back. He smelled fresh and earthy.

"I think that's my song, Ian Roi."

*I have always found that mercy bears
richer fruits than strict justice.*

Abraham Lincoln

CHAPTER 33

"YOU'VE BEEN VERY QUIET, AMARYLLIS. How was your first day of school?" William licked his fingers. "Did you talk yourself out at recess?"

Amaryllis looked up from her dinner. Allen was scooping a second helping of potatoes onto his plate. Iris looked like a milk-drenched lamb as she chewed a piece of bread over and over.

"It was fine." She tried to smile. "I guess I'm just tired like Iris."

"Was Alice in school?" Eileen held her breath.

Amaryllis shook her head.

Allen's humph was audible. "None of the Davies kids were there. No wonder, with the things people were saying about them." He swirled the butter in his potatoes.

"What were they saying?" William asked.

"Nothing worse than they said 'bout you." Allen scowled. "They say anything else, I'll take care of them, I will."

"Allen Williams," Eileen gasped. "You best not be getting into fights or your father will thrash you."

"Why were your mates talking about me?" William

paused with his fork in the air.

"They're just a bunch of sheep farts in a jam jar." Allen scooped potatoes into his mouth. "They think you're causing trouble for their dads. Said you were striking something." He shrugged his shoulders.

"Close your mouth when you're eating," Eileen reminded him.

"How can I close—"

"That's enough." William stopped his son. "Finish your dinner and get your chores done."

———————

"Your father's right; you've been very quiet this evening." Eileen took the dripping bowl from Amaryllis's hand. "Are you sure there isn't more to it than first-day fatigue?" She wiped the bowl dry and watched her oldest child out of the corner of her eye.

"I think I'm just tired."

"But maybe there is something else?"

Amaryllis looked at her mother, then back at the dishwater. She carefully slid the dishrag down the blade of the bread knife.

"There was talk. Allen was right."

"About Alice?"

"Not quite. ... Maybe. ... Yes." Amaryllis sighed, and her face turned red.

"Amaryllis, something's wrong. Tell me." Her mother's voice draped her like a soft blanket. "What happened?"

Amaryllis looked up at her mother and burst into tears. "They said things about you and me. Owen said I was like Mrs. Davies."

"Oh, dear girl." Eileen held her daughter. Dishwater

dripped down the back of her dress and tears damp-
ened the front. "Is it because of the Benefit meeting?
I'm so sorry, sweetheart. I was just trying to help those
poor women."

"I know, Mum." Amaryllis stepped back and wiped
her face on her sleeve. "It wasn't just the Society Meeting. I'm afraid I wasn't very ladylike last time I went
swimming."

Eileen raised her brows.

"Nothing like that, Mum!" Amaryllis turned red.
"I ... I smarted off to Owen. Now he's angry and I
suppose he's getting revenge. He thinks I'm sweet on
Dennis Byrne because I took up for him. He says I
love foreigners, prostitutes, and who knows what else."

"Sounds like the right people to love if you ask me."
Eileen hugged her daughter close. "Don't worry. We'll
get this all worked out."

———◆———

Eileen walked into Shotton Cross with her head
high. If children were saying something at school, it
was only because they had heard it at home first. She
would not let it get to her. She knocked on the first
door like a judge's gavel.

The door cracked open and Doris peered out. Children's voices floated out of the house.

"Good morning. Would you like to buy some fresh
fish? Can't beat the price." Eileen smiled and pulled
the cover back from the fish.

Doris looked down the street each way, then
motioned Eileen to come in.

"I'll take four big ones if you have them. Henry was
just saying yesterday he'd like some fresh sea trout."

The young woman pulled her change purse out of a table drawer. "How much are they?"

"Three shillings for four. Would you like me to take them back to the kitchen for you?"

"Oh, that would be lovely. Can you stay for a cup of tea?"

"No thank you. I need to sell the rest of these and get back to the farm. Rutting season is starting, and with William at the colliery it takes a lot of my time."

"You're sweet as my old nain's biscuits to take care of things at home so Mr. Williams can help out our men. I know some people are upset, but not everyone is." She looked down and smiled. "Here's an extra shilling for the Benefit. I hear there's going to be a bathhouse soon."

Eileen's mouth dropped open. She followed Doris to the kitchen, glad for the time to gather her thoughts.

"Yes, Mr. Jones is putting up some of the money. Cardiff will put some up as well. It's terribly generous of you, Doris. Every little bit helps." She set the bucket of fish on the table and took the money. She slipped it into her pocket and then reached for the fish. "You know some of the money goes to help the widows in Shotton Cross too."

"Christian charity has been known to change lives in more ways than one. I don't know where I'd be if I lost my husband." A child appeared from behind the door. She hid in Doris's skirts. "Let me get a bowl for those fish."

———◆———

The afternoon passed quickly. No one else invited Eileen in, but several women bought fish and added "a little extra for the Benefit." There were still some who slammed the door, even a few who made crude remarks, but generally people were kind. Even Catherine managed to throw in an extra shilling.

———

The autumn sun was high in the sky now. Eileen had a few fish left, held back for Constance. She pushed open the gate and started up the walk. Singing came from the open window. Eileen stopped to listen for a moment. When was the last time she had heard Constance singing? Had she ever?

"Constance?" Eileen pushed the front door open. "It's Eileen."

"Come in," Constance's voice rang out from the front room. "I'm up to my elbows in wash water."

Eileen stepped into the house. The smell of vinegar and wood oil was strong. The entrance was filled with furniture stacked against the wall.

"You know it's not spring, right?" Eileen asked, maneuvering her way to the front room.

Constance laughed and looked over her shoulder. She was teetering on the edge of a kitchen chair. A ratty old blouse and a patched skirt clung to her bony frame. Wisps of hair escaped the kerchief wrapped around her head.

"I missed the spring cleaning this year." A cloud darkened her spirit for just a second. "I thought I better get on it now or I'll be too far behind." She grinned, the sadness replaced with sunshine.

"You're certainly feeling chipper." Eileen couldn't help smiling. "It's better than Christmas to see you like this."

"Can you stay for tea? Just let me finish washing down this wall and then we can sit and visit."

"I'd love to. I brought you some fish, not as many as before, but enough to help you with dinner. I'll go put them in the kitchen while you finish up."

———————

Eileen poured a bit of cream into the strong black tea. She'd have plenty of energy to finish the chores when she got home now. Constance passed a plate of lemon shortbread. Eileen nibbled the biscuit while her friend put the water pot back on the cookstove.

"Something has happened," Eileen said. "I was worried when Allen told us the children weren't in school."

"Something has happened, quite right." Constance nodded as she smoothed her skirt to sit down. "Something startling, and wonderful, and unexpected." She giggled like a schoolgirl.

"Tell me," Eileen begged.

"Enoch Evans has been visiting me for a while, since his wife died." She slurped the hot tea. "At first it was laundry or helping with the children, but then he started bringing us food." She blushed. "He said if I would cook for him, he would bring enough for me and the children as well."

"That was very generous." Eileen put down the biscuit and nodded for Constance to continue.

"Quite." Constance scooted forward in her seat. "I told him I was happy to help without the food for us, but truth be told, we needed it. All three boys eat like there's a famine coming. I can't keep up. Thanks for the fish too." She squeezed Eileen's hand, remembering why she was there.

"As my mother always said, *'Bydd y plentyn yn tyfu, ni fydd ei ddillad'*—'The child will grow, his clothes will not.' I have trouble keeping one boy fed; I can't imagine three of them." Eileen shook her head and lifted her teacup.

"Yes, so Enoch kept bringing food and then he'd pick up the meals after work. The stack of dishes flowing between our houses was never-ending. Finally I invited him to bring his children and come for dinner." She couldn't look Eileen in the eyes. "It was forward, I know, but it just made sense."

"Of course it did. It wasn't forward at all." Eileen crossed her legs and leaned her arms on the table.

Constance squeezed Eileen's hand again and smiled like a child at the candy counter. "Soon Enoch was coming every evening. I kept the babes when he had to work night shifts. The children get along so well." She sighed. "One thing led to another." She trembled all over. "He asked me to marry him, Eileen! Me, getting married! Can you believe it?"

Eileen hollered and jumped out of her chair. The two women hugged and cried and laughed. They were too happy to talk, rocking back and forth, holding onto each other like long lost friends.

"What do the children think?" Eileen stepped back and looked at her old buttie.

"They're excited, just like me." Constance stood on her toes, ready to blast through the ceiling if gravity should let her go. "That's why they aren't in school. They went over to Enoch's to help him get the house ready for us. His house is a *tai-unno*, remember? Much too small for all of us. He's adding another room for the boys, and Alice will room with the babes."

"Oh, Constance, I'm so happy for you. Enoch is a

lucky man to get you. When is the wedding?"

"Two weeks. I'm cleaning out the house so I can move by the end of the month. Then the kids will be back in school."

"Alice too?"

Constance nodded.

"Amaryllis will be so glad to hear it. She could use a friend." She hugged Constance again. "I better get home. Sheep need a shepherd, you know."

———————

Eileen stopped under the oak tree to rest in the shade and think. How differently the day had ended than she had expected. She sold all the fish, received support for the Benefit, and discovered God had her friend taken care of. She was sure all the rumors and lies would end now.

From her vantage point Eileen could see the town spread out behind her and the rutting rams charging in front of her.

It's always like that: moving from one thing to the next—a never-ending cycle of life, death, and life again. If only we could learn to live the life more than the death ...

*When Thou callest me to go through the
dark valley, let me not persuade myself that
I know a way round.*

John Baillie

CHAPTER 34

THE GIRLS CAME RUNNING DOWN the lane as soon as they saw Amos's wagon.

"Papa! Papa! You're back." Their hair flew behind them as they ran beside the wagon.

Amos laughed and reined in the donkey. He reached down to pull each girl up on the seat beside him. He clucked to the donkey and they jolted as the wagon started. The girls laughed and bounced on the seat.

"Did you bring us something?" asked Jemima, the oldest. "Mama said you're bringing us toys."

"Better than a toy." Amos smiled sideways at her.

"What is it?" she squealed.

"You'll have to wait and see." Amos hurried the donkey toward the barn.

Malaki stood in the doorway of the house holding the baby as Amos passed. Amuz was big enough to wave now, his chubby arms flying when he saw his father. Amos pulled up next to the barn and handed the reins to the hired man.

"Come on, girls." He swung them down from their perch. "Let's see what Mama thinks of your presents."

The children ran ahead of him, calling for their mother to come out of the house. Malaki laughed and stepped out onto the sandy pathway. She set Amuz down and he took a few tentative steps. Amos ran and caught him up in his arms.

"What a big boy you are." He tickled the boy's stomach. "Thought you might have to walk to Jerusalem to get your papa, did you?"

"Papa brought us presents." Jemima grinned and pulled on her mother's sleeve. "He said you'll like them."

"Oh, he did, did he?" She stroked the girl under the chin, then looked at her husband. "And what might these presents be?"

Amos gave the baby back to Malaki and reached in his pocket. He pulled out the little scripture boxes from the Temple booth. He handed each girl a box and then placed another in Malaki's hand.

"This one is to save for Amuz for when he is bigger." Amos kissed her hand and closed it around the box.

"What is it, Papa?" Elizabeth asked, trying to open the tiny package.

"A whisper from God himself." Amos picked up the little girl and held her close.

Malaki watched as Amos showed the girls how to open their tiny treasures and pull out the scrolls inside. He read each scripture to them.

"You'll be able to read it yourself soon." He tugged Jemima's long hair.

———◆———

"The girls liked their scripture boxes." Malaki lay next to Amos, her head resting on his chest. "Weren't you able to find the carpenter? Next to the wall?"

"Yes. I found him." He slid his arm around her and brushed her hair with his fingers.

"Why didn't you get a toy for the children, then? There was plenty of money from the wool." She lifted her head enough to look at him.

Amos licked his lips and inhaled through his nose. It was a sigh she understood.

"What happened?" She put her head down again and reached for his hand.

"You don't need to worry about what to wear to the king's fall banquet." He tried to laugh and squeezed her hand.

"Oh, Amos. Not the king." She jumped up in the bed.

Amos rearranged the covers, then pulled his beard trying to decide how much to tell her. *Might as well tell the truth.* He shrugged and related the whole story.

———————

"You're very quiet." Elroi was helping Amos treat the sheep for flies.

"Long week." Amos applied the ointment while Elroi held the sheep around the neck.

"Your father is well?" Elroi watched Amos's face. Deep lines formed across his brow.

"Healthy, yes." Amos nodded, dipped into the bowl, and smeared another ewe.

"That is an answer." Elroi pursed his lips. "But it isn't the answer you hold at the back of your tongue."

Amos straightened up. He eyed the head shepherd. He always knew more than Amos wanted him to know.

"Father defended idolatry." His voice was low, the

words painful. "He doesn't have any idols in his house, and he still goes to the Temple, but ..." He stared across the meadow dotted with late-spring flowers.

"But?" Elroi let the ewe go and shook the tension from his arms.

"I shouldn't be surprised. King Uzziah is the same." He raised an eyebrow at Elroi. "He doesn't see how he can remove all of the idols from the land, so he just plans to keep the royal places and the Temple clean. How can he not know that's the beginning of the end?"

Elroi spit and crossed his arms. He stroked his beard, thinking. "Why is it that the fattest and healthiest sheep are the ones that seem to get cast on the hillside?" Elroi watched the lambs frisking in the corner of the field. "I'll tell you why: they get comfortable."

"Mm." Amos followed Elroi's gaze.

"Their wool is long and sleek, their bellies full. They find a little hollow that caresses each curve of their bodies and they fall asleep. Before they know what happens—phew—they end up on their backs gasping for air and begging for help." Elroi threw his arms up and flailed the air.

"King Uzziah is cast?" Amos wrinkled his nose.

"He's certainly fat and sleek. It's only a matter of time."

Elroi grabbed the next ewe that passed. Amos smeared the greasy mixture on its face and stepped aside.

"If it's inevitable, why do I feel the need to say something?" Amos straightened up again.

"Sheep need a shepherd, even the fat, healthy ones. God is calling you to be his voice. You've heard him; you know you have." Elroi lifted his chin. "The question is: Are you going to obey?"

"Malaki …" Amos looked away.

"She'll understand. She was a shepherdess, and now she's a mother. She'll understand."

———◆———

"I don't understand." Malaki sat across from Amos at the dinner table.

"I just need some time away from here, time to listen." Amos put down his bread. His leg jiggled with nervous energy.

"Listen for what?" Tears filled her eyes.

"I think God is calling me, Malaki. I'm pretty sure of it, actually." He reached across the table and took her hands in his.

"Where will you go? How long will you be?" Her chin quivered, and the pools of misery overflowed.

"Valley Grove. I should check on Kediah and the new trees. Leah must have had the baby by now. You'll send a present?" He tried to smile.

"Yes, of course." She swiped at the tears that fell in a stream down the valley of her nose. "You'll come home soon?"

"As soon as I can. Elroi is going with me. It'll be alright." He winked. "Maybe I can find a toy for the children this time."

I tremble for my country when I reflect that God is just:
that his justice cannot sleep for ever....

Thomas Jefferson

CHAPTER 35

"WHAT'S THIS?" WILLIAM PICKED UP a paper on Edward's desk.

"Last night's report. The engineering supervisor didn't have all the paperwork done, so Glenn asked me to type it up for the records." Edward cleared his throat. "As if it matters what I type."

"What do you mean?" William looked over the paper.

Edward shrugged his shoulders and shook his head. He took another paper and placed it in the typewriter. "You know better than I do." Edward nodded toward William's desk. "Seems like you do a lot of carbon work of your own."

"Just trying to stay on top of everything. Mind if I look this over?" William held the paper over Edward's growing stack.

"Just make sure it gets back here." Edward patted his desk.

William nodded and crossed the room. Morning light streamed through the window behind his chair. He sat down to compare notes. Glenn's scribbles from the last shift were concerning. The surface fans were having some electrical glitches. The reverse ventilation switches were faulty.

William bit his lower lip, trying to sort out exactly where the discrepancies fell. Engineering noted a few missed transversals, but the supervisor wasn't concerned. The percentage of misses was within the safety regulations.

"I'm heading down the pit to check a few things." William stood up. "I'll be back in an hour or so."

Edward raised his chin and looked sideways at William. "Might check with the day manager about maintenance on Pit Twelve."

"Quite right." William nodded.

———◆———

The moan of the engine lowering the cage into the darkness chafed William's nerves. He jumped as the bottom stopped against the pit floor. He snapped the carbide lamp until it lit, the metallic smell burning his nostrils. He walked out the open side into the darkness.

Men called to each other between stalls. Equipment droned and squealed, echoing off the damp walls. William waved to the crew in Michael's stall and headed for Pit Twelve. He stooped his shoulders to walk through the low passages.

The beam of light filtering in front of William's face scattered like gunfire in the night. It ricocheted off the rock walls, the men's equipment, and the glitter of coal dust on the floor. William took a deep breath and pressed on.

"How are you doing over here?" William asked as he approached the day manager in Pit Twelve. "Everything right as rain?"

"Only if you like downpours that flood." The man's voice sounded plenty angry. "I've been calling for clean-up since last Tuesday. Look at all this dust." He kicked at the floor.

"What are they telling you?" William squatted to the floor and ran his hand through the thick layer of coal dust.

"Say they're working overtime in Seventeen. Ever since the collapse, that's all I hear. I've got live men right here who need help." His voice raised over the men working nearby.

William nodded and looked around. He heard the ventilation fans grind to a halt. "I'll check into it right away." He made a note on his clipboard. "Let me check with engineering on some other things first. I'll get back to you this afternoon."

The manager huffed and nodded. Disgust carved his face with a scowl deeper than the caverns of Snowdonia.

———————

"When will the beams be replaced?" William pressed the head engineer. "Coal dust isn't all that's filling the floor in Twelve. It has to be taken care of now."

"We haven't got the manpower. Jones is pushing for larger production every day. The new areas are taking all our energy; there's no time to fix the old spots."

"You think you're short of manpower now, wait until there's an accident." William threw his hands in the air. "Production numbers will be zero if we get shut down."

"As if that could happen." The engineer snorted.

"Oh, it can happen—in the blink of an eye, I tell

you." William snapped his fingers. "Get men over to Twelve before lunch."

William strode away, feeling like a sheepdog in search of a foundering ewe.

———

"How was your day?" Eileen kissed the air between them. "I guess you were in the pits today."

"How can you tell?" He pulled off his shirt and dust flew into the air. "Is it the dust or the smell of hellfire and brimstone?"

"Dinner is ready. I'll bring you a bucket of hot water out back. Yell for Allen while you're there, will you?"

William walked to the fold and searched the barn for his son. He should have been back by now, but his pup, Major, was not in the pen either.

"Allen!" William cupped his hands to his mouth and called across the hillside.

He heard barking and knew they were on the path from the brook. Soon Allen came driving three yearlings ahead of him. William waved when the boy looked up.

"Hello, Dad!" Allen called as he neared the gate. William went to open it. "These three hooligans were dashing around the countryside like it was springtime. They must've found a hole in the east meadow."

"No problem rounding them up?" William pulled the gate shut behind them.

"Not with Captain and Major around." Allen smiled. "Major's really getting the hang of herding." He scratched his dog behind the ears.

"That's because you treat him right." William put his hand on his son's shoulder. "And he sees that you respect the sheep too. A dog takes his cue from the shepherd first."

———◆———

"You seemed pretty worked up at dinner." Eileen situated her head on the pillow. The outline of her husband's face was barely visible in the darkness.

"Mm."

"Want to talk about it?"

"Not sure how much I can." William sighed. "It's getting worse, Eileen. Men are in danger—real danger."

"Why doesn't the Commission close the place down until it can be righted?" She sat up on an elbow.

William moved his head to look at her, then turned back to the ceiling. His hands were clasped across his chest, and his thumbs beat a quick rhythm as he said, "They may not be getting the true state of affairs. If only I could get Mr. Jones to respect the men. He's so concerned about output numbers—production, production, production. We could produce more if he would let us take the time to make repairs, clean the lines, sort it all out. Those men would be devoted to him if they were treated like people instead of serfs."

"He needs someone to talk to him on level ground. All he knows is being in charge."

"Yes, but who in Shotton Cross is on the same level as Granville Jones? He owns everything and says what everyone else can own."

"Well," Eileen drawled. "He doesn't own all the sheep in Shotton Cross. Maybe you could talk to him as a shepherd."

William was quiet, thinking. An idea was working its

way across the meadow of rutting rams.

"You may be right." He rolled over and kissed Eileen. "You're one smart woman, Mrs. Williams."

Christ … have mercy on us and give
us the courage to suffer.

Dorothy Day

CHAPTER 36

THE GREY MORNING LIGHT WAS quiet, stealing across the countryside. The sun pounced like a cat hunting warblers, and the birds flew when they heard its first rays. William loved witnessing the dawn of each new day.

He swung his tommy box beside him and thought about last week's meeting with Granville Jones. It had gone as expected. He'd left the gate open in his presence, but Jones wouldn't go in. William had done what was right; he knew that.

He stopped to watch the rams charging each other. Only a few of the yearlings were still fighting for their place. The others knew where they belonged in the herd. Eileen would turn them out with the ewes today.

The rams' horns crashed against each other with such force that they shook their heads to regain balance. The yearlings eyed each other, backed up, and charged. The sound vibrated through the air and into the ground. Then the ground shook. A violent blast reverberated in William's ears.

He ran toward Shotton Cross.

———

William could see the mayhem from the top of the hill. He scanned the streets from his vantage point, headed east toward the river, and ran with all his might.

Women were screaming. The slag heaps had shifted again and taken out three miners' houses. People were digging desperately, racing against time and terror. Glenn and Edward stood on the stairs waving to William as he raced toward the chaos.

"What happened? Was it Twelve?" William huffed trying to catch his breath.

"No, Fifteen." Glenn put his hand on William's shoulder. "The explosion knocked out the power. The fans aren't working."

"The backup?" William turned as the firemen sprinted by. "What about the generators?"

"We're working on it, but William …" Glenn looked at him. "The power is out all over. We can't get the men up in the lifts. We might be able to run them manually, but it's going to take awhile to get everyone out of there."

"Some are coming up, though? How many? Who?" His thoughts flew faster than his words. "Do we have masks for everyone?"

Glenn shook his head. There hadn't been enough breathing apparatus for years. The men all knew it. They worked under the assumption that if everything went wrong, they were dead anyway, breathing apparatus or no. That's how things were at Shotton Cross Colliery.

William paced on the stoop.

Clarence appeared at the bottom of the steps. "The

cages are going down, Mr. Williams. Do—"

"Thank God. I'm coming." William took the stairs two at a time, and the men crossed the courtyard. "No one is being asked to go." He looked around the group of men.

They all nodded. There was no question that they were going. It was what miners did for their own. They climbed onto the lift, as many as it could hold.

William could smell it as soon as they touched bottom: fear. He knew the smell from butchering hogs. An animal knows when its time is up; these men were sure they were finished.

William flipped on his light. Pit Fifteen was completely obstructed. Rubble littered the floor. The earth creaked and moaned, shifting under its own weight. Men and rats were pouring out of the other passages hoping for air, for life.

"Where are you from?" William asked each man as he loaded them onto the lift.

Most were from Fourteen. They were broken, battered, suffocating, but alive. The signal was given, and the lift began to rise.

"Looks like Fourteen is going to be alright." William took charge. "You three see if you can find anyone else in Fourteen. You six go down Thirteen. I'll take Twelve."

"I'll come with you," Clarence said. "The damp gets strong in Twelve."

William nodded. The men turned to their assignments and walked into the unknown.

———————

The mine was dark like a cold midnight lake. The

ripples of men moving rocks twenty yards away was a light of its own.

"Hello! We're here. We're going to get you out of there!" Clarence yelled. He looked at William. "You alright?"

William stared at the wall of rock. Men were depending on him to get them out of there. Fellow soldiers, comrades in arms, bombed by the enemy, were waiting for him.

"Williams." Clarence was pulling on a boulder.

William shook his head and took a deep breath. He joined Clarence and pulled the boulder away from the pile. A shaft of light appeared from inside the collapsed passage. They heard a shout echo on the other side of rock.

When the opening was big enough for men to slip through, they sent the first man out. His arm hung loose at his side. He was pale but talking.

"You made it," William said. "Head for the lift. It's making runs manually, but you're going to get out. You'll be home soon."

Men stumbled out of the mound of rock and debris. Broken arms, a shattered foot, lots of coughing and choking, but William began to relax. They were getting out; he could go to the surface on the next lift.

"Is that everyone?" Clarence asked a straggler.

"Billy's stall isn't out yet. The damp is thick." The man gasped and collapsed.

"Take him," William said to Clarence. "I'll check Billy's stall and be right behind you." He motioned the men on and covered his mouth with a wet rag.

William slid through the hole that had poured forth broken lives. On the other side was only darkness and poisonous gas. William kept his hand on the slick wall and followed it to Billy's stall.

Billy was an experienced collier. He was working with his grandson, teaching him the ropes. *He'll have everyone sheltered. It's going to be fine.*

"Hello? Can anyone hear me?" William called.

"Here ... here." A faint moaning caught William's attention. "I can't see."

"It's alright. Your light is out. I'll be there in a minute. It's going to be alright."

William felt his way along the wall as his light began to flicker. He tapped the helmet he wore, but the light didn't increase. Another of Jones's ideas to save money: used equipment, outdated and in disrepair.

He stopped when the wall opened up. He could see men backed against the wall.

"The damp is too strong; we have to stay up, boys." It was Billy, encouraging his men to keep standing. Poison swirled around their feet, threatening their lungs and their lives.

"No one has a light?" William glanced around the group. "That's alright; you can follow me. Billy, you take the back and make sure they stay up. You're the best miner I know."

"You heard him, boys. Follow Williams. He's a war hero; he'll get you out of here. Go on with you." The older man pushed them ahead of him. "I've got your back."

William walked faster, heading home like a shepherd with sheep at the end of the day.

"Cover your heads!" Billy shouted as the floor shook and the ceiling gave way.

It was another explosion.

William swept pebbles and dirt from his chest. The explosion had knocked him backward. His feeble light swept the area in front of him. It was blocked solid.

"Is everyone alright?" William looked behind him. "Are you there, Billy?" Wooden beams and boulders blocked the back. It was a total cave-in. "Billy?"

"There's no one else." It was a young man, a boy, blown against the wall by the force of the explosion. A wooden beam lay twisted at his feet. "We're going to die." His voice quavered.

"No." William crawled to him. "We have to stand up. They'll get to us. They know we're here."

William strained to move the beam. He tried to lift the boy. He cried out; his leg hung limp like one of Iris's rag dolls.

"Lean on me. I'll hold you up." William bent over and lifted the boy onto his back. "What's your name, son?"

"Dennis. Dennis Byrne."

My native land is a slave of heathenism, men's
god is their belly, and they live only for the present.
The richer a man, the holier.

Saint Jerome

CHAPTER 37

"MASTER AMOS." LEAH STOOD WITH the door half-open. "Was Kediah expecting you? He didn't tell me." Her face was pink.

"No, it's a surprise visit." Amos and Elroi stood in the afternoon sun. "Can we come in?"

"Yes." She blinked and nodded her head. "Yes. Of course. You just startled me." Crying came from the back room.

"I see the baby is strong and healthy." Amos smiled as he walked into the cool house.

"Babies." Leah groaned as she closed the door behind the men.

"Twins?" Elroi laughed. "A double blessing."

"Mm. So they keep telling me." She waved the men on into the kitchen. "I can't offer you your favorites today, Master Amos. I've been a donkey in a mudhole ever since the boys were born."

"We'll just take some water. Thank you, Leah." Amos sat at the table along with Elroi. "Where's Kediah?"

"In the orchard." She ladled water into cups and handed one to Amos. "He's been caressing those saplings like a concubine." She handed the other cup to Elroi. "If they don't grow better than those sons of mine, I'll be a scandalized woman."

Amos laughed and took a drink. The cool water washed the road dust from his throat.

"Kediah is devoted to you." Elroi raised the cup to his lips. He swallowed. "That's why he works so hard." He put the cup down. "May I go to the babies?"

"Yes." Leah started for the hallway.

"I can find them." Elroi motioned for her to sit. "You take a break for a minute." He handed his cup to her and disappeared down the mosaic hallway.

"Kediah hasn't been ignoring you, has he?" Amos rested his elbows on the table and sighed. It had been a long journey from Tekoa.

"No." She tried to smile. "Twins was more than I expected. Kediah is a good man. He works hard for you and me both, Master Amos."

"Good." Amos looked around the room. There were more dishes than two people should have used. "And the Moabite caravans? He isn't adding that to your workload, is he?"

"There haven't been many this winter. I think they heard that you bought their trees." Leah frowned.

"Trouble?"

"No." She shook her head and stood. "I better start something for dinner. Kediah will be glad you're here."

"I'll just go find him—make sure he's working as hard as his wife." Amos winked and stood. "Elroi, are you ready?"

Elroi's sandals padded down the hall. "Always."

"Kediah!" Amos waved through the leafy branches of the orchard.

Kediah was in the eastern acreage talking to some men. They were measuring the trees. Kediah turned when he heard his name.

He spoke to the men, then quickly headed for Amos. The men watched from a distance.

"Master Amos." Kediah was breathing heavy. He wiped sweat from his face. "I didn't expect you. Is everything alright?"

"Just checking on my new trees." Amos jerked his head toward the men. "What's going on?"

"An Israelite, my lord. Down from Bethel." Kediah turned his back on the men. "He's looking for good sycamore fig wood for his house. I told him you might be interested in a deal."

"Israelite, huh?" Amos smoothed his beard. "Why does he want my trees? There's good lumber in Israel."

"He's been traveling and seen the houses in Egypt. Says he wants sycamore wood for the walls." Kediah shrugged his shoulders. "I guess all the upper class use sycamore in Egypt."

"Quite a bit," Elroi agreed. "I've been around." He grinned at Amos's raised eyebrows.

———

"My man tells me you're in the market for some lumber." Amos extended an arm to the older man. "I'm Amos of Tekoa."

"Eliakim, son of Samuel of Bethel." He grasped Amos's forearm. "Kediah said you may be willing to sell some of your trees."

"There might be some I could let go. I've started

replacing them a few acres at a time. How many are we talking?"

The two men talked business, walking through the wooded acres and choosing trees that met both men's criteria.

"It's for a summer house in the mountains." Eliakim strolled, hands clasped behind him. "It gets so hot in the summers. Don't you think so?"

"I like the heat." Amos smiled at Kediah. "Makes the figs taste that much better."

"Still, you aren't here all summer." Eliakim stopped to study a tree. "Tekoa must be cooler."

"I spend most of the summer in the mountains anyway. My first love is shepherding."

"Sheep?" He sniffed in disgust. "Smelly, dirty work. Surely a man as rich as you leaves that to the shepherds."

"Where would you be without the shepherds?" Amos's eyes narrowed. "Even our father Abraham was a shepherd."

"Yes." Eliakim cleared his throat. "Well. So that should about do it. When can you deliver?"

"Kediah, do you think you can get enough men to fell the trees this week?" Amos turned to the young man.

"Yes, my lord. We can get them loaded and in Bethel within the month."

"Good." Eliakim rubbed his hands together. "You'll send Kediah along with the lumber?"

"Perhaps you should go, Amos." Elroi stepped between the men.

"No. Kediah can be spared for a while. He'll be back before harvest." Amos tipped his head and studied Elroi, then turned back to Eliakim. "Leah is cooking dinner. Come back to the house and we'll make the final arrangements."

———•———

Eliakim's servant man stood beside the table anticipating his master's every need. Leah waited on the table while the babies slept in the corner. Kediah sat at the table with the other men.

"The meal was delicious, Leah." Amos wiped his mouth and brushed crumbs from his beard. "Thank you."

Eliakim looked from Amos to the woman and back again. "I'll retire early this evening so we can get started before the sun rises." Eliakim then addressed his servant: "You can bed with the animals after you feed them."

"The house is large, Eliakim. Surely there's a room for him?" Amos looked at Leah.

"The pallet is still in the back room, my lord." She took his plate. "I keep it ready for passing guests."

"No." Eliakim held up his fingers. "He'll sleep in the barn where he belongs."

———•———

Amos steadied himself with his shepherd's staff. The ground was shaking. A river of people rose from the valley below. The sun grew dark and the cries of the people echoed off the rocks above.

Amos looked across the valley. A fiery altar stood against the hillside, casting shadows over the people below. In front of the altar Eliakim measured each person's offering, his finger lying heavy on the scale.

"Sit."

Amos heard a voice and turned. There was a table of colorful bowls filled with ripe figs. Amos pulled out a chair and sat down. The Lord sat across from him.

"What do you see, Amos?" his voice whispered above the cries of the people.

"Ripe fruit." Tongue-tied for the first time in his life, Amos struggled for words.

"That's right." The Lord nodded. "The time is ripe for Israel. I will pick them and scatter their bodies. Their hollow songs will turn to wailing. ... Silence!"

The cries of the people below quieted. Amos blinked.

"Hear me." The Lord stood, towering over mountain and valley, his shadow spreading across the entire land. "You who stamp out the life of the poor and needy, cheating them and then buying them for payment, I will not forget your wickedness."

Amos slipped off the chair and fell at the Lord's feet.

"A famine is coming. Not an absence of food, but a famine of words. You will look for me, straining to hear my love songs, but you will only encounter silence."

"No." Amos gasped and sat up in bed. He held the covers in his fist, his fingers pale in the moonlight. "No, Lord. Please don't leave us."

Crickets chirped outside his window. Amos crossed the room and looked out. The fig trees stood at attention in the orchard. An owl called from far away. Amos sighed and went back to bed.

———

"You look awful." Elroi sipped his tea.

"Rough night." Amos stumbled to the table and sat down. Leah placed a cup of tea in front of him. "Thanks."

Oil lamps cast shadows on the early-morning breakfast. They could hear Eliakim moving around in his room.

"Want to talk about it?" Elroi set down his cup.

"I think ..." Amos looked Elroi in the eye. "I think the Lord appeared to me last night."

Elroi never flinched. Leah dropped the carrot she was chopping.

"He said a famine is coming. A famine of words, not food or water. People were dying, looking for him, but he wouldn't answer." Amos blew across the hot tea, trying to gather his thoughts. "He said Israel is a bowl of ripe fruit—fruit to be scattered abroad. None will be left."

The room was silent, a reminder of the nightmare.

"Good morning." Eliakim came into the kitchen. "We'll be heading out soon." He held his hand up to Leah and shook his head. "We'll eat on the road. We need to get going. Where's Kediah?"

"You know ..." Amos stood up, hitting his knees on the corner of the table. "I think I'll meet you in Israel after all." He winced at the pain shooting through his legs.

"Wonderful." Eliakim smiled like a lion after the kill. "I'd rather do business with you. Servants can't be trusted. Cheats in my experience, all of them."

Leah huffed and turned to the work counter.

Amos, Kediah, and Elroi waved to the men as they started north on their donkeys.

"I better get to work." Kediah headed back into the barn. "You'll be staying a few more days?"

"No." Amos watched the donkeys disappearing over the hillock. "I better go tell Malaki that I'm leaving for Bethel."

"Glad I'm not you." Kediah shook his head and kept walking.

———————

The trip to Tekoa was longer than ever. The late-spring sun beat down on Amos's head and drained him of energy and enthusiasm.

"You're worried." Elroi rode next to him.

"Yes." Amos nodded. He never took his eyes from the road.

"Let's stop here for a rest." Elroi pulled the donkey to a stop.

They sat on a large rock near the road. Elroi pulled out a basket of fruit that Leah had packed for them two days ago. He took a piece and passed it to Amos.

Amos took the fruit, but he didn't eat any. He stared at it. A tableful of ripe figs flashed through his mind.

"How can he abandon all of us?" Amos asked.

"Abandon?" Elroi swatted gnats that swarmed the overly ripe fruit.

"The Lord. I know it was him in my dream." Amos looked at his friend. "He said Israel is a basket of fruit and he's going to dump them out and scatter their bodies far and wide."

"Fruit, huh?"

Amos stared down the road. A caravan was headed toward them. Dust flew from their wagon wheels. Life continued for everyone else.

"The thing about fruit ..." Elroi waited for Amos to look at him. "The thing about fruit is the seeds."

Amos opened his mouth, but nothing came out.

"Even rotten fruit has seeds that someday will grow into more ripe fruit. The Lord has never abandoned his people. God will keep his promise to David."

For there is no defense for a man who,
in the excess of his wealth, has kicked the great
altar of Justice out of sight.

Aeschylus

CHAPTER 38

"FATHER, SOME PEOPLE ARE HERE to see you." Etta motioned some men into the dining room and then sat down to breakfast.

Granville Jones wiped the Welsh rarebit off his mouth. He wadded the napkin and threw it on the table, saying, "It's awfully early in the morning for a business call, boys."

"There's been an accident. Several shafts have caved in. Men are trapped underground."

"Which shafts?" Jones pushed his chair back.

"Pit Fifteen started it. Twelve followed. Most got out of Thirteen and Fourteen uninjured."

"Thank God." Etta breathed a sigh of relief.

"A lot are sure to be lost." The man frowned at Etta. "Williams went down to help. He hasn't come back up. One of the foremen said he went into Twelve before the collapse."

"Good. Good." Jones nodded.

"Father! That's terrible." Etta stared wide-eyed, a pup recognizing the cruelty of the world.

Jones looked at his daughter. He blinked a few times.

Why was Etta out of bed this early anyway?

"What are you doing up so early?" he growled, low and menacing.

"I have a Shotton Cross Benefit meeting this morning." She blinked again. "But, Father, why are you glad Mr. Williams is trapped?"

"I'm not glad. Good Lord, girl." He cleared his throat, thinking fast. "Williams is a war hero. If he's in the mine, he'll get everyone out. He knows what he's doing."

"Oh." Etta nodded slowly. That made sense. "Good."

"I'll be there soon. You boys go on back and get the rescue started." He dismissed the men. "I just need to check some things with the Commission. I'll call them from here."

"Quite right." The men turned for the door. "We'll let the office know you're on your way."

———— • ————

Etta knocked on the library door. She could hear her father shuffling papers and slamming drawers. It grew quiet.

"What?" came his voice.

"I wondered when you will be leaving. I'd like to go help if I can," Etta said through the heavy door.

"You don't need to be down there getting in the way." He sounded angry.

"But can't I do something to help? Mother wants to as well."

"No. Now go and scratch!"

———— • ————

Dust flew behind Jones's car as he slid into the parking space at the colliery. He jumped out of the car and climbed the stairs in one fluid motion.

"Mr. Jones is here. He'll get things moving!"

Granville Jones heard the engineer's cry, but he raced into the office.

"Edward, get Charles Hughes on the phone. That man's a sheep fart in a jam jar if there ever was one." He walked into his office and slammed the door.

"Sir, the rescue team from Flint is on their way to help," Edward called from his desk. "Hughes isn't answering."

Jones stormed out of his office and crossed the room in three strides, stopping in front of William's desk. He stood with his hands on his hips, legs spread. He surveyed the contents without touching anything. Pens, writing paper, carbon paper. Nothing was out of the ordinary.

"Sir, are you ready to meet with the rescue team?" Edward stood by his desk. "The explosion was nearly two hours ago now."

"Where are they?" Jones rubbed his chin.

"They've been digging on Fifteen."

"What?" Jones turned to look at the office clerk. "Fifteen. Good. Yes, Fifteen." He took another look at William's desk, then walked out of the office.

———◆———

News traveled fast. Colliers from all over the countryside had already come to help with the disaster. Nitroglycerine had exploded in a nearby shaft, causing Fifteen to collapse for more than fifty feet. The vibrations set off a ripple effect deep in the ground. The heavy fall released methane gas, and the rescue workers didn't have enough masks to keep everyone below safe.

Oxygen was running low. Everyone's heart wanted to believe, but time was running out. Their reason was in full combat with hope.

———•———

"Did you hear the explosion or feel it first?" A reporter was taking notes in the makeshift infirmary of the school building.

Pallets were laid out on the floor, and the desks shoved against the wall. A few people murmured words here and there, but silence reigned as the hours crept by at a snail's pace.

"What do you remember?" The reporter moved to the next pallet.

"Nothing. Darkness." The boy was barely a man. "Dad was beside me. He shoved me against the wall, held me up while we felt our way along the shaft."

"Did your helmet light go out?"

The boy blinked at the reporter. His words made no sense. Tears trickled out the edge of his eyes and down his temple. He tried to brush the burning memory away, but it stuck in his ears. The explosion, the falling rock, the breaking of bone ...

The reporter didn't give up: "Which pit were you working?"

"Twelve."

"Everyone got out?" He made a note.

"No." The man–child shook his head. Why couldn't he wake up? "The support beams were weak farther back. Couldn't nobody help those fellows. Nobody." He turned his head.

"What do you mean the beams were weak?" The

reporter leaned forward.

"I could hear them screaming." Tears continued to flow. "God save their souls."

A woman moved to the bedside. She washed his face with a cool rag and held his hand. The reporter walked away.

———◆———

The afternoon sun was bright, unaware of the disaster below the earth. Eileen stood near the mouth of the pit with the other wives. The women steeled themselves against the possibilities. Every passing hour meant less oxygen, less hope.

"Do you mind answering some questions?" A man in a dress shirt stopped beside Eileen. "I'm with the *Cambrian News*."

"What kind of questions?"

"What's your name? Who are you waiting for?" The man held his pencil ready.

"My husband." Visions of William—holding the children, returning from war, leading the sheep home—wandered through her mind.

"His name?"

"William. William Williams." She took a breath and returned to the present. "He's over the day shift. He wasn't supposed to be down there. They say he went down to get people out as soon as it happened." She half smiled. "That's William, always trying to save people."

"Is he helping dig them out now?"

"I don't know what he's doing." Her eyes filled. "He got trapped in Twelve when it collapsed during the second explosion."

"Twelve? I hear there were weak spots in Twelve. Know anything about that?" He watched her carefully.

Eileen shifted her weight and looked away. "I know William had concerns. He went to talk to the owner—Mr. Jones—'bout a week ago."

"Why didn't he pull the men out of there? Until it could be inspected ... fixed?"

"Granville Jones would be the man to answer that." She crossed her arms and nodded her head toward the office. "He's been in there on the phone all day."

———————

"Mr. Jones?" The reporter knocked on the door and walked in.

Granville Jones looked up from his desk. He had been dealing with colliers, firefighters, rescue workers, and wives all day. And now who was this clean-cut man in city clothes?

"Yes?"

"Greg Ellsworth with the *Cambrian News*. I have a few questions about the accident, especially in Twelve."

Jones raised an eyebrow but said nothing.

"I hear there were concerns about the safety of the shaft. Some are saying there wasn't enough support; that it was weak." He stood ready to write, shoulders back and self-assured.

"Who said that?" Jones gripped the edge of the desk.

"It's all over the town."

"It is, is it? And how would the town know what was going on in Twelve?"

"The women seem pretty certain it was in disrepair." Ellsworth cocked his head and watched the other man begin to boil.

Jones eyed the reporter. "It was the Williams woman, wasn't it? She's got no proof of anything."

"Who is the Williams woman?" Ellsworth wet his lips, enjoying the hunt.

"Get out of my office. I've got business to take care of. Go on with you!"

The reporter nodded once and slipped the pad of paper in his pocket. "I'm only the first of many. Better get your story straight." He turned and walked out.

Justice and power must be brought together, so that whatever is just may be powerful, and whatever is powerful may be just.

Blaise Pascal

CHAPTER 39

AMOS AND MALAKI WALKED ACROSS the pasture. Lambs jumped from rocks and chased each other. Mother ewes eyed the couple and called their children home.

"I don't understand why Kediah can't go." Malaki took his hand. "You've already been gone so much."

"I hear an echo. It bounces off everything I do." Amos grasped for words, looking for just the right stone to bring down this bear. "I hear it when I calculate my records. It drives with me to Tekoa. Am I part of the problem? Do I do enough to help the poor, to honor God?"

Malaki let go his hand and embraced her husband. "You can't change the world, Amos. You do what God commands and let it be."

"But that's part of the echoing." He wrapped his arms around her and watched bees fly over the wild rose. "The dreams are from God. He has set me up to make a difference. He's commanding me to go to Israel and I must go. It would be disobedient not to."

"What if something happens to you, Amos? What

about me and the children?" She leaned back to look in his face.

"I don't know if I will return, Malaki, but I know I have to go." He pulled her back into him and rested his chin on her head. "Elroi will be here. He'll care for you like his own."

———————

The donkey tripped over some rocks and Amos grabbed its mane to regain his balance. A large rock caught his foot and gashed the side open. Amos dismounted and sat on a boulder to wrap his foot.

"Where're you headed?" Two men were walking south. They stopped in front of Amos.

"Bethel." Amos tied off the wrapping and placed his foot gingerly in his sandal.

"We live in Bethel." The men smiled. "I'm Jethro, and this is my brother, Gad."

"Amos of Tekoa." Amos stood to shake their hands. "You're going the wrong way for Bethel." He pointed south where they were headed.

"We've been doing some carpentry in Bethel, but the wages aren't so good." Jethro shrugged. "Thought we might try our luck in Jerusalem on one of the king's projects."

"What makes you think they'll pay more in Jerusalem?"

"Not more." Jethro laughed. "Just pay. Those rich boys are rich 'cause they don't bother to pay anyone."

"What do you mean?"

"We're tired of fighting them, but at least we have some legal recourse," Gad said. "Their servants just have to take what they can get."

"Why are you going to Bethel?" Jethro looked at the expensive saddle on Amos's donkey.

"I have some business to take care of. A man bought some lumber from me."

"I hope you were paid before delivery." Gad slapped his brother on the back.

"Good luck." Jethro waved as the two men turned down the road.

———————

It was late when Amos got into town. The sun was going down and he was looking for a place to stay. He followed the wall around the border of the city until he came to a tavern. The evening lamps were already lit, and the crowd was rowdy.

Amos entered. A woman stood behind a counter pouring glasses of ale and wine.

"Have you any rooms for rent?" Amos leaned on the counter.

"How many nights?" She eyed him but kept pouring drinks.

"Three ought to be enough." Amos turned as the crowd cheered.

A shaggy-haired man was held down on a table-top while wine was poured into his mouth. The man spluttered and spit the wine back out. Another draught was poured, and the crowd clapped and yelled.

"What kind of party is this?" Amos turned back to the woman.

"One of those high and mighty Nazirites. Think they're better than the rest of us." She spit on the floor. "They aren't anything special." She carried a tray of drinks to the table of partiers.

Amos watched as another round of drinks was passed among the people. The woman came back with an empty tray.

"Three nights, you say? I can do that. Pay up front."

Amos poked through his bag of coins and handed over the money. She slipped it into her cloak pocket and pointed to the back of the house.

"Go around outside. There's a room over the back shed. You can bed there." She placed more cups on the tray and started filling again.

Amos watched as the shaggy-haired man was again tortured and jeered. He went out to the donkey and pulled his staff from the saddle. *"No good shepherd leaves his staff behind,"* he could hear Elroi saying.

Amos reentered the public house and rapped the staff on the stone floor. The crowd ignored him. He walked up to the group and slammed the staff on the tabletop, just missing the drowning Nazirite's head. The crowd jumped back.

"That's enough!" Amos looked at each one. "Let him go."

"Who are you?" A burly, pock-faced man poked Amos in the chest.

"Amos of Tekoa. Now let him go." Amos never flinched.

"And why should we listen to you? Some quarter-shekel shepherd from nowhere." He snapped his teeth at Amos.

"Because it would be wise. We shepherds are famous for destroying lions, bears, and giant fools." He stepped closer to the man.

The crowd hooted and egged them on. The man tried to throw a punch, but Amos blocked it with his staff and then shoved the butt of it in the man's gut. He fell at Amos's feet.

"Let the Nazirite go," Amos repeated.

The Nazirite slipped off the table and slunk out of the tavern. Amos turned to follow, but the crowd jumped him.

"I have his money bag," one yelled.

"We'll teach you, you filthy shepherd."

Amos knocked several heads with his staff, but the men landed punches of their own. He was beginning to fall when a strong hand lifted him to his feet.

"Go home, all of you." A man in a bearskin skirt and girdle silenced the room.

The men threw back the last of their drinks and walked out, giving a wide berth to the bearskin man.

"Thank you." Amos rubbed his jaw and looked at the man. "Amos. Amos of Tekoa." He held out a hand to the man.

"Micah." He shook Amos's hand. "The Nazirite you saved found me. You could have been killed. What were you thinking?"

"I was defending a man of God. There's nothing to think about."

"Not many around here believe that." Micah looked around the empty room. "Are you staying here?"

"I was, but they took my money bag." Amos went to the woman at the counter. "I'll need my money back for the room."

"Don't know what you're talking about." She grabbed a broom and started sweeping up the night's mess.

"Come on." Micah opened the door to the street. "You can stay with me."

Amos smelled fried bread. He opened a swollen eye and peered around the room. Now, in the morning's light, he could tell that it was more than sparse—crude, some might say. His straw pallet in the corner touched both corners of the wall. Micah, the bearskin still around his waist, was cooking over a brazier in the middle of the room. A table, a chair, and a bed were the only other furnishings.

"You're awake." Micah looked up from the pan at the brazier. "Probably feeling worse for wear."

Amos sat up as every muscle screamed. He stretched, then leaned against the wall. "I haven't fought off wild animals in many years." He chuckled. "I'm more of a business shepherd these days."

"What brings you to Bethel?" Micah handed him a cup of water.

"Business." Amos sipped the water. It was a cool stream in a desert land. He sighed. "I sold some lumber to a man here. I've come to settle with him."

"Who's the man?" Micah sat on the chair.

"Eliakim, son of Samuel."

Micah nodded once and sighed. He looked out the open door.

"Do you know him?" Amos asked.

"I do. I've had some dealings with him since I arrived."

"Can you tell me how to get to his place? It's a summer house he's building."

Micah went back to the brazier and flipped dough over. It spat on his wrist and he rubbed the burn.

"I can." He walked to the table for a plate.

"You don't say much, do you?" Amos grinned.

"Better that way." Micah stabbed the bread and put

it on a plate for Amos. "You can make your own judgments."

The road Micah pointed to went straight up the hillside and through a forested area. He assured Amos it would be safe in the daylight. Bandits weren't much of a problem here. It was the citizens you had to worry about.

Amos found the construction project by midmorning. The lumber from Valley Grove was stacked in a clearing. Carpenters were planing the wood into thin panels to line the walls of the stone house.

"Amos." Eliakim walked out of the structure. "I thought that was you coming up the mountain."

Amos raised an arm in greeting and dismounted the donkey.

"What happened to you?" Eliakim stopped in front of the donkey. "Were you in a fight?"

"The Bethel Welcoming Council." Amos pointed to the lumber. "I came to settle our account."

"Lovely wood it is, too." Eliakim was all smiles. "Let me show you the house. The carpenters just started putting in the paneling today." He stepped aside for Amos to walk up the path.

The air was cooler here, and Amos could see why Eliakim had chosen the spot. Bethel lay below, the road to town curving through the valley. The dampness of the undergrowth in the forest beyond filled the air with an earthy aroma. Amos breathed deeply.

"This is the entryway. My wife wanted a mosaic floor like the ones in the king's palace." Eliakim and Amos stepped inside. "A man's home tells the world who he is, doesn't it?"

"Often." Amos kept walking to the room beyond.

The tour was accented with tidbits about where each material came from: Syria, Lebanon, Egypt, even Spain. Eliakim seemed to be trying to outdo himself. Finally they ended back outside, and Amos could breathe again.

"It's very nice, Eliakim." Amos stopped outside the back door. "I'd like to get finished here, though. I'm anxious to get back home."

"Oh, I don't have money here." Eliakim circled his arms around the clearing. "No, too dangerous."

"Well then, where should we go to get it?" Amos rocked on his toes, trying not to get angry.

"Come to my house for dinner. My town house." Eliakim smiled. "My cook is the best in the city. She'll put your little Leah to shame."

"How do I get there?" He ignored the verbal punch Eliakim tried to deliver.

———————

The city house was more extravagant than the summer home. Eliakim met Amos at the front. Palm trees fluttered above the roof, extending a welcome to the expansive courtyard inside. A pool with two geese was the centerpiece.

"Come in, Amos. Come in." He stood in the hallway while the servant girl closed the door behind Amos. "My wife is waiting to meet you. We'll feast by the pool this evening."

The dinner was delicious; Amos couldn't deny it. He asked to tell the cook himself, but was assured his compliments would be passed on.

"You know, you could do a lot of business around here." Kediah looked across a plate of sugared figs. "Some of my neighbors stopped by this afternoon and were pleased with the wood you sent. You could be a regular around Bethel."

"No." Amos shook his head. "I've sold all the lumber I'm selling. I'm in the fig business, not the lumber business." He sat back in the cushioned chair. "Besides, I don't want anything more to do with Bethel."

"What's wrong with Bethel? This is a major city." Eliakim looked like he'd just stuck his hand in a hornet's nest.

"A major city with some major sins." Amos said it before he thought it through.

"Is this about the bandits that robbed you?" Eliakim relaxed.

"There weren't any bandits." Amos sat up straight again. "Men were assaulting a Nazirite and forcing him to drink wine." He smacked his hand flat on the table. "I was defending him when they beat me up and stole my money."

"Just some foreigners having fun, no doubt." Eliakim waved it off. "You were in the wrong part of town."

"They were Israelites or I'm not a Jew." Amos clenched his fist. "And it wasn't just the fight. I've seen servants mistreated; some workers even told me their wages were withheld." Amos leaned forward. "So if you don't mind, I'd like my money now."

"Of course." Eliakim motioned to the manservant to bring the payment. "But I'd like to prove to you that Bethel is a good city. Come to the altar with me tomorrow. You'll see. We serve the same God. You'll like Bethel, I'm sure."

We should never desire to be over others. Instead,
we ought to be servants who are submissive to
every human being for God's sake.

Saint Francis

CHAPTER 40

"WHEN IS DADDY COMING HOME?" Iris whimpered as Eileen lay her down in the bed next to Alice. "I want Daddy."

"Shh. You sleep here awhile with Alice, and when you wake up, you can have a special breakfast with scones and honey." Eileen pulled the cover up to her little girl's shoulders. "Good night, my little flower." She kissed Iris on the forehead, but the girl was already sleeping.

"Thank you, Alice." Eileen's voice cracked.

"She'll be fine. I've taken care of little ones for a long time now." Alice smiled and curled up next to the small bodies in her care. "You go help, and as soon as Mr. Williams comes up, we'll be there to celebrate."

Eileen grabbed Alice's hand and smiled through the tears. Life had been unfair to Alice since she was a tot, but here she was encouraging, smiling, offering help. *She's just like her mother, doing what needs to be done and moving on.*

"Are you ready to go back?" Constance whispered from the doorway.

Eileen swept the hair from Iris's face one last time and then turned to face the night.

"Set it over there. Thanks so much." Eileen was directing the other women. They were bringing hot tea and coffee, biscuits and scones, sandwiches and pasties. Tables were laid out near the workers so they could be refreshed whenever they came aboveground.

It was the first official work of the Shotton Cross Benefit Society. Eileen took charge so that she wouldn't have to think about what might be going on below her. It was even harder when she started thinking about what might *not* be going on below her. Busy hands cleared the mind and strengthened her resolve to believe the best.

"Strong coffee for the men." It was the owner of the Italian café. "It will make them do the work of ten men."

"That's so thoughtful. You're a good neighbor, Mr. Lorenzo." Eileen smiled at the old man. "Antony will want it when he gets up here."

Mr. Lorenzo nodded. His son was in Fifteen, deep in the shaft. The outlook was grim; it had already been nearly eighteen hours.

"Let me help with that." Etta took the old man by the arm and led him to the table with all the drinks.

"Thanks, Etta." Eileen's smile faded before she finished speaking.

She put her fists in her apron pockets and took a deep breath. The night was dark and quiet except for the sound of the lift bringing tired men up and taking tired men down. Time was not on their side.

"God is here with us. He knows the pain and fear." Constance put her arm around Eileen. "William is going to be fine. They all are."

Eileen nodded and blinked back the tears of fear and distrust.

———◆———

Generators restored light to the pit mouth about midnight. It was a momentary victory. The ventilation fans still couldn't be reversed. The switches were bad, and none had been found even as far away as Flint. Cardiff was sending some engineers to work on it, and even Swansea was sending men, but the clock was ticking.

Eileen sat on the stairs of the office building, watching the scene. Two women handed drinks to the men as they stumbled to the table. It was Constance and Etta, working together. No one noticed, but Eileen saw. They held hands and prayed together as the last of the men walked away. Catherine Smith and the other wives joined them.

Disaster has a way of polishing the glass and letting us see clearly. Eileen wiped her eyes. It was a glimmer of hope in a deep darkness.

There is a saying among children, that
"Sometimes one is hanged for speaking the truth."

Joan of Arc

CHAPTER 41

A MOS AND ELIAKIM WIPED THE dust from their feet as they entered the stone center of town. The morning's rays were just coming over the treetops. Sunbeams danced in the clearing like children on a holiday.

Crowds gathered in familiar groups, chatting about the summer harvest, marriages, and strangers in the area. Amos felt every eye on him. *Are you sure about this, Lord?*

Another dream had haunted his night. Sheep scattered across the hills of Israel. They ran from rabbits and bears alike, never knowing what truly endangered them. Amos tried to gather the sheep before they plunged into deep crevasses, but a voice in the valley shadows cautioned him: *"They have run from me; you will not gather them. Strike them with your staff."*

Shrine prostitutes stood at the edge of steps leading to their quarters. Baal worshippers mingled with those offering sacrifices to Yahweh, Lord of the Israelites.

"I thought you said we worship the same god?" Amos's wide eyes gave away his concern.

"Oh, I don't go there." Eliakim turned Amos away from the Baal shrine. "The Lord's altar is up here."

They passed a family selling their daughter to a woman for a pair of sandals and a cloak. The mother cried like a dog being beaten by its owner, but the father would not relent.

"She'll have food there and a warm blanket at night," the father said as he wrapped his arm around his wife's shoulders to shield her as the child was led away.

"Eliakim, how is the summer house coming along?" An older man approached them.

"Fine, fine. The sycamore panels are the perfect thing." Eliakim took Amos by the elbow. "Amaziah, this is Amos of Tekoa. Amos, this is Amaziah, the priest."

Amaziah smiled. "Ah. The rich shepherd I've been hearing about. You fight like a warrior, from what I hear." He laughed. "Some of my men were looking rather sheepish, if you know what I mean."

"You must mean the brutes that forced wine down a Nazirite and then stole my money." Amos felt like a brick oven on Thursday, his anger rising in the heat. "Their own shepherd hasn't taught them very well."

Amaziah's eyes widened. He pulled back his hand of peace. "I'm sure you don't mean to say that I have done anything wrong."

"No, of course not." Eliakim moved between the men. "Amos, tell Amaziah what you mean."

"This altar was holy when Abraham erected it and called it the house of God, but you have pushed God out of the house and hidden him in a well shaft." Amos's voice vibrated off the walls of the shrine. "You draw him out when it suits you and drown him when it doesn't."

"What is this treachery? Eliakim, why did you bring this man here?" Amaziah pulled his beard in anger.

"I …" Eliakim rubbed his chin.

"Don't blame the sheep for what the shepherd has failed to do." Amos couldn't stop now. The crowd hushed and watched him. "Your people withhold wages from the workers and force them to sell their children for a set of clothes. The Lord will repay Israel by sending her away without food or clothing."

"How dare you admonish me!" Amaziah stepped closer to Amos and raised his voice. "Israel is a great nation blessed by God himself."

"This country will fall, everyone from the king to the man in that prostitute's bed." Amos stood face to face against Amaziah.

"Get out of here, you seer—you foolish Judeans who believe you're better than the rest of us. Seers like you should stay to advise your own pitiful king."

"I am no seer. I'm a shepherd and a dresser of figs. But God called me to Israel to warn you." Amos turned to look at the crowd, then faced Amaziah again. "And since you don't believe my words, this holy altar will be torn down and your wife will serve as a shrine prostitute to feed your own."

Amaziah struck at Amos but he stepped out of the way.

"You're swinging in the air, Amaziah. Tell your king what I said." Amos turned to Eliakim. "I'm leaving, and I won't return. I suggest you do the same."

———◆———

Amos flung his leg over the donkey, anxious to leave

Bethel as soon as he could. Threatening the king could lead nowhere good.

"Wait." Micah approached him. Twenty men followed on his heels. "Take them with you. They aren't safe here. The people don't want to listen. They need to escape."

"You're prophets?" Amos looked down from the donkey.

The men nodded and huddled closer together. They were sheep, but he wasn't their shepherd.

"I'm a shepherd. I fight wild animals to protect my flock." Amos looked over their heads into the distance of a field and a fight. "A lion once approached, circling my sheep in the middle of the night. I called to the others to wake and help me, but they didn't rouse. The lion came looking for a sheep, but now he had decided that a shepherd would do nicely."

Amos looked back down at the men standing around his donkey. They were scared. The lion was roaring and circling the group.

"I clubbed that lion and yelled for the others like my life depended on it. Because it did." Amos smiled at Micah and the other men. "Sometimes you need another shepherd to rescue you. Stand and fight this lion together. The Shepherd of us all will hear your cries. Perhaps he will relent and rescue."

*I am not afraid of an army of lions led by a sheep; I am
afraid of an army of sheep led by a lion.*

Unknown

CHAPTER 42

"LEADING, FOLLOW PATHS OF ROCK," William sang. Dennis leaned heavily on his back, but William braced himself against the wall and kept the boy out of the firedamp. "Follow, leading gentle flock."

"Hello!" A voice called out in the darkness.

William stopped singing. Had he really heard someone?

"Hello?" came the voice again. "Where are you?"

"Here! We're here!" William called in the darkness. His light had gone out hours ago.

"We're coming. Keep talking."

"How many are you?"

"Six."

"Where've you been?"

"We had to dig through the rock to get out. Lost everyone else, but we're here. Where are you? Sing to us."

"Sing with me, boy." William shook Dennis. "Calling, hearing lamb's sharp cry. Hearing, calling lest he die."

William could hear the labored breathing of the

men. They turned into the stall where he and Dennis were standing against the wall. Everyone grasped hands in the dark.

"I'm William Williams. This is my young friend, Dennis Byrne." William felt each man as he introduced himself and Dennis. "I'm glad to see you."

"Williams? You're the supervisor?"

"Yes. And you are?"

"Roberts. You're the reason we're here to start with, I'd wager." The voice sounded angry. "But how'd you come to be down here?"

"I came to help people get out. Fifteen is where the major explosion caved in. There's no one left there." He shook his head in the darkness. "I knew Twelve was in bad shape, so I came to clear everyone out."

"Too little, too late," another man growled. "Now we'll all die down here thanks to you."

"I'm sure you think so, but I was trying to get you out of here before the explosion. I've sent for the Commission to look into things at Shotton Cross." William boosted Dennis up again. "Are any of you hurt?"

"Jenkins broke his arm. Rest of us are scraped and cut. We've got to get some air," Roberts answered, terse words washed with vinegar.

"The last cave-in filled the shaft," William said. "The air's bad, but not so bad here in the stall." He tried to think. "Maybe we could take turns clearing the rubble. Dennis here has a bad leg and can't stand. Jenkins, do you think you could hold him up while I help the others dig?"

"Aye, I can. It's my wrist what's broke."

The men shuffled in the darkness finding each other, stepping on feet, feeling along the wall. Once Dennis was braced against Jenkins, the other men groped the stall until they found their way to the passage. It was twenty feet to the pile of rock and wreckage.

"The damp is heaviest on the left. Be sure to keep your head up." William started throwing rocks to the left.

"You don't get to tell us what to do." Roberts pushed William against the wall. "You do what you're told and don't cause any more trouble."

"If that's the way you want it."

"That's exactly the way we want it. Ain't it, boys?"

————◆————

The men took turns digging in the blackness. A mountain of hatred lay before them, and a valley of fear behind. Roberts had been in a cave-in once before. He knew to keep working, keep digging, keep living.

"Time to switch, fellas." Roberts breathed heavily.

"We're never going to get out of here." One of them fell to his knees.

"You found me, didn't you?" William pulled the man up. "We have to let them know we're here."

"How do we do that?" Roberts scoffed. "Morse code on the walls?"

"Some of us did that in the war." William felt along the rock ledge. "There's nothing to signal on, though."

"Hello?" Jenkins called from the stall. "The boy isn't breathing so well."

"I'll come help," William called back. "Think of something to signal with while I'm gone."

William stumbled back to the stall, noticing immediately that it was filling with poisonous firedamp. He lifted Dennis onto his back.

"We've got to get out of here. Go on and see if you can help with the digging." William took the boy from Jenkins. "I'll try hoisting this young man higher somehow."

Jenkins's steps faltered in the darkness. "Where are you, boys? I'm losing my sense of direction."

"Here." They called along the shaft. "We're getting closer. We can hear something."

William put Dennis on his back and started for the rock pile. "We're going to make it. Sing, boy! Sing!" William jostled Dennis, but he cried out in pain. "Sorry, Dennis. I'll sing for both of us."

William's song echoed in the chamber. Soon all the men had picked it up.

"Haven't heard that song before," Roberts said. "Where'd you learn it?"

"Africa. The shepherds sang it in the fields at night."

"What were you doing in Africa?" Jenkins tossed one rock at a time, his broken wrist held against his ribs.

"The war." William looked around. "It was a dark place too."

"I need a break." Roberts lay against the rock pile. "I'm too old for this anymore. I'm done if we ever get out of here."

"We'll get out, and it'll be better. I know you don't believe me, but I did inform the Commission. Things are going to be different." William wheezed.

"Leading, follow paths of rock," one of the men started singing. "We're close now. Let's sing them the rest of the way."

"That's how we bring the sheep home." William smiled in the darkness.

"I hear them, boys; I hear them!" Roberts cheered.

"Calling, hearing lamb's sharp cry. Hearing, calling lest he die."

A tiny beam of light broke through the gloom.

Punishment is justice for the unjust.

Saint Augustine

CHAPTER 43

"WE'RE UP TO NINETY-NINE, MASTER Amos." Jacob broke the membrane around the lamb's nose so it could breathe. "Come on, little one." He rubbed the wet lamb.

"It'll make it. That ewe comes from my prized stock. King Uzziah approved her mother." Amos watched as the lamb tried to lift its head.

The ewe lay in the pen. She had shown early signs of labor. Jacob had made a special pallet for her in the straw and slept nearby all night. It had paid off. The lamb began to bleat, and the mother licked it dry. Soon the ewe was breathing heavy, again in the pains of lambing.

"It's small, but I think it will make it now." Jacob stood beside Amos and watched the miracle unfold. "Some warm milk and they'll both be fine."

"You're a great shepherd, Jacob." Amos clapped him on the back. "Elelbet would be so proud."

Jacob rubbed his chin and sighed. It had been nearly a year since the old man's heartache had become unbearable. Elelbet never forgot the horrors his children had faced. He died of a broken heart.

"He was as happy as he could be here, Master Amos.

Thank you for that." Jacob kept his eye on the ewe.

"He was my brother." Amos cleared his throat. "I'll be at the house if you need me."

Amos turned to go. The barn doors swung shut. Dust and straw filled the air as the walls of the barn shook and part of the loft fell. The ewe cried out as the last of the contractions brought another little ram to the world.

"Earthquake!" Amos crossed the barn like a drunken soldier on leave. "Malaki!" He threw the doors open but then caught his hand in between them as they quickly slammed shut again.

The shaking lasted nearly two minutes, with Amos staying put inside the barn doors. Powerful earthquakes were not uncommon in Tekoa, but this was a terrible tremor. From the crack in the barn door, Amos could see the stone house buckling. His heart stopped until the trembling was over.

"Malaki!" Amos threw his shoulders into the doors and sent them flying open.

Children came running out of the house. Jemima carried Amuz, and Malaki was on their heels. They met under the shade trees.

"Are you alright?" Amos felt over Malaki's body, the swollen melon under her cloak was safe.

"I'm fine. I'm fine." She kissed his face.

"Mama threw me under the bed." Amuz stuck out his lip.

"Just as she should have." Amos laughed. "Everyone is safe?"

"Yes." Malaki nodded and gave him another kiss. "What about the men?"

They looked together at the barn. Part of the roof was going to need repair, but it was still standing, and

Jacob was already walking around the perimeter assessing the damage.

"I better take the men into Tekoa and see if they need help." Amos kissed all his children. "You help Mama get everything cleaned up. I'll be back as soon as possible."

———

A few places in the city wall would need repaired; Amos could see that as they approached Tekoa. People were staying out of the buildings as smaller tremors continued to rock the land.

"Amos, so good of you to bring your men to help us." Mattathias wrung his hands.

"We're all family." Jacob lifted stones and handed them down the human chain as they dug out the mayor's home. "I'm sure you would do the same if we needed help."

"You know I'd be the first to help you." Mattathias handed over another rock. "I've always liked you Gileadites."

"Men needed. Men needed." One of the king's soldiers rode into town. "The king requires all men who can work to go to Jerusalem." He kept on riding through the streets making his announcement.

"Jerusalem must have been hit hard." Amos put his hands on his hips. "The damage was worse the closer we came to Tekoa. The earthquake must have started in the north."

"You'll need supplies," Mattathias said.

"Yes, food and water, but rope and donkeys and wagons more." Amos was thinking out loud. "Jacob, take your brothers back to the house. Get all the rope we have and bring the donkeys and wagons, even the old mare. Stop at Elroi's and tell him what we're doing. Ask if he can check on the sheep until we get back."

"Yes, sir." Jacob handed over the last rock and straightened himself. "Come on, boys. You heard Master Amos."

———

Amos pulled the donkey to a stop within Jerusalem.

Jacob came alongside him and said, "Whoa." The wagon creaked like rusty hinges in an old door. "Looks pretty bad, my lord."

"I have family here. My father and brother live near that broken section of the wall." Amos pointed to the eastern block of wall that leaned precariously over the road. "We'll start there." He clicked his tongue and the donkey pulled the wagon through the streets of Jerusalem.

Amos could see his brother's house. He took a deep breath. The house was intact. Fear had stalked him from the time he'd left Tekoa. But there was his father, giving orders as always, while servants and citizens alike picked up the pieces of their lives.

"Amos." His father smiled and held his arms wide. "You've come to help."

"Yes." Amos hugged his father and kissed his cheek. "I brought my shepherds to help, as many as I could spare." He motioned for Jacob and his brothers to come near.

"It could have been worse. I hear Israel was hit very hard." The old man tittered and shook his head. "God has sent his vengeance on their wicked ways."

"And Jerusalem hasn't escaped unscathed." Amos

looked around him.

"Make way. Make way," the king's attendants called as the king clopped through the streets on a white stallion.

"Amos?" The king stopped his horse. "Amos of Tekoa. What are you doing here?"

"Yes, my lord." Amos bowed and then looked at the king sitting atop the tall horse. "I've come to help."

"You didn't seem so eager to be here the last time we spoke." King Uzziah raised an eyebrow.

"Obedience to the king is not surpassed by obedience to the Lord." Amos nodded. "But I know the Lord will restore David's fallen city. He'll repair the broken walls and restore its ruins."

"You're a good man. May the Lord make his face shine upon you." The king patted the horse's neck. "It's lambing time, though."

"My shepherds can handle whatever comes their way." Amos smiled and lifted his chin. "I have the best shepherds in the land."

"We'll see about that when the wool tax is due." The king laughed and chirruped to the horse, then trotted onward.

"It looked like Hananiah's widow needs some repairs down the street," Amos said. "We'll start there." Rebuilding was going to be a lot of work. A widow's house seemed the right place to start. Amos took hold of his donkey's reins. "Come on, men. I'll lead the way."

*"But sooner or later you'll grow up and realize that
Profit is the only god this world worships."
He leans in close for emphasis, engulfing me
in the incense of his cologne. "And all
gods demand sacrifice."*

From The Sacred Year by Michael Yankoski

CHAPTER 44

"MUM! MUM!" AMARYLLIS SHOOK HER mother. "They're singing Daddy's song."

Eileen lifted her head from the step where she was sleeping. The sun was above the horizon. Pink clouds hemmed the sun's blue skirt. Women were shrieking and men cheering as a lift rose with new miners from below.

Eileen jumped from her stoop. She wrung Amaryllis's arm. Last night's anxious thoughts flew away on the morning breeze.

"When I see him, I'm going to beat him senseless and kiss him to death all at once."

"Come on, Mum." Amaryllis pulled her mother by the hand. "They've found him. I heard them."

Eileen and Amaryllis ran to the group by the pit's mouth. The lift rose again with another man. His arm was held against his side.

"We made it. Thank God; we made it."

A cheer rang out. The man stumbled off the lift with

help and it started back down again.

"Where were you? Were you in Twelve?" Eileen called above the clamor. "Did you see my husband? William Williams."

"Yes." The man nodded. "He's coming up next. He and a boy ... Dennis."

Amaryllis's mouth dropped open. "He found Dennis. He took care of Dennis, like I asked." Tears filled her eyes.

Eileen rubbed her daughter's cheek with her thumb. She understood young love, first love. William was her own first love.

———

Cars raced into the parking area near the office building. Men jumped out before the cars were stopped. Their doors slammed in rapid fire, sounds of shot after the trigger was already pulled.

"Jones! Where is Granville Jones?" A man in a suit scanned the crowd.

"In the office." A collier pointed to the stairs.

The men from the cars tore up the steps. They were dogs on a hunt, and they smelled their quarry. Voices rang out from inside the office. A constable pushed Granville Jones ahead of him.

"I ... I didn't know anything about it," Jones was spluttering, his face red and splotchy. "I can get you the records."

"We've already seen your records." The man in the suit stood at the top of the stairs. He looked across the crowd. "Where's William Williams? Is he here?"

"He's below. Trapped in Twelve," someone yelled from the crowd.

The man walked down the stairs toward the voice. The crowd moved aside, making a path toward Ian Roi Bugail.

The man stopped beside Ian Roi and asked, "You know Williams?"

"I've known him all his life." Ian Roi nodded and smiled. "A better man would be hard to find."

"That's right," several spoke up.

The crowd murmured agreement.

Eileen stood near the mouth of the pit, waiting for the lift. She could hear it coming closer. Her stomach flipped, and she grinned like a schoolgirl.

The gears of the lift ground to a halt, and several men carried William off the lift. Another two men had Dennis on a gurney.

Eileen's smile froze. It couldn't be.

The men began to sing as Ellen's screams filled the air.

William was tending his sheep in the fields of Forever.

Right is right, even if nobody does it. Wrong is wrong,
even if everybody is wrong about it.

G. K. Chesterton

CHAPTER 45

"DAD SAYS TAID WAS A war hero."

"He was." Amaryllis held the small hand beside her. Visions of her husband returning from war were faded and dim. "He saved twelve men in Poland."

"Wow." The little boy looked at the wooden statue of a collier. "Teacher says colliers were heroes too."

"Mm." Amaryllis nodded. "Especially your great-taid."

"Why?" He looked up at his grandmother. Her short hair was more salt than pepper. "Did he save someone in the mine?"

"He saved an entire village, but he gave his own life."

"Why would he do that?"

Amaryllis looked over the hillock to the river below. The evening sun glinted off the water. Sheep bleated on their way back to the fold.

"There was a shepherd boy who went to London to see what he could see." Amaryllis spoke from far away. "One foggy night he met a man on the Tower Bridge. The man saw a hazel staff in the boy's hand."

She looked down at her grandson, so young, so innocent. "The man asked where the boy got the staff, and the boy told him it came from the wood on the hillside in Wales." She stooped down to look the boy in the face. "The man offered to show the boy an amazing thing if he would take him to the hillside.

"The man and the boy raced back to Wales as fast as they could go. On the hillside the man led the boy into a cave." Amaryllis's eyes smiled. "Do you know what was in the cave?"

"A hazel tree?" The little boy watched his grandmother closely.

"No." She shook her head. "It was a chamber full of knights. 'Are we needed?' the prince of the knights called out, but the man said, 'Not yet.'" A tear rolled down Amaryllis's cheek. "'I'm leading the fight, and more are behind me.'"

OTHER BOOKS BY TRACI STEAD

———•———

The Potter of Paradox:
Book One of The Spirit Series

The Doctor of Dunstable Plains:
Book Two of The Spirit Series

Devotions of a Gerbil

———•———

For FREE resources or to read more by Traci visit
www.TraciStead.com.

ABOUT THE AUTHOR

TRACI STEAD IS A CHRISTIAN author and teacher. Her books are a mixture of biblical and contemporary fiction. Her weekly blog promotes her passion to make the ancient relevant. God is and always has been closer than you might imagine.